Also by James Castagno

Octavia and the Greek Key

Lady of the Lantern

Dance of the Red Panel

THE FUGITIVE SERIES

Witness to Terror
Out of Tunis
Out of Naples

James Castagno
Three Novellas

Witness to Terror, Out of Tunis, and Out of Naples are works of fiction. All characters, businesses, places, events or incidents either are the products of the author's imagination or used in a fictitious manner. Any resemblance to actual persons, living or dead, or actual events is purely coincidental.

WITNESS TO TERROR

There is no witness so terrible and no accuser so powerful as conscience which dwells within us.

–Sophocles

I
THE HUNTERS

Carabinieri Captain Angelo Randi and U.S. Marshals Service Inspector Joe Costa, in official-looking dark suits, walked into the opulent bar at the Hotel Majestic, not far from Villa Borghese in central Rome.

The government sponsored conference on terrorism had ended thirty minutes earlier, and Angelo knew Joe felt as he did. The presentation impressed neither of them.

Angelo motioned to the ornate vaulted ceiling and the large black leather bar stools. "Impressive isn't it?"

Joe raised his eyebrows and nodded.

They slipped onto chairs at the end of the bar and loosened their ties. The bartender, wearing his uniform of a short white tux jacket and black bow tie, stepped up to take their order.

"Rémy Martin XO for both of us," Angelo said.

The conference was a waste of time, Angelo thought. An overabundance of politics, interwoven with European Union political correctness, turned him off after the first half hour. *A full day, time better spent tracking fugitives... wasted.*

"All bullshit. From the opening remarks, to the end," Angelo said.

Joe shrugged. "Affairs of state, nothing classified and no practical ideas on how to fight terrorism. We should have known."

The bartender set two perfectly filled crystal snifters in front of them and walked away.

Angelo rubbed his goatee. "Each month thousands of people from North Africa are given a free trip here, courtesy of the Italian Coast Guard. They don't carry Al Qaeda or ISIS identification cards. Thank God most of them go to northern Europe."

"Look at what my country is going through on the Mexican border. If the Middle East abutted our southern states, we'd be up to our asses in them. Who knows, we may already be." He lifted his glass. "Here's to yesterday's raid. The conference sucked, but at least we took five hardcore killers and a bomb maker off the streets," He tapped his glass against Angelo's and both sipped the expensive spirit.

Angelo set his drink on the bar and shook his head. "You had September eleventh... we've been lucky."

Joe took a deep breath and raised his eyebrows. "Hate to say it, but the day will come. The EU politicians won't turn anyone away. That decision will come back and bite them in the ass."

"Depressing, isn't it?" Angelo said as he tapped a fingernail against the crystal. "The sad part is they don't call us until after it's over, and the guy's hiding to keep his ass out of jail." He stared at Joe and rubbed his fingers across his goatee. "You never told me why you left Witness Security to chase wanted men around the world."

"Ten years dealing with psychopaths. Most of them would do anything to save their skin and remain free. Loved every minute spent working witnesses, but outwitting someone who doesn't want to be caught is more fun."

"Didn't you work at your headquarters?"

"Yeah, but the International Desk wasn't exciting enough, I wanted to get back on the street. Last year, when the Department of Justice announced the opportunity to come here and help you start the Fugitive Task Force, it didn't take me long to send in my application."

"Having family in Italy must have helped."

"No, but speaking Italian did." He took a short drink. "Let's talk about something more interesting. When are you going to introduce me to your wife's cousin?"

"Which one?" Angelo asked.

"The flight attendant you told me about last week. Why did you say she should have been a model?"

"Oh yes." Angelo raised his eyebrows. "Nina."

"Why modeling?"

Angelo smiled. He knew Joe wasn't a womanizer and had a strong connection to his family in Boston and the small town south of the Amalfi coast. "All the women in her family are taller than my wife."

"I wouldn't call Sofia short."

"No, but she looks up at Nina. How tall are you?"

"Six feet, two."

"Nina's three inches shorter."

"Wow." Joe's eyes brightened.

Angelo tilted his head and smiled. "Do you think my secretary has pretty eyes?"

"Mia? Hell yes, they're beautiful... she's beautiful."

"Nina's eyes are the same color, but a shade lighter."

Joe turned towards him and sat erect. "Why the hell are you waiting? Invite both of us to dinner so I can meet her."

"She's in London, but I know she wants to transfer back to Rome. I'll ask my wife."

II
THE PALESTINIAN

With all the pieces now in place, Saleh al-Filistini knew the western world would cower at the strength and boldness of those fighting the infidels. American soldiers throughout Europe would soon realize they met their match.

The sparse furnishing in the Milan apartment fit his goal to keep himself and his Saudi wife as inconspicuous as possible. The metropolitan area's large population of Middle Easterners aided him in maintaining a low profile. His slight English accent attracted little attention in the multicultural city.

He dropped onto the old couch, turned on the lamp and set a large manila envelope on the unfinished wooden coffee table. Saleh focused on Pasha, a man in his fifties in traditional Arab garb, sitting in a chair across from him.

Pasha's hands, folded on his lap, drew Saleh's eyes. The left hand, comprised of two fingers and a thumb, and the right, four scarred fingers and a thumb bent from multiple broken bones, made him shiver. *The hazard of being a bomb maker.* Saleh adjusted his shirt and leaned back. "How long have we been planning this?"

Pasha wiped sweat from his forehead. "More than one year."

When the sheik first proposed the mission to the terrorist leaders in Iran, Saleh had his doubts the operation was possible. His Al Qaeda boss in Tehran silenced him and supported the sheik in the same way a puppy would submit to its mother's demands. For the next six months, Saleh dampened the man's enthusiasm, bringing up the logistical problems and possible political ramifications of a bold bombing on mainland Europe. In spite of his misgivings, the day was at hand. He pressed his lips together and nodded to himself. *Finally, those left in the mountains along the Afghanistan border will get what they want.*

"The car is ready?" he asked Pasha.

"Yes. I finished it last night."

"Did you use the plastic explosive?"

Pasha continued to nod as he spoke. "Yes, Semtex... one kilo in a suitcase. It's easy to form and safe." He gazed around the room.

"Is something wrong?"

Pasha lowered his head and studied the square blue and white floor tiles. "I'm worried. We must be careful. This is Italy, not the streets of Kabul or Baghdad."

"You've done your job well, Pasha. You'll be gone before it happens. Remember to tell Nassem I will call him when I see the color of the bus."

Pasha's eyes remained on the tiles and he did not respond.

The Iraqi bomb maker was not someone Saleh wanted to befriend. The man scared him so much he no longer went to the small apartment where Pasha assembled the components of the bomb. He spoke of his destructive devices with the same loving words he used to describe his own children.

"You'll be rewarded, they transferred the money yesterday." Saleh lifted the envelope from the coffee table. "Put this in the car. Don't let Nassem see it."

"Why do you want to keep it hidden from the boy?"

"There's no reason for him to know who is on the bus." He pushed himself up from the couch.

Pasha stood, adjusted his calf-length thawb and took the envelope. "Peace be with you." He scurried out the door.

Saleh focused on the floor as he paced the living room. He pulled a cell phone from the pocket of his pressed slacks, dialed a number and waited.

Tomorrow's bold undertaking, hatched in the caves of Afghanistan, taxed his knowledge of operational planning. He had rehashed the details in his mind many times. *Flawless.* He knew Akram would pass the information to the sheik, waiting for word in the northern tribal area of Pakistan.

The ring on the phone stopped, and he listened to the voice asking the caller to leave a message. "We're ready, Akram. Tomorrow the world will hear and fear us."

###

The next morning, Saleh parked his black BMW at the side of a narrow two-lane mountain road overlooking a small Italian town, and reached for the binoculars on the passenger's seat.

He climbed from the car, set the field glasses on the roof and leaned against the door. A sense of calm and ease came over him as he relaxed his muscles, drew in a breath of fresh mountain air, unbuttoned his sports coat and loosened his tie.

During the past three months, he'd spent considerable time searching for the perfect location along the route. Every Tuesday the bus took the same mountain road out of the Southern Limestone Alps known as the Dolomites. Four times in the past, he parked in the same spot and watched the bus enter one side of the community and leave from the other. The village had a single road leading through it. *One way in, one way out.*

Saleh raised the binoculars and focused on the winding two-lane road leading into the left side of the town.

He scanned right, over the red tiled roofs, and picked up the road as it emerged from behind a large church steeple topped with a golden cross. Two hundred yards from that side of the village, he focused on a two-door faded blue Fiat, parked along the side of the road.

At no time in his life had killing himself entered Saleh's mind. *How can the boy want to end his life?* Too many young, uneducated fanatics spent their days studying in a radical madrasah. *Without them, Al Qaeda could not flourish and we would have no martyrs.*

Saleh focused the binoculars on the car window.

Nassem's seventeenth birthday was weeks away, and he did not regret the decision he had made. Soon his family would be honored on the streets and in the marketplaces of Kabul.

He wiped his forehead and pulled his sweat-soaked shirt away from his skin. Reaching over the steering wheel, he repositioned the cell phone on the dashboard. His eyes darted across the interior of the car and settled on the passenger's seat. A wire ran from a small plastic cylinder with a red button, to a suitcase on the back seat. He raised the deadly device and stared at it. When his hand shook, he returned the cylinder to the seat beside him.

Staff Sergeant Tony Drago, a member of the 173rd Airborne Brigade Combat Team out of Vinceza Italy, sat behind the driver of the faded yellow tour bus with thin white stripes snaking their way across the front and along the sides. It eased around sharp curves on the two-lane road heading into the small town.

Thirty-four American soldiers, in uniform, occupied the seats behind Tony. The last week of mountain training with members of the Italian Army's 4th Alpini Parachutist Regiment had left them exhausted, and eager to get back to their base and routine duties. Most men dozed, but a few talked, or read newspapers and books while he gazed out the window. *Another two hours of boredom in a bus that looks like a ripe banana.*

He glanced at the driver and wondered how difficult it was to keep the bus on the proper side of the narrow winding pavement. The man, whose legs seemed too short to reach the pedals, tapped the brakes as they approached the edge of town.

III
THE FATAL DAY

Saleh's heart thudded in his chest as he lowered the binoculars and watched the yellow tour bus descend a hill from the left and disappear behind buildings at the edge of town. *Soon it will end. The news of Al Qaeda's terror will flow from Italy to Scandinavia.*

He removed the cell phone from his pocket, dialed a number and raised it to his ear. In the back of his mind, he debated if he should talk to the boy. "It's a large yellow bus. Be ready. It will soon pass you," he said into the phone and ended the call, not giving Nassem an opportunity to speak.

Saleh set the binoculars on the hood of his car and leaned against the fender. Crossing his arms over his chest, he kept his eyes on the right side of the town where his target would exit. His gaze moved to the Fiat, parked a short distance down the road.

###

Nassem adjusted himself in the seat and focused on the rear-view mirror. *The man on the phone must be somewhere nearby.* Movement on the road in front of his car caught his attention. A bus with large yellow stripes across the front sped towards him. He furrowed his brow and glanced back at the mirror. *Thought it would come from behind me.* As he lifted the cylindrical detonator from the passenger's seat, he shrugged and locked his eyes on the approaching target. *He said yellow... that's it.*

###

Saleh shook his head when he realized he had been staring at the road exiting town for over two minutes. Pushing himself away from the fender, he glanced at Nassem's car and spotted a tourist coach approaching the Fiat from the wrong direction.

A sinking feeling grew inside him as he grabbed the field glasses and raised them to his eyes. It took a few seconds to focus on the bus and the large yellow stripes on the front and sides. *It's almost the same color.* His mouth fell open, face contorted, and he dropped the binoculars. He struggled to remove his cell phone from his pocket and press the green button twice. With wide eyes locked on the bus speeding toward the Fiat, he held his breath, and listened to the phone ring. "Answer it!"

Nassem jumped in his seat the moment the phone rang. He reached to grab it, looked at the bus and lowered his hand. *I know... I see it.*

The coach did not slow down or move closer to the right edge of the road.

Nassem raised the detonator to his chest and glanced at the ringing cell phone. When he looked back at the bus, he saw the driver staring directly at him. As soon as it came alongside his car, he screamed, "Allahu Akbar" and pressed the red button.

Saleh flinched when he saw the bright flash of the explosion. "No!" He raced around the car, jumped in, and sped toward the small town.

He stopped at the side of the road, thirty meters behind a yellow tour bus. Saleh got out, stood beside the door and glared at a group of American soldiers, milling around a flat tire at the front of the bus. After he lowered himself back in the car, he stared at the men in uniform. "Today you were lucky. I was not."

Saleh slammed his fist onto the steering wheel, his lips pressed into a fine line. *Two motor coaches... almost the same color... coming from opposite directions. How could this happen?* "I hope it was empty and not full of Italian pensioners." He knew there would be no second opportunity to kill the Americans. He made a U-turn, and five minutes later, pulled onto the road to Milan.

IV
TRAGEDY

Staff Sergeant Drago and two soldiers turned away from the bus driver, cussing in Italian at the flat tire. "Look at that," Drago said, pointing to a cloud of smoke rising above the buildings at the far side of town.

A Municipal Police officer got out of his compact Alfa Romeo, stepped to the center of the street and looked at the smoke.

"What the hell happened?" a nearby corporal asked.

A wide-eyed private held his hand out and shook it. "Damn ground vibrated."

Drago glanced from side to side and frowned. "Sounded like something exploded." He scanned the crowd of soldiers and located Lieutenant Rickter. "You hear that, sir?"

"Yeah," Rickter said and pointed at the police officer. "Find out what happened."

Drago trotted to the officer. "Excuse me."

"Yes."

"Do you know what happened?"

The officer looked at the smoke. "I'm going to find out."

"You're alone, can I go with you?"

"Yes." He headed to his car.

Drago turned and yelled. "Lieutenant, I'm going with him."

###

The patrol car stopped five feet from a gaping hole in the pavement. Both men momentarily froze in their seats.

"Something exploded," Drago said.

Twisted car parts lay in the street and white sheets of paper littered the ground. A motor coach leaned against the far side of the ditch. Black smoke rose from a massive hole in its side.

The police officer and Drago leapt from the car and ran toward the wreckage.

Drago stopped at the edge of the road and his mouth fell open. He held an arm out to stop the police officer.

"Mother of God, what happened?" the officer asked. He pointed at two small bodies lying in the grass. "Children."

Drago scanned the massive hole in what used to be the side of the bus and clutched his stomach at the sight of young broken bodies inside the wreckage. "They're all children."

The officer raised a trembling hand to his forehead. "How did it happen?"

Images of the damage he had seen caused by improvised explosive devises in Afghanistan shot through Drago's mind. He dropped to one knee and glanced at car parts and an engine in the road. He turned and locked his eyes on jagged metal bent inward along the edge of the hole in the coach. "A car exploded beside the bus." A charred paper beside him fluttered in the breeze. He picked it up and saw half the page covered in Arabic writing. Drago folded the paper and shoved it in his pocket.

The officer squatted next to him and covered his mouth with his hand. "How could a car explode with such force?"

Drago rose. "It couldn't. This was a car bomb." As he and the officer walked past the wreckage, he picked up another page. "Here, it's written in Arabic. I think you need to call your headquarters." They reached the back of the bus and looked at the words written below the rear window.

Drago's mouth fell open and his eyes widened when he read the bold black print. "Holy shit!"

V
REALIZATION

Saleh stepped into his apartment and marched to his computer on the coffee table. He dropped onto the couch, opened the laptop and hit the power button.

Twelve months of planning and surveillance wasted. There had never been another bus on the road during the times he watched the American soldiers returning to their base in Vicenza. *Why didn't Nassem answer the phone? That bus came from the wrong direction, he should have known.*

He typed an Internet address into the browser. The screen flashed to the World Caliphate website, and he focused on the words in the middle of the screen, reading them aloud. "A martyr has given of himself and destroyed infidels in Italy. Slay them wherever you find them, for persecution is worse than life without honor." Muscles stiffened, and he slammed his fist against the table. "Couldn't they wait to tell the world? The soldiers are still alive. A meaningless operation." Saleh took a deep breath and shook his head. Many times in the past he had seen the fools who maintained the website jump to conclusions that later turned out to be untrue. He closed the computer, leaned back and thought about the time and energy he and Pasha had wasted. *Something will be on the news.* He picked up the television remote and sat up to watch the state-owned RAI News 24 channel.

A video panning along the side of the smoldering wreck came on the screen. The raw footage showed firefighters spraying water on the bus. The video moved past the hole in the side of the bus and reached the back. An unfocused view of writing below the large back window appeared. The camera zoomed in and the fuzzy words became clear. Saleh thrust himself forward and read the words. "Centro Islamico, Milano, Italia." His eyes widened as his face turned to a mask of terror. "May the Prophet be merciful... what have I done?"

A female voice broke the silence of the broadcast. "Authorities estimate there may have been over thirty Muslim boys, nine to thirteen years old, and an unknown number of adults on the bus from the Milan Islamic Center. RAI News is waiting for a statement from the leading Iman in Milan."

Saleh's hands flew to his chest, and he gasped. Sudden coldness entered his core and his heart raced as the word 'children' repeatedly slammed into his head. A wail, that didn't sound human, poured out of his throat.

Most Fridays he visited the Islamic Center to pray. He knew the Iman and many Muslim faithful who frequented the end of the week service. For the past two years, he had purchased the uniforms for the youth soccer team. *I may have killed friends, destroying the dreams of families.*

The front door creaked opened, and he heard his wife and brother-in-law speaking.

"Thank you, Musa," Zarina said.

"I'm your brother... no need to thank me. I'll see you tomorrow."

The door closed and Zarina, wearing slacks, a long sleeve blouse and light jacket, stepped into the living room. She removed the hijab covering her head, let her black hair fall over her shoulders and glanced at the television. "What are you watching?"

Saleh did not respond nor turn his eyes from the TV.

She sat beside him and raised her eyebrows the second she saw his face. "What's wrong?" She glanced back at the television.

A tear slid down his cheek and he took her hand. "We need to pray for the children."

"What children?"

"Why must we try to kill everyone who does not follow Islam? We are destroying ourselves Zarina... we are destroying a great religion."

Zarina blinked and squinted. "Why are you talking this way?"

Saleh thrust a finger at the newscast. "Pasha's bomb killed Muslim children. The bus is in pieces." He lowered his head and focused on the floor. "It's time to stop the madness."

Zarina squinted and tilted her head. "Pasha returned to Baghdad... what Muslim children?"

"I did it Zarina!" He said as he leapt from the couch. "The mission I planned for over a year failed. The Afghan boy set off the bomb next to a bus carrying children from our Islamic Center." He walked away from her. "Leave me, I must call Tehran."

Zarina covered her mouth and ran to the kitchen.

Saleh pulled his cell phone from his pocket, scanned his contacts, tapped the screen and turned on the speaker.

After the third ring, Akram answered. "Peace be with you, Saleh."

"And with you, Akram. We are cursed."

There was a pause before Akram spoke. "I saw the news on the television. Everyone will understand this was not what you intended. Sometimes mistakes are made in the name of Islam."

Saleh's empty hand made a fist as blood rushed to his head and his face reddened. "Mistake? Over thirty Muslim boys died. We killed them... remember that, Akram."

"Maybe you should have been more observant."

Saleh glared at the phone. *I was and I see what is happening.* "The Prophet sent a message, a sign of what our future will bring."

"Often the innocent must die."

Saleh's fist tightened. "No, Akram. These were our children. Listen to yourself."

Akram sighed. "Listen to what I..."

"You said innocent! That means the boys were pure and uncorrupted by evil."

"Why are you shouting at me?"

Saleh forcibly exhaled and drew a short breath, his voice softened. "You are not listening. Those young lives mean nothing to you. I now know who is evil and corrupt."

"It is your duty to do what we ask and support our cause."

"I thought it was, but we kill our own people, defile our religion, and destroy its future."

"That is not what we do, Saleh. Our purpose and goal is to bring Islam to the world."

"By force?" Saleh yelled. "No. I'm not here to destroy our youth. It's not the life I want for myself. I will no longer do this, I'm finished."

"You are our leader in Southern Europe."

"Find someone else, I can't live with the pain we inflict on innocent families."

Akram hesitated. "My friends and I will not allow you to leave us."

Saleh heard the subtle threat in the Al Qaeda's leader's voice. He opened his fist and stared at four curved marks of blood his fingernails had brought to the surface of his palm. "You can't stop me, Akram. No one can. The Prophet produced peace from the cruelty of war. It's time I help him."

VI
THE PAPERS

Carabinieri Captain Angelo Randi brushed a piece of lint from his dark uniform and sat in a padded chair in front of Colonel Giuseppe Aldo's ornate oversized desk. He ran his hand through his black hair and glanced at the four rows of medals and a parachutist badge on Aldo's uniform. On the wall behind the desk, hung a framed photo of the colonel's father, a Carabinieri officer that helped arrest Benito Mussolini, in July 1943.

The colonel has good taste. Although Angelo had been in the office many times, the size and elegance of the furnishings impressed him. The round hand-forged iron coffee and end tables, next to the large couch, held slabs of rare black marble, no longer found in the Tuscan town of Carrara.

Aldo rubbed a hand over his shaved head, leafed through photos of the destroyed bus, raised one and shook it. "Tonight there will be riots in the major cities of the Middle East."

Angelo shifted his stocky frame in the chair and nodded. "It was not intentional, they hit the wrong bus. They'll do everything in their power to turn their mistake into an advantage." He handed Aldo a piece of paper with a burned corner. "This is Al Qaeda's statement I told you about," he said handing his boss a second page. "Here's the translation."

Aldo read the sheet in Italian and shook his head. "The children didn't have a chance. Their bus came down that road at the wrong time."

"And the American soldiers were lucky their bus had a flat tire," Angelo added.

Aldo handed the paper in Arabic back to him and shoved the photos across the desk. "We need answers. You and Inspector Costa get everyone in the fugitive squad on this case. It's out of the ordinary since we don't know the identity of the people who did it, but your men are good at digging up information. Call your American contacts at the embassy and find out what the CIA knows. Tell Costa to set up a meeting. Al Qaeda tried to hit the bus full of American soldiers, their Justice Department will want to get their hands on whoever did it."

Angelo slid his chair back.

"Take whatever resources you need and find the bastards." Aldo raised the translated page. "I'll have this copied and released to the press. The world needs to know they killed their own children."

That afternoon at the U. S. Embassy, Angelo sat across the conference table from FBI Agent Robert Duffy, in a room with no windows and bare walls. His partner, Inspector Joe Costa, had called earlier and said he'd be with the American ambassador in Milan, and wouldn't be able to come to the meeting. Duffy wasn't Angelo's first or second choice to meet. He was the only agent available.

Angelo opened his briefcase and removed copies of pages printed in Arabic and Italian.

"Since American soldiers were the target, we'd like to work with you on this," Duffy said.

Angelo cocked his head to the side. "Who do you mean?"

"The Bureau... the FBI."

"You?" *The one they jokingly call 'The Kid' behind his back?*

"Yeah."

The young FBI agent grated on Angelo's nerves. All the other American agents had many years of service with their respective agencies and were veterans of complicated international investigations. Robert graduated law school and joined the FBI four years ago. The young man could not stop talking about the wonders of the FBI and the heroics of his uncle, the Executive Assistant Director for Science and Technology.

Angelo pressed his lips together and nodded. "Joe Costa helped us set up our task force, and he's already involved... but of course. I'll ask Colonel Aldo to get you clearance."

The door opened and a wiry gray-haired man, carrying a pair of glasses and a thick folder, entered the room. Angelo, well aware of the man's reputation, never met him, but had heard the stories of the beautiful female Russian agent he convinced to defect.

The man nodded. "Hi, Robert."

Angelo and Duffy stood.

The man extended his hand. "Captain Randi, I'm Al Provitti."

"Please, call me Angelo."

"Sit and we'll get started." Al said. He slid a folder, stamped in red with CIA Top Secret, onto the table. He peered over the glasses perched on the tip of his nose.

"Angelo leads the Carabinieri Fugitive Task Force," Duffy said.

"Yes. I've worked with his boss."

"I hope you can help us," Angelo said placing his hand on the two pages in front of him. "These are the papers found near the bus. We need all the information we can get."

"I have copies of those," Al said pointing to the papers. He tapped the folder in front of him. "This should give you a good start... sources redacted. Do you know Josef Alfano... a section chief at your government's External Information and Security Agency?"

"A.I.S.E.? Yes, I spoke to him once."

"He and I share information. He has copies of everything I'm giving you. I believe it's best if you get your information from him. Please understand, I don't want to step on anyone's toes in the Italian intelligence community."

"Yes, and I respect that. I'll call him."

"Is Inspector Costa and your task force involved?" Al asked.

"Yes. Colonel Aldo told us to make this case our top priority."

Al removed the contents from the folder and pushed the papers across the table.

Angelo looked at the documents. "Our people think they used the explosive Semtex. Any way to find out where it came from?"

Al raised his eyebrows and shook his head. "It wouldn't matter. Czechoslovakia sent so much of it to the Middle East it's as common as shit under a fly's feet."

Angelo hid his smile. "Have you intercepted any communications?"

"Not yet. They're staying quiet. I'm sure you saw their website before they changed it. They're now blaming the Italian government."

"The Prime Minister will not stay quiet."

"I don't blame him," Duffy said. "He needs to schedule a news conference as soon as possible."

Angelo noticed Al roll his eyes.

"Good idea," Al said.

Duffy doesn't get it... he never does, Angelo thought.

Provitti handed him a business card.

He glanced at it and raised his eyes to him. "Military Attaché?"

The CIA Station Chief repositioned his glasses on his nose and shrugged. "Everyone needs to be called something. Military Attaché sounds better than cook and bottle washer, and it has immunity attached to it. I'll speak with Alfano and tell him to expect your call."

VII
CARMINE AND THE TEENAGER

Along the dark street, two of Akram's men sat in a black car, parked under a tree twenty yards from the entrance to Saleh's apartment. The man in the passenger seat held a folding stock AK-47 rifle and listened to the drone of the motor.

They scrunched down when a white Smart Fortwo rolled past and parked in front of the apartment. A young woman, and a Middle Eastern man, got out and walked to the front door. She shoved the key into the lock.

"Now, before they go inside." the passenger said.

The driver slipped from the parking spot with the lights off, stopped in front of the apartment and the shooter raised the weapon. Ten shots, in rapid succession, shattered the silence along the street.

Zarina spun around at the sound as bullets slammed into Musa, the doorframe, and the side of the house. He grabbed her blouse as he fell, ripping it and exposing her shoulders and red bra.

Zarina's face contorted. She yanked the hijab from her head and screamed, sinking to her knees beside him.

Tires squeals and a car sped down the street.

She wiped her cheek, not realizing she was spreading his blood across her face. "Musa, get up." Her pulse raced and heart pounded when she saw him gasp and his head fall to the side. "Musa! No!" She lowered her head to his chest.

###

Saleh, standing in his living room, recognized the unmistakable sound of gunfire and ran to the front of the apartment. He yanked open the door and froze when he saw his wife on her knees leaning against her brother's red stained shirt. He pulled her away from Musa. "Have you been shot?"

"No, my brother!"

He glanced at tears mixing with blood on her cheeks and his eyes widened as he focused on her exposed hair, bare shoulders and bra. "Get in the house and close the door," he said pulling her to her feet.

Zarina pushed him. "No, Musa..."

"Cover yourself," Saleh yelled. He shoved her into the apartment and slammed the door.

His Italian neighbor, Carmine, with his teenage son, ran to Saleh's side. "We called the police," the teenager said. He glanced at Musa. "Holy Jesus, look at the blood."

Carmine squatted and pressed two fingers against Musa's bloody neck. "I'm sorry. I think he's dead."

Saleh looked down the street when he heard the fluctuating wail of a siren. A police car, with two flashing blue strobe lights on the roof, sped toward the house. Behind him, the door opened and Zarina stood in the doorway sobbing. With one hand, she held a scarf covering her hair. The other hand clamped the torn fabric of her blouse against her neck. Tears flowed over smeared makeup and blood.

Saleh stared at her and tightened his jaw. "Go inside the house!" He forced her into the apartment and pulled the door closed.

Two officers from the Italian National Police ran up the walkway. The tall one arrived first and the short man followed, barking orders. "Move out of the way... everyone get back."

The tall officer stepped beside Musa and looked at his body. He turned and glared at Saleh. "Who lives here?"

Saleh placed his hand over his heart. "I do."

The officer turned to Carmine. "Who are you?"

"We live next door. I work in a medical clinic." He pointed at Musa. "I checked. He's dead... no pulse."

The officer looked at Saleh. "Your name?"

"Saleh... Saleh al-Filistini."

"Do you know this man?" He pointed to the body.

"He's my brother-in-law."

Both police officers looked to the street as a black Alfa Romeo, with a blue flashing light on the dash, pulled to a stop.

Carabinieri Lieutenant Massimo Scopise, in his distinctive dark uniform, approached the apartment. His driver raced around the car and followed five feet behind his boss.

Carmine and his son stepped away from the body.

Massimo looked at the tall police officer and nodded. "Good evening, Franco, we received a call. Did anyone see this happen?"

Franco snapped to attention. "Yes, sir, the dead man's brother-in-law, Saleh."

Saleh shook his head. "No, my wife did, she's in the apartment." He leaned to Musa and touched his head. "Peace my brother."

"What is your full name?" Massimo asked.

"Al-Filistini, Saleh."

"Please tell your wife to come out." He turned to his driver. "Call this in to headquarters."

Massimo stared at Saleh and waited for a reply. After ten seconds he said, "Get your wife."

Saleh shuffled his feet. "She's Muslim, she must stay in our home."

I'm in no hurry, Massimo thought looking into Saleh's eyes. He spoke in a low confident tone. "You speak with a British accent?"

Saleh's eyes darted to Musa and back to Massimo. "I went to school in London."

"Then understand, you are in Italy, and you are subject to the laws of the Republic. Where are you from?"

"Palestine."

Massimo leaned toward him. "In Gaza would I have to abide by their laws?"

"Yes."

"Then I suggest you get your wife."

Saleh pushed open the door.

A woman stood in the hall with glassy eyes and smeared makeup. Her long sleeve blouse, buttoned to the neck. Wrapped over her head and around her neck, a scarf, covered her hair. She held a red cell phone at her side.

Saleh took a deep breath. "Please, can we go inside the house?"

Massimo followed Saleh and the woman to the couch. He remained standing, pulled out a pad and pen and scribbled notes. He looked at her. "Your name, madam?"

"Zarina."

Massimo tilted his head forward, focused on her and raised his eyebrows.

"Al-Ansari... Zarina al-Ansari," she said.

"And the man shot is your brother?"

"Yes," Saleh said.

Massimo turned to him. *He's in control.* His eyes lingered on Saleh, then turned back to Zarina. "What is your brother's name?"

"Musa Gafar al-Ansari," she said.

Massimo took his time. "Did you see who killed him?"

"No."

"Your husband said you did."

"I was standing with him, when someone shot from a car." She sobbed and placed a hand over her mouth. "He fell in front of me."

"Why would anyone want to kill him?"

Saleh slid close to his wife. "She wouldn't know that."

Massimo rubbed his goatee and stared at Saleh. "Mr. al-Filistini, I am speaking to your wife."

Saleh raised a hand. "People in Iran want me killed."

"Then why did they kill him?"

"I don't know."

Sure he does, he doesn't want to tell me. He noticed Zarina's eyes open wide, and she adjusted her position on the couch, her lips pursed.

Saleh glanced at her and turned to Massimo. "My wife knows nothing about it."

She stared at him and tightened her jaw.

Massimo thought the couple odd. In past dealings with Muslims, they cooperated for fear it would affect their immigration status and they may face deportation. *He must have a resident permit, he doesn't seem concerned.* "Why should I believe you are telling me the truth?"

Saleh's eyes narrowed, and he clenched his teeth. "Call the CIA, MI-6 or your A.I.S.E. Ask them if they have heard the name Mohammad Halabi."

Zarina's eyes widened and a seething look of disgust came over her face as she turned away.

The moment the words came out of Saleh's mouth, Massimo concluded he would not be leaving the house soon. *This guy must be someone's spy.* He motioned to a nearby chair. "May I sit?"

Saleh nodded.

Massimo dragged the chair to the coffee table and noticed Zarina's demeanor had turned from sorrow to anger. He made notes on the pad.

VIII
MOHAMMAD HALABI

Angelo leaned his high backed leather chair away from the desk, folded his arms over his chest, and stared across the office. Two padded chairs and a small couch surrounded a low table in front of his desk. *We always know who we're looking for, where the hell do we start?*

The telephone rang. "Hello." He listened a moment. "Yes, Mia, bring it here."

When his secretary entered the office, he smiled. *Single and a beautifully built man magnet.* He knew she realized most men and women sensed her presence when she walked into a room, but Angelo was different. She was one of his wife Sofia's many cousins.

She handed him a two-page report and sauntered out.

As he read the report, his eyes stopped on the name Halabi. He dropped the pages, lifted the phone handset and tapped two numbers. "Mia, this report is dated yesterday. When did it arrive in our office?" His gaze slid from side to side as he listened. "Okay. Find Lieutenant Scopise... he's in Milan. Get him on the phone."

Al Provitti sat at his desk in a windowless office and picked up a folder stamped 'Top Secret' just as the phone rang. He hit the speakerphone button. "Yes, Julia."

Al trusted his secretary with his life. She had never failed him. Although she could have retired a year ago, he considered himself lucky she loved her job and wanted to remain in Rome.

"General Alfano is on the line," she said.

"General?" He heard Julia chuckle. "Put him through."

"Go ahead, sir," Julia said.

"So, you're a general now?" Al said as he leaned back and clamped his hands behind his head.

"I thought by now you would have received the news. Did the CIA lose contact with the outside world?" Alfano asked.

"Josef, you're not political enough to be a general."

"That's true. It would be nice but I'm happy with my present position."

"What can I do for you?"

"Nothing, but I received a report from Milan and I can make this the best day of your life."

Al smiled. "Are you going to introduce me to Miss Italy tonight?"

"I'm no fool, I'd keep her for myself. But I know someone you are dying to meet."

"This has got to be good. Whom might that be?"

"Al Qaeda's man in Southern Europe... Mohammad Halabi."

Al laughed and leaned forward. He directed his soft voice toward the speakerphone. "Damn Josef, this may be the best one you ever pulled."

To survive in the job, those in the intelligence services needed to have a good sense of humor. Al's Italian counterpart had the reputation of a man who could convince a Ferrari owner to trade his legendary sports car for a Volkswagen.

"You're blowing smoke up my ass. No one knows what he looks like."

"You're correct. Only the photo of his back while sitting with bin Laden outside a cave, but I am now looking at a copy of his Italian driver's license."

Al sat up in his chair. "You serious?"

"We should have him in custody by the end of the day."

A thousand questions bounced around Al's brain. *How the hell did they find him?* "Do we get to talk to him?"

"Consider this call your invitation."

"Call me when you get him and we'll meet."

"I will." Josef ended the call.

Al hit the speakerphone button and dialed. "Julia?"

"Yes."

"Get someone near the top at the Directorate of Intelligence on the phone."

"Which office?"

"Any of them... No! Terrorism Analysis."

"Sir, it's almost midnight in Washington."

"I know... it's important. I don't want to talk to the Duty Officer. Tell him to get a person well above his pay grade out of bed. Make sure he has a STE secure telephone and get his number. I'll call him... no wait. First get me the Mohammad Halabi file, then make the call."

IX
THE DISAPPEARANCE

Angelo made it from Rome to Milan with ten minutes to spare. He met Lieutenant Scopise just before a group of officers approached the apartment they knew to be rented by Saleh al-Filistini, also known as Mohammad Halabi.

Earlier in the day Angelo talked to Massimo on the phone. The lieutenant explained that he hadn't recognized the name and didn't know an arrest warrant had been issued for Saleh in the name Halabi. After Saleh mentioned the intelligence agencies, he assumed the guy worked for one of them.

Angelo and Scopise walked to the side of the building and leaned against the wall near the door. Both men watched an officer thrust a ram against the deadbolt and step aside. Five officers rushed into the apartment.

Two minutes later, an officer came to the door "They're gone. It looks like they were in a hurry."

"Talk to the neighbors, get as much information as you can," Massimo said.

Angelo frowned and shook his head. It wasn't their fault. Someone at Carabinieri headquarters had taken their time forwarding Massimo's report. The name Mohammad Halabi wasn't well known outside the intelligence community. He had recognized it because of the old wanted fugitive file. *Why would he identify himself and then leave? It makes little sense.*

Angelo pulled his cell phone from his pocket and dialed. "He's not here. Find out if he has a car."

"Are you going back to Rome?" Massimo asked.

"Yes."

"I'll make sure everyone in Milan knows he's wanted."

###

Akram, and Gafar Muhammad al-Ansari, Zarina's father, sat at a cheap makeshift desk in a tiny Tehran street level office. Stains marked the walls where old posters and papers had once hung. A stack of magazines and newspapers lay on a square wooden table across the room.

Akram looked at Gafar's traditional Saudi Arabian dress. A cord circlet held a diagonally folded cloth on his skullcap.

"When do you return to Riyadh?" Akram asked.

"As soon as possible. We're waiting for the Italians to release Musa's body. My family needs me."

"Did you hear anything more?"

Gafar looked at the floor and shook his head. "Nothing. My wife is worried about Zarina."

"How could Saleh be so stupid?" Akram asked.

"Stupid?"

"Two different buses... soldiers and children. All he had to do was look."

"I was speaking of Zarina, not Saleh. She must not be hurt. Those who killed my son cannot hide from me forever."

"Did you try to call her?"

"Yes, the phone is disconnected."

Akram knew losing one of his sons had dealt a blow to Gafar's family. *Praised be Allah, no one told him I sent the two men to Saleh's house.* "I am sorry about your son. Those who killed him were not competent. I've contacted my best men in Italy. They're discreet and efficient, and will soon find him."

"What about the bank account?"

"If he moves the money, I'll be notified and told where it went."

Gafar leaned over the desk and stared at Akram. "The sheik wants him found."

"Doesn't he understand we're trying?"

"Yes, but the longer it takes, the more trouble we both face. Why did I agree when she married an educated refugee?"

"Your daughter made a better life for herself. She is not hiding with the tribes in North Waziristan."

"Palestinian... why a Palestinian?" Gafar asked himself.

"She has always had her own mind."

Gafar stared at him. "My family will find those who murdered Musa. I do not want Zarina harmed. If she is hurt, people will die."

"You have my word, Gafar. Saleh is the target. Continue trying to call her."

X
ROME IS SAFE

Normally a six-hour trip, it took Saleh five hours to drive to Rome. He and Zarina sat on the couch in the living room of a hotel suite on via National near Piazza Repubblica in central Rome. Saleh stared at the wall across the room. Without turning his head, he sensed her glaring at him.

"I still don't understand why you gave the police that name... have you gone mad?" her voice tight with anger.

He looked at her and thought about how he had explained himself hours ago. Another argument was not what he wanted. "Everything is different now. It's time to stop killing."

"You can't quit. You're abandoning our cause."

"When I saw the newscast of the children, I knew the prophet had spoken."

Zarina raised her voice. "The prophet was a fierce warrior."

She's starting again, calm yourself. "Yes, I know, but he was also a teacher."

Zarina slid away from him. "You'll dishonor your family."

"What family, they're all dead."

"Because of you, my father will die."

"Gafar knows the right people, nothing will happen to him."

"What about my sister and my other brother?"

"Those men were after me not Musa. The rest of you are safe. You know he died because someone believed I was the one standing with you at the door."

Zarina tilted her head and stared at him.

"It was a sign, Zarina, just like the children."

A knock on the door startled them. Saleh jumped to his feet, reached for her hand and pulled her from the couch. "Go in the bedroom." He waited for her to close the bedroom door. After he looked through the peephole, he relaxed, and opened the door, blocking the entrance to the room with his body.

A hotel employee leaned on a serving cart. "Your food sir, may I bring it into your room?"

"No, I'll take it." Saleh pulled the cart into the room and closed the door.

Zarina stepped from the bedroom and followed him as he pushed it to a small circular table. He lifted a bottle of water from the tray on the cart. "I'll be back in an hour."

She grabbed his arm and glared at him. "Where are you going, you can't leave me here alone?"

He took her hand and patted it. "Don't leave the room or answer the door. I won't be long. We need to get the money out of the Swiss account before Akram takes it. The bank's not far."

On his way to the door, Saleh picked up a briefcase setting beside the wall.

Angelo and Duffy sat in chairs beside the low table in Angelo's office. He handed Duffy a sheet of paper. Colonel Aldo had told him the Fugitive Task Force and the Counterterrorist Group would find al-Filistini. Until the request from the FBI received approval, he was to spoon-feed them information. Based on Aldo's words, Angelo knew it may take a while for the paperwork to reach a Lieutenant General exercising overall control over the Regional Commanders. *Inspector Costa is working with us, what more can the American Justice Department ask?*

"Where's Costa?" Duffy asked.

"He's working with a few of my men."

"So you think this guy al-Filistini's driving a black BMW."

"That's what the neighbors said."

Duffy scanned the page. "Why would he give the lieutenant the name Halabi if he planned to run?"

"I don't know. Assuming we're right that Al Qaeda sent men to kill him, he had to get out of that apartment. When he gave us that name, he may have been thinking about talking, but reconsidered. If Provitti's friend Josef Alfano is correct, and Saleh's friends in Iran want him dead, we need to find him first... alive."

"And convince him we're the only ones who can keep him that way. Why don't I get one of our SWAT teams over here?"

Angelo raised his eyebrows. *All we need is a bunch of cowboys with guns on our streets.* "Such a proposal would need approval at the highest level of the government. You and I will retire before that happens. We'll find him." *Call your uncle, he'll fix everything.*

Mia stepped into the room carrying two demitasses of espresso and set them on the table in front of the two men. "Hello, Mr. Duffy."

"Please, Mia, call me Robert. You get more beautiful each time I see you."

He doesn't stand a chance, Angelo thought.

Mia smiled. "Thank you." She walked to the door and stopped. "Angelo, are you and Mr. Duffy going to be long?"

"No."

She nodded and stepped from the office.

Duffy sighed and raised his eyebrows.

"She's still not married," Angelo said.

"I'm not the marrying type."

Angelo shrugged. "Then you have no chance with her."

"Maybe dinner, we'll see."

Angelo laughed. *The guy is acting like Giacomo Casanova and his name doesn't even end in a vowel.* "Dinner, possibly, but you can forget dessert. So, back to our missing Palestinian. By tonight, every police officer in Italy will look for him."

Saleh returned the hotel room, set down his briefcase, and eyed the cart of untouched food. Zarina, on the couch, held the television remote and bounced between channels.

"You didn't eat?"

"The pasta isn't good. You said it wouldn't take long. Where were you? It's been two hours. Did you get the money?"

"No. It will take a day to gather that much cash and the bank in Zurich must approve the withdrawal. They said the day after tomorrow."

"Can we go for pizza?"

"Why don't you eat the food I ordered?"

"I don't like it."

Saleh felt a headache coming on, took a deep breath and shook his head. "I'll get pizza." He headed toward the door.

"Nothing from the hotel... a good one," Zarina said.

###

Saleh strolled out the double doors of the hotel and stopped to let a deliveryman, carrying three large bags of coffee, pass in front of him.

Every muscle in his body tensed at the sound of automatic rifle fire. The bags erupted, spewing dark beans across the sidewalk. The deliveryman spun and crumbled in front of him, blood seeping from the man's body. A split second later Saleh dove to the ground at the second crack of rifle fire.

Bullets ricocheted off the sidewalk, tore into the hotel door and shattered windows. Saleh's face contorted in terror as he low-crawled across pieces of glass, threw himself against the door and into the hotel lobby.

He jumped to his feet and raced past a stunned clerk and a screaming couple kneeling on the floor in front of the check-in desk. On his way up the three flights of stairs, he wiped his blood splattered hands on his shirt.

Saleh burst into the hotel suite. Crushed coffee beans clung to his pants around the rips in the fabric at his knees. "Zarina!"

She ran from the bedroom and stopped. Her eyes widened and hand covered her mouth. "What happened? You're bleeding!" She tightened her hands around his arm.

Saleh yanked his arm away, ran to the bedroom and picked up a towel from the bed. He wiped his hands and face, threw the towel on the floor and snatched open dresser drawers. With both hands he scooped up his clothes and threw them on the bed. "Pack your bag, we need to leave."

Zarina stared at him with her mouth open. "Are you bleeding? Your pants are ripped."

He grabbed his suitcase from the corner and shoved the clothes into it. "Someone tried to kill me, but it's not my blood."

"No one knows we're here!"

"Get your clothes! Akram knows."

An hour later they had avoided the police by going out the back service entrance of the hotel. They settled into a single room in a two-star hotel, near Piazza Navona and the Pantheon.

Zarina tapped her fingers on the wooden armrest of the one chair in the room and stared at Saleh sitting on the bed.

"Have you noticed anyone follow us from Milan?" he asked.

"I wasn't watching."

He understood why. She had been in a vile mood since they left Milan and dozed for most of the trip. She hadn't looked at him more than twice since they walked into the new hotel room. "You don't seem to be concerned that people are trying to kill us."

She stepped to him and took his hands. "Don't say that. I am concerned. We should call my father and ask for his help."

To him, the tragedy in the mountains meant more than a mistake. To her it was part of their quest to rid the world of infidels. *She thinks Akram and her father will again trust me. No reason to argue.* "Do you still want pizza?"

"Yes."

"What do you want on it?"

"You know what I like. While you are out, try to move the car closer to the hotel."

Saleh slipped on his shoes and headed to the door. "I'll be gone thirty minutes, stay in the room."

###

He walked out the hotel door and looked in both directions. No parking spaces were available near the entrance. Motorbikes took up more area than they needed. When he and Zarina arrived at the hotel, he had noticed a pizza restaurant at a nearby corner. He turned in that direction.

Saleh returned to the hotel room carrying a large pizza Margherita and set it on the low desk. "I bought your favorite."

Zarina, pulled the chair in front of the box. "Thank you."

"I don't understand how they could have known we came to Rome? Akram must have called all his men living in the city. We might recognize them if we pay more attention to the people around us," he said.

"What are we going to do?" she asked between bites.

He sighed and shook his head. "I don't know. We can't stay here long. I think somewhere in the country will be safer." He took a slice from the box.

"Did you move the car?"

"No." He stepped to the window overlooking the front of the hotel and pulled back the curtain. "All the parking spaces are taken. Maybe later."

"We need a plan, Saleh. There's no reason to move from hotel to hotel when we can find someplace safe. Why don't we leave Italy and go to Saudi Arabia?"

The piece of pizza in his hand stopped at his mouth. He stepped beside her and returned the wedge to the box. "Your father has been working for Al Qaeda since before your birth. He has too much to lose. I'm the last person he wants to help."

"What about me? Does what I want matter to you?"

Saleh sat on the edge of the desk. "Do you want to leave?"

"What do you mean?"

"Go back to Saudi Arabia... alone?"

Her body stiffened, and she reached out to touch his hand. "No, Saleh. My duty is to stay with you."

He kissed her on the cheek and grabbed the slice of pizza. *Finally she's being reasonable.*

They passed time watching television. Saleh looked out the window every thirty minutes checking for an empty slot to park his car. At half past ten, he saw a vacant space. He grabbed his keys. "There's an open spot to park, I'll move the car." He left the room and scurried down three flights of stairs. As he stepped out of the hotel, he paused and looked in both directions. A man sat in a chair, and talked on a phone, near a doorway fifty feet down the street. He watched him for a full minute, but the guy didn't look in his direction.

The tension in Saleh's body ebbed away, and he headed up the street past the motorbikes. When he reached the scooter at the end of the line, he heard a loud pop and saw smoke flow from the plastic travel box on the back of the bike. A fiery hole grew in the side of the box.

Saleh's muscles tensed, and his heart fluttered, as an icy chill ran down his spine He had seen it happen many times. A defective or damp blasting cap or detonator failed to set off the explosive and caused it to catch fire. The sound of a metal chair clanging against concrete made him turn. The man who had been on the cell phone, ran down the street and disappeared around a corner.

With short backward steps, he eased away from the bike keeping his eyes on the flames shooting from the hole in the travel box. He spun around and bolted to the hotel door.

XI
THE SUMMER HOUSE

Saleh and Zarina took less than an hour to leave the hotel and reach the SS-5 roadway, snaking its way toward the mountains near Tivoli, east of Rome.

Zarina focused on the dark road stretching out ahead of the BMW. "Where are we going?"

Saleh ignored her.

"How can we stay in Italy? We need to go to Riyadh."

Saleh turned and looked at her. "You are wasting your time, Zarina. Forget about Riyadh, forget about your father. Akram, and your father's friends, would like nothing more than to see me dead." He clamped his teeth together and took a deep breath through his nose.

"Even if his best friend asked, my father wouldn't hurt my husband."

The car rounded a curve and Saleh stiffened when he spotted the blue flashing lights of a police car at the side of the road. He glanced at Zarina.

They passed a traffic officer examining a parked motorcycle. As they went by, Saleh looked in the rear view mirror and held his breath when he saw the officer looking in their direction.

"Is he coming?" Zarina asked.

"No."

She focused out the windshield and pointed to a white and black street sign. "The town of Tivoli Terme is five kilometers." She turned and snapped at him. "This is the way to Musa's summer house."

"No one will think we went there."

In the rear view mirror, Saleh glimpsed flashing lights. "The police are behind us."

Zarina's eyes widened, and she glanced out the rear window.

When the officer's patrol car pulled behind them, Saleh slowed and waved for him to pass. High beam headlights flashed twice, illuminating the interior of the BMW.

The options Saleh had available raced through his mind. *I can't keep going. He'll use his radio.* He thought of no reason the officer should recognize him or the car. The Italian authorities would want to talk with him after he mentioned the name Halabi, but he didn't think they would pass the information to the local police. *What does he want?*

Saleh removed a Browning High Power semiautomatic pistol from the center console and transferred it to his left hand beside the door. He pulled to the side of road, stopped, and lowered his window.

The police officer approached the side of the car. "Good evening. The rear light on the left side of your car is not working."

"Sorry, I didn't notice."

The officer squinted and nodded. "Are you British?"

"Yes."

"This car has an Italian license plate."

"It belongs to a company owned by a friend."

"Is he Italian?"

"Yes."

The officer leaned to the window, looked at Zarina and nodded. "Good evening," he said, and looked back at Saleh. "May I see your identity documents?"

Saleh pointed at the glove-box. "Get our passports." He kept his left hand against the side of the door and turned to the officer. "Would you rather see my license?"

"No, those will suffice." He examined the two United Kingdom passports, scanning the entry and exit stamps of various countries. Leaning over he pointed at Zarina "And Zarina is your wife?"

"Yes."

"You both travel to the Middle East often."

"Business... imports to Italy, and to visit friends."

The officer handed him the passports. "Please repair the light tomorrow, Mr. Harrington."

"I will."

"Drive carefully, good night."

Saleh watched him walk to his car as he turned the BMW back onto the road and drove away.

Zarina exhaled. "I thought we would have to kill him."

Saleh's eyes lingered on her. *Too many years helping her father... no qualms about killing people.* "Why take the life of an innocent man?"

Zarina ignored his question.

Saleh stopped the car near the front door of a weathered stone house built on a deserted hillside. The headlights illuminated a dead plant in a clay pot beside the entrance. He left the lights on and they walked to the pot. Saleh shoved dirt aside, removed a plastic bag with a key in it and unlocked the door.

Zarina stepped inside the foyer, turned on the lights and set her handbag on the floor. She looked at drop cloths covering the furnishings.

"Uncover everything. I'll get the bags," Saleh said.

He returned with two suitcases, and the briefcase, and shook his head when he noticed Zarina, still standing in the foyer staring into the house. "Why are you doing nothing to help us?"

"I hate this place. Musa said he wanted to sell it."

He moved past her and entered the living room. "It's safe here, and you can cook what you want. I'll go to a market tomorrow."

Zarina slid beside him and took his hand. "Why are you doing this?"

"Have you listened to a single word I've said?" He raised his hands. "If you don't know by now, you'll never understand!"

"We worked so hard."

Saleh berated himself for not remaining calm. "I can no longer fight for Islam if it means killing more Muslims, especially children. How many lives and families are we to destroy in our lifetime?"

She stepped back and glared at him. "It's not only Muslims that die."

"How many must? A hundred times more than Jews or Christians?"

"We can't hide forever."

He reached out, held her shoulders and steadied his voice. "The Italians may help us."

Zarina shoved him. "Are you out of your mind? The Italians will kill us because of what happened to the children." She strode from the room.

XII
FIND HIM

Gafar and Akram sipped tea in the small office in Tehran.

"I don't think he's given the Italian authorities any information. Maybe he wants to go his own way," Gafar said.

"I told him we wouldn't allow it. My men tried to kill him at the hotel but Sky News reported that the Mafia killed someone. I think they were told what to say, it wasn't him."

Gafar took a deep breath. "Your men must be more cautious. There will be consequences if we keep killing people in Italy."

Akram tightened his jaw. "Do not question my resolve. I've spent many hours on the phone talking to our friends who know him. We'll find out where they moved."

Gafar didn't back down. He glanced at his fingers tapping against his knee and looked at Akram. "I didn't question your resolve. Your plans may open the eyes of the Italian government. How many more of their citizens will die before he's killed?"

"You're naive. We will kill as many as it takes to save ourselves."

Gafar leaned over the table. "The decision is yours. Kill as many as you want but remember what I said about my daughter. Tell your men to be very careful before they shoot."

###

Al and Josef alternated paying the bill for their biweekly outings in downtown Rome. A year earlier Al proposed they meet away from the office to discuss anything they didn't want put on paper or being recorded. They also used the time to discuss the tribulations of life with teenage children.

Today's meeting, four days since the last, was out of the ordinary. Al had received printouts of intercepted communications, and that morning sent them to Josef's office.

They walked to a table at a sidewalk café not far from 'il Vittoriano', the monument to Victor Emmanuel II, hated by most Romans. Al knew Josef picked the spot because he loved the view of the magnificent white marble structure and its matching bronze statues of the goddess Victoria in chariots drawn by four horses, high atop the building.

"Coffee?" Josef asked.

"Yeah."

A young waitress stepped to the table and Al stared at the tattoo on her neck, two inches below her ear.

"Two coffees," Josef said.

The girl spun and hurried into the café.

Al shook his head. "Why would a girl have an ancient insignia of Rome tattooed there?"

Josef smiled. "S.P.Q.R., The Senate and the Roman people. She must study political science at the University of Rome."

Al rolled his eyes. "Kids. You read the Tehran telephone transcripts I sent you?"

Josef nodded and raised his eyebrows. "Yes, interesting. I've been tracking down the Italian numbers called."

"We both need to make sure the information doesn't get into the hands of law enforcement authorities too soon," Al said. "If they pick up people, the calls will stop."

Josef nodded. "I know you won't share it and neither will I. I didn't think they'd be this careless."

"If we wait long enough, and they continue to bullshit with each other, we'll have a list of their entire organization in Italy."

"When that time comes, people will scream." Josef raised his eyebrows. "A few of the numbers are attached to important names with good reputations."

Ms. SPQR slid two espressos on the table and dropped four packets of sugar. "Something to eat?"

Al handed her two Euros. "No thank you."

"Call if you want anything." She walked to the café door.

Once she was out of earshot, Josef leaned over the table. "Have you heard anything from..."

Al's phone rang. He raised a finger and answered it. "Hello... right now?" He glanced at Josef, pursed his lips, and continued his conversation. "Cause a commotion... keep him occupied." He began to turn toward the street but stopped. "Okay, when we leave, we'll take a look." He ended the call.

"What was that about?"

Al raised his hand. "Don't react. Someone followed us. We're being watched."

"How do you know?"

"Two of my agents have been keeping an eye on me."

"What do you want to do?"

Al grinned. "Finish our coffee, get in your car and drive away."

"They'll follow us."

"It's one man. He won't be able to follow. My people will take care of him."

"Where is he?"

"Across the street... in front of the news stand. When we walk to your car, we should be able to see him." Al rubbed his temple. "They'll keep him busy, but it would be great if you can have someone pick him up?"

"What do your men look like?"

"One is female... long blond hair and easy to pick out in a crowd."

"I'll call from inside." Josef marched into the café.

Al downed his coffee and tapped his fingers on the table while he waited for him to return. He knew the chances of the man being connected with the Halabi case were slim but not impossible. *Love to pick all that information from his brain.*

Josef approached the table and sat. "Two Carabinieri are a block away. They'll handle it."

Celeste Starr pushed her almost white blond hair over her shoulder and slipped her hand under her partner's arm. She and Brice Knox enjoyed keeping an eye on their Station Chief boss. *This is more exciting than being stuck in the office. Walk around and act like tourist.*

Brice unfolded a street map and walked a crooked path along the sidewalk. She remained at his side, holding his arm, and watching a short Arab beside a newsstand.

With his face buried in the map, Brice stumbled into a motorbike, knocking it off the stand. "Damn, my knee," he grabbed his leg and plopped on the overturned bike.

She leaned over him and slid a thin blade into the front tire. "Are you hurt?"

The Middle Eastern man ran to the motorbike and tried to lift it. Brice did not move as the man attempted to pull him off the bike.

"Move, that's my bike, I must leave."

Celeste seized his shirt and slung him aside. "Stop hitting him, he's hurt!"

Two Carabinieri, strolled toward the commotion.

Brice stood. The man pushed him and yelled. "Get out of my way."

The taller Carabiniere confronted him. "Leave that man alone." His deep voice startled people nearby, and they moved aside. He turned to Celeste.

"My name is Vincenzo. Is there a problem?"

"He assaulted my husband and shoved him into the motorbike. I heard him speak English," Celeste said.

Vincenzo glared at the man. "Why did you push him? These tourists are guests in my country."

The man replied in Arabic.

Vincenzo turned to his partner. "What did he say, Paolo?"

"I think it was no."

"No!" He glared at the man. "You think we're stupid? I saw you push him."

Again, the man muttered in Arabic.

"That time he said yes." Paolo said. "He confessed. If he has proper immigrant papers, I'll buy you dinner."

Vincenzo stepped close to the defiant Arab. "Give me your identification documents."

More Arabic mumbling.

Paolo smiled. "No, again. He said you're stupid."

Vincenzo spun the man around and clamped handcuffs to his wrist. "I think you better come with us." He held the short chain between the cuffs, looked at Celeste, and grinned. "I am sorry this happened while you are visiting my beautiful country."

She smiled and handed him a business card. "Thank you Vincenzo. We're staying at the Palace Royal Hotel, near the Spanish Steps."

Paolo nodded. "If we need more information someone will call. Enjoy your vacation in our Eternal City."

Josef pulled his Alfa Romeo into the stream of heavy traffic.

Al fidgeted with his seatbelt as both men fought to control their laughter.

"I almost laughed on our way to the car. The guy didn't know it was all a setup." Josef said.

"Laugh, I came close to pissing my pants."

Josef furrowed his brow and attempted to stop his smile. "Let's plan to go out for coffee again tomorrow."

"Stop it, please."

"You want to talk to him," Josef asked.

"Hell yes. If someone in Al Qaeda sent him, he may be loaded with information."

Josef grabbed his cell phone. "I'll find out where they're taking him."

XIII
IT'S OUR DUTY

Saleh and Zarina ate dinner at the dining room table.

Zarina pushed her food around her plate and took a deep breath. "How long will we stay here?"

Saleh stared at her and paused before he spoke. "Are you worried about our future?"

"This isn't the way we should live. I want things to be like they were."

"Before what? Before the children died, and the prophet sent me a message? Or before I told Akram I am finished killing for him?"

"Before all of it!"

"Please try to understand," he said setting his fork on his plate. "What I did was wrong. Nothing can be the same after my plan failed and killed those Muslim children."

Zarina threw her head back and locked her icy gaze on his eyes. "Muslims have struggled for centuries... why do you say it's wrong?"

"Tell me, Zarina. Why have we struggled for so long?"

"To bring Islam to the world."

Saleh nodded. "It's our duty, just as it's the duty of every religion to spread the word of their faith."

Zarina raised her eyebrows and smiled. "Then how can you say it's wrong?"

"It isn't wrong. Each day Muslims, Christians and Jews work hard to gather more followers."

"Saleh, you're making no sense."

He knew he could control the conversation. *She is smart, but a follower and thick headed.* He shook his head. "That's because you haven't heard what I've been saying." He reached to take her hand, but she slid it to her lap. "I watched those children die."

Her gaze bounced around the room and she pounded her small fist on the table. "It was an accident. Why can't you accept that?"

"No, it was a sign."

"What sign?" she yelled.

Finally. Once she became emotional, he could lead her around in circles by answering her question with a question. "How many people will follow Islam by force?"

"I don't know."

"How many of our Muslim brothers should we kill because they are not fundamentalist and follow the prophet's cousin?"

Zarina raised her voice. "I don't know." Tears formed.

"Would it be better to train children to be doctors... or Martyrs?"

"I don't know, Saleh!"

He slammed his hand on the table startling her. "Don't you understand? We kill people... then demand that those we allow to live respect us and honor our teachings. Is that the way to bring people to accept Islam?"

Zarina shoved her chair away from the table with such force it fell. "They must convert!"

Akram's cell phone sat on the table in front of him. He planted his elbows near it and listened to Gafar on the speaker.

"What is being done?" Gafar asked.

"Two men have crossed into Italy."

"Are they going to the house?"

Akram hesitated and looked at the ceiling. "Yes. First, they'll go to a garage we rented in a nearby town. A car and weapons are there. I told them to take whatever time is necessary."

"Did you explain to them that my daughter is with him?"

Akram shook his head. Their leaders didn't care about Gafar's daughter and neither did he. Saleh needed to die before he talked. *No reason to tell this Saudi my men plan to blow up the house.* "Yes, I did."

"Their lives depend on her not being hurt." Gafar said.

Angelo sat next to Joe in straight back chairs in front of Colonel Giuseppe Aldo's desk. He had warned his American partner before they arrived that the colonel was not in a good mood. Neither man moved nor diverted their eyes from their boss.

Aldo stared at them for a full fifteen seconds without blinking. "I like you Inspector Costa, your work has impressed me." His eyes moved to Angelo. "I gave you the job of organizing and running the Fugitive Task Force because of your skills and tenacity. I did not bring both of you here to threaten you, only to... as the American's say, light small fires under your asses." His eyes paused for a moment on each man. "How did he register in a hotel, in the middle of central Rome, without us knowing about it?"

"He and his wife registered with British passports," Angelo said.

Aldo looked around his office shaking his head. "This is not America, Angelo. People don't shoot automatic weapons on the streets of our cities."

"Yes, sir."

Aldo placed both arms on the desk and leaned forward. "You and Inspector Costa will be busy and lose a lot of sleep. I don't care what it takes. Find him before someone else dies."

"One of our agents will get lucky, sir." The moment the words came out of Angelo's mouth he realized his mistake.

Aldo glared at him. "Luck better have nothing to do with it, Captain Randi. Take him into custody before his Al Qaeda friends kill him."

Joe sat forward in his chair. "We now have three names he uses and a complete description of the car, including the tag number."

Aldo looked at Joe and raised his eyebrows. "I suggest you and Angelo go to church tonight and pray he doesn't have more names on different passports, or a second car."

"We'll find him, sir," Angelo said. "When we do, we have plans to make sure no one can get to him."

"First you need to get your hands on him. Both of you may want to light a candle before you pray. What can I do to help?" Aldo asked.

"We want to ask Witness Security in America for help. A request from someone with a little more influence than Angelo and me would get a quicker response," Joe said.

Aldo grinned. "I have the name of just the man. Now get to work."

Both men walked out and Joe cornered Angelo in the hallway outside the colonel's office. "I haven't been that uncomfortable in years."

Angelo took a deep breath and exhaled. "That was nothing. You should see him when he's angry."

Joe smiled. "Pick a nearby church and we'll go there now."

###

Ahmed and his brother Jafar each carried an RPG 7 rocket-propelled grenade launcher as they snaked their way down the hillside behind Musa's country villa. Both men wore tan clothing to blend in with the color of the ground on the hillside. They crouched and moved through the moonlit night seeking the best concealment in the trees and brush.

It had taken them less than twenty four hours to get into Italy, pick up the weapons and a car at a garage outside Rome.

When they reached a point fifty meters from the house. Ahmed raised his arm to stop Jafar. "Here, we're close enough. We'll wait until after midnight, they'll both be asleep." He raised a pair of binoculars.

Saleh leaned back on the couch and removed two British and two German passports from the briefcase, He looked at the photo on each document and stared at the floor. *How did they find us in Rome? Akram knows the car. That's it, the car.* He looked up and saw Zarina standing in the bedroom doorway watching him. "I think I know how they found us."

"What do you mean?"

"After I spoke with Akram, he must have had someone put a tracking device on the BMW. All he would need to do is turn on his computer and it would show our location. We may need to leave here, but we're safe for tonight. I'll check the car in the morning."

Zarina walked across the room. "Do you believe he would do that?"

"Yes. We're a threat to him, and his followers."

"Why don't you check it now?"

"No. There's not enough light."

"It's late, Saleh. Are you going to sleep tonight?"

He threw the passports into the briefcase and closed it.

"Will you change your mind and contact my father?"

"I want us to be free of all this. Calling your father isn't the answer."

"It's been our life for many years. We were happy."

At times during their marriage, Zarina played the part of a helpless wife to get her way. It may work with a stranger, but Saleh had seen her ploy too many times.

"Yes, but think. What life have we had? Going out to enjoy ourselves, without being cautious, is out of the question. Wouldn't you be happier with friends who did not look over their shoulders each time they go shopping?"

"It's always been this way. We've sacrificed our lives for our cause."

Saleh stood and pulled her to him. "It's time to think of ourselves and our future, not our past life." He looked into her eyes and thought about the many years of happiness they had shared. *I should have made this decision a long time ago.* "Come, we'll go to bed and talk about..."

An explosion ripped open a wall. The force of the blast, knocked them to the floor and filled the room with smoke, dust, and debris.

"Saleh!" Zarina screamed.

He looked toward the sound of her voice and saw his briefcase through the haze. He crawled toward it and saw Zarina, in a fetal position against the wall, her hands clamped over her ears. Saleh grabbed the briefcase and dragged it to her side. "Get up! We need to get out of this room." He pulled her to her feet and shoved her through the bedroom door just as a second explosion brought down a section of the ceiling and knocked them to the floor beside the bed.

XIV
DECISION TIME

Early the next morning, Saleh sat at the kitchen table and watched firefighters scurry from the section of the house destroyed by the explosions.

He looked at Zarina and saw a tear slide down her cheek. *If I'd stayed in Milan and waited for the police to check the name Halabi, I'd have more bargaining power. Why was I so stupid?* His eyes came to rest on the set of handcuffs attached to Zarina's right wrist and the chair. A handcuff, locked in the same fashion as hers, kept him from raising his left hand above waist level.

A police officer, with a red cross on his sleeve, bandaged minor cuts on their arms.

Saleh glanced at the huge officer guarding them from a position near the door and watched as a sergeant stepped into the room.

"Who are your important friends?" the sergeant asked.

Saleh glanced at his wife and turned to him. "What important friends?"

"The people who are keeping you out of jail."

Saleh shrugged. "I have no friends with that power."

The sergeant rolled his eyes. "Sure you don't. No one ever admits they have political connections." He shook his head on the way out of the room.

Zarina looked at Saleh and raised her eyebrows. "What did he mean?"

He focused on the center of the table. The only person he knew with political friends in Italy was Akram. The thought of the old man's reach, all the way from Iran, terrified him. A whisper into someone's ear and a thousand Euros in their pocket was all it would take. "If he meant Akram, we'll be dead before tomorrow night."

Three men in expensive looking suits walked into the room. Saleh's eyes locked on them. *Local police officers don't wear tailored suits. Who are they?*

The one with black hair and a goatee walked up and stood in front of him. "Should I call you Saleh al-Filistini or Mohammad Halabi?"

Saleh took a second before he replied. "al-Filistini."

"May I call you Saleh?"

Saleh nodded.

The man turned to Zarina and stared at her for a full five seconds. "And you, madam, are Zarina al-Ansari from Riyadh, Saudi Arabia?"

Her eyes widened, moved to Saleh and then back to the man. "Yes."

"May I call you Zarina?"

"Yes."

"I am Carabinieri Captain Angelo Randi." He had decided to keep everything as formal as possible for the time being and motioned to the young man beside him. "This is Inspector Gino Palma of the Italian State Police." He pointed to the third man. "Inspector Joe Costa from America's U.S. Marshals Service." He looked from Zarina to Saleh and paused. "Both of you are lucky, and Akram's men are incompetent."

Saleh hid his surprise by biting the inside of his cheek and saw Zarina stiffen. "I don't know anyone named Akram."

Angelo's eyes lingered on him and he smiled. "We did not come here to lie to you. A man in Rome told us a different story. He said you worked for Akram and were once good friends." He turned to Zarina. "Is that true Zarina?"

Saleh held his breath. *These men are not fools.* He glanced at Inspector Costa. *Why is an American here?* "My wife knows nothing of this."

"I doubt that," Angelo said. "We will discuss her future later. We came here today to spend only a short time with you. In the next few minutes, you will make a single decision."

"What if I'm unable?" Saleh asked.

"It should not be a problem, it's simple."

Saleh looked into Zarina's terror stricken eyes before turning to Angelo. "I may need to speak with my wife before I can give you an answer."

"Discussing it will not be necessary."

Saleh took his time digesting everything Angelo had said. His life was about to change but he couldn't be sure if it would be for the better.

Angelo leaned toward him. "Shall we meet tomorrow to discuss your future, or should I tell the officers outside to find you both accommodations in separate prisons?"

Zarina's body tensed. Her free hand clutched Saleh's arm, her eyes filled with tears, and focused on his face.

He looked at her small hand and covered it with his to calm her. "Are you saying you will not take us to jail?"

Angelo nodded. "Not today... and maybe not tomorrow. You will make that decision for me."

Saleh felt Zarina's hand squeeze his arm. "And after that?"

"Your future decisions determine what I will do. For now, you must decide on jail or limited freedom in comfortable surroundings."

"Where will you take us?" Zarina asked.

"You'll go to a house with my men."

Saleh glanced at Zarina and looked back at Angelo. "Where?"

"The location doesn't matter. It's a house where you'll be safe."

Saleh tilted his head and pressed his lips together. "Can we discuss..."

Angelo raised a hand to stop him. "I need your answer. Now."

Saleh rubbed his chin and stared at Angelo. "We'll go to the house. I think you and I have much more to discuss."

Angelo turned to the officer standing in the doorway. "Remove their handcuffs."

###

Early the next morning, Joe walked into his office at the U. S. Embassy and nodded to Gino Palma, leaning against the couch armrest. "Hi Gino."

A large plaque of a United States Marshals badge hung on the wall, and a carved wooden nameplate on the desk identified Joe Costa, Inspector, United States Marshals Service.

Joe took a seat in front of Gino. "Angelo's on his way."

"From what I've seen, Angelo's tough," Gino said. "I wouldn't want to make him my enemy, but al-Filistini may think he's important enough to push him around."

Joe grinned. "Behind his back we call him 'the bull', but I wouldn't say that to his face. He can handle Saleh. He'll play the guy like a church organ."

They heard a knock on the door and Angelo, in a Carabinieri uniform, entered.

"Good morning," Joe said.

Angelo nodded. "Gino... Joe."

Angelo sat beside Gino. "A few minutes ago I verified your government approved our request for assistance. Soon we'll see if your Witness Security Division will help us hide al-Filistini. Gino will handle the case in our Program."

"Who did you meet with?" Joe asked.

"The Deputy Chief of Mission and Al Provitti. The ambassador received the approval message an hour ago. Al said the intelligence community supported the request one hundred percent." He smiled. "Colonel Aldo agreed with our plan with one exception. He wants you to handle the American side of the case and not someone new from Witness Security. He wants no one else around Saleh and said your ten years' experience working the program is sufficient."

Joe pondered Angelo's words and was about to speak when he continued.

"The intelligence services realize Saleh is loaded with information and they want to get it. Everyone agreed he will be more comfortable in America, and much more willing to talk if he isn't locked down in an Italian safe house."

Joe shook his head. "There's one big problem. WITSEC is protective of their business. They won't welcome an outsider, even one with my experience, back into the fold as a part time Witness Security Specialist. They may not go along with it."

Angelo grinned. "Aldo made it clear. If they don't agree to let you handle the case, there will be no American involvement. He doesn't trust many people; you're one of the few."

Joe raised his eyebrows. "He told me he did, but I thought he was blowing smoke up my ass. I guess he was serious. I still need to contact my boss and have him speak to someone at the Justice Department."

Angelo laughed. "You're not listening to what I'm saying, Joe. Colonel Giuseppe Aldo gets what he wants. It will happen. You're supposed to get a call by five this afternoon."

Joe shook his head. *How powerful can Aldo be?* "The chief of WITSEC will be mad as hell."

"Maybe, but he'll hide it and walk around his headquarters with a smile on his face. The Minister of Foreign Affairs already called your Secretary of State."

Joe avoided the petty politics that worked their way down the ladder in every organization administered by a political appointee. *If Aldo made this happen at that level of our government, I won't have to worry about anyone screwing with me.*

Gino scooted to the edge of the couch. "When do you want us to explain our programs to him and his wife?" he asked Angelo.

"Today."

Joe nodded. "We'll need a few hours. Did you tell him it's voluntary?"

"Not yet. I don't think there will be a problem."

Joe shook his head. "He may refuse the program."

Angelo grinned and raised his eyebrows. "When I finish telling him about the prison he's going to, he'll agree. I've never taken you to visit any on them. Before this thing is over, I'll get you a private tour of San Vittore in Milan... built in 1880, and the Poggioreale in Naples... built in 1905."

"They still use them?"

Angelo nodded. "They've made a few upgrades but they're nothing like your country club penitentiaries."

XV
THE RATS OF POGGIOREALE

Saleh and Zarina sat close to each other on a love seat in a one-bedroom apartment with no windows and a solid metal entry door. He peered around the living room and stopped on the telephone on the end table next to him. *No numbers to dial... why is it here?*

They had arrived yesterday in a blacked out van and were blindfolded before they walked to the apartment. Once inside and free of the blindfolds, he saw the surprise on Zarina's face. It wasn't the worst place they'd stayed.

He and Zarina had taken their time and walked through each room. The bedroom had separate beds, the living room spacious, and the kitchen well stocked with dishes, pans and food. Two things bothered him. *There's no windows to look out, and I can't hear any sounds from beyond the walls.*

Zarina clutched her handbag and pulled it closer to her side. "This isn't a house."

Saleh nodded. "Whatever it is, it's secure."

"What do they want with..."

The telephone rang.

Saleh looked at her as he lifted the handset. "Yes." He whispered Angelo's name. "Yes, we are." He hung up the phone.

Both looked at the metal door when they heard a deadbolt turn.

Angelo stepped into the room and motioned to a chair. "May I?"

Saleh nodded. "Please."

He moved it closer to them, took a seat, and looked at Zarina. "You have a cell phone that does not work?"

"Yes." She removed a phone from her purse and handed it to him. "After my brother's murder, my husband told me to throw away the SIM card. I went to the bathroom and flushed it down the toilet."

Angelo slid open the back, examined the empty SIM card slot and returned the phone to Zarina. "Did you sleep well," he asked.

"No." Saleh said.

Angelo shrugged. "No view but it's much nicer than the Poggioreale Prison in Naples. For many years we tried to clean that place up, but the rats have been there longer than the Italian government."

Zarina glared at Saleh.

"These accommodations are comfortable," Saleh said.

Angelo smiled. "Good. Today you will need to make another decision about your future."

Saleh stared at the Carabinieri captain and pondered. Somehow, he needed to gain more control by bargaining with them. *They want information from me, but I want things from them.*

"If you and your wife wish to stay alive you will need the help of my government, and the government of the United States."

Zarina repositioned herself and crossed her arms. "What can the Americans do for us?"

"Along with Italy, provide for your safety. You should feel secure knowing two great countries will use their resources to make sure you continue to breathe fresh air. Your own people are trying to kill you. You know that don't you?"

Her jaw tightened, and she glared at Angelo. "What will you ask of us?"

"For now, Zarina, your responsibility is your husband's welfare, nothing more."

"And me?" Saleh asked.

"We want every piece of information you have in your head. You must agree to truthfully answer the questions of those we bring to interview you."

"Who?" he asked.

"A.I.S.E., the CIA and law enforcement."

Zarina's shoulders drooped. Saleh touched his temple and closed his eyes for a moment He opened them and stared at Angelo. "If we do what you ask, we'll be dead the next day."

"If we wanted you dead, you would be cell-mates with the rats in Naples."

Saleh took a deep breath and shook his head. "No one can insure our safety."

"The people who will help you are professionals. They can make you disappear and reappear as a married couple any place on earth." Angelo clasped his fingers together and studied his two captives for a few seconds. "Shall we begin so I can make the appropriate arrangements, or would you like me to arrange transportation for you to Naples?"

Saleh pursed his lips. *This won't be easy.* He looked at Zarina, tilted his head, and turned to Angelo. "I need to speak with my wife."

Angelo stood and nodded. "If you agree, lift the telephone. Someone will answer and I will send in Inspector Palma and Inspector Costa to explain the arrangements. Please don't take long to decide." He crossed the room, pulled open the heavy door, and stepped out. The deadbolt snapped into place with a loud clank.

Zarina's hands trembled. "You can't do this. I don't trust them."

"What choice do we have?"

"They're asking you to betray our cause, our families."

Saleh took her hand. "If we go to prison, it will take Akram one day to have us killed. We need to listen to what they propose and decide what is best for us under these circumstances."

###

Joe and Gino sat in a room outside the secure apartment and watched Angelo pace the floor.

"Think he'll take the deal?" Joe asked.

Angelo stopped and smiled. "When I told him about the large rodents at the Poggioreale his wife didn't look happy. I thought she would vomit on the floor." He shrugged. "Naples has a problem with the garbage collector's union. It wouldn't surprise me if the rats paid union dues."

"That's the place you want me to visit?" Joe asked.

"It's one of the oldest prisons in Italy. The capacity is fourteen hundred, but in the past year the population rose to two thousand nine hundred. Most of the prisoners are locked in their cells for twenty-two hours a day."

Angelo's playing hardball, Joe thought. If that prison was any sign of what Saleh and his wife faced, he didn't doubt they'd agree. "I guess he..." His cell phone beeped, and he looked at the text message. "The Witness Security Division accepted the case. We leave in three days from Sicily."

Angelo smirked. "Talk to him. Make sure he accepts our offer. I'm going for coffee." He stopped at the door and looked at Joe. "I'm glad we have time to plan before we leave. Can you be in my office tomorrow afternoon at four?"

"Sure, is anything wrong?"

"No. A new development... slight change in our organizational structure."

Joe watched the door close and turned to Gino. "You'll be mad when you hear this." He continued reading the text message. "Approved, date and time follows. You and Captain Randi depart, on a C-141, out of Sigonella Naval Air Station in Sicily. Destination, MacDill Air Force Base, Tampa, Florida."

Gino stiffened in his chair. "What about me?"

"It's not all bad." Joe said and continued. "Inspector Palma will be the primary contact person in Italy. Arrangements will be made for his arrival at Marshals Service headquarters next month."

"A trip to Florida would have been better, but at least I'll get to see Washington," Gino said smiling. "Let's talk to them."

Saleh raced across the room to answer the ringing telephone. "Yes... Please come in."

Gino led Joe into the apartment. Both men held briefcases.

"Mr. al-Filistini, we met. I'm Inspector Gino Palma, and this is Inspector Joe Costa. We are both Witness Security Specialists. Inspector Costa works for the American Department of Justice."

"Here in Italy?" Zarina asked.

Joe nodded. "Yes."

"We're here to answer your questions. If you agree to the terms of our programs, both of you are required to sign the documents." Gino said. "Shall we sit?"

Saleh pointed at a round table and four chairs near the kitchen.

Both Gino and Joe removed thick folders from their briefcases and dropped them on the table. Everyone took a seat.

"Before we talk about protection and services, there are things you should know," Gino said.

"Our programs are voluntary, both of you must agree to the rules," Joe said. "It is critical both of you understand that if you violate these rules you will be terminated from the programs, and protection will stop."

Saleh raised his eyebrows. "Terminated?"

Gino smiled. "It means removed from the program and nothing more."

"If my wife doesn't agree, can she return to Saudi Arabia?"

Gino shook his head. "That's not an option. We'll arrange for her to be moved to a jail and held to face charges in an Italian court."

Saleh glanced at Zarina. As far as he knew, they couldn't charge Zarina with anything. "What charges?"

"Suspicion of terror association and subversion. Ask Captain Randi for the details, he has photos that may explain our decision," Gino said.

Zarina's shoulders slumped forward. "Will I ever see my family again?"

"No." Gino said.

She shook her head and stared at the ceiling. Tears rolled down her cheeks.

Saleh took his wife's hand. "I have money in a bank account."

Joe raised his head. "Where?"

Saleh hesitated. *They'll take it... no, they don't know the name.* "Zurich."

"How much?" Gino asked.

"Almost a million Euros."

Neither of the investigators reacted. "Ask Angelo. He has friends who can help you securely transfer the money," Gino said.

Saleh glanced at Zarina's trembling hands on her lap.

"Will I have to testify?" he asked Joe.

"That's up to government officials in America and Italy. The aspects of your criminal case are not the concern of witness security."

"Our role is to keep you alive, move you to a safe place, establish your new identity, and help you assimilate into a community." Gino said. "Testimony is not a requirement for protection. Let's begin."

Saleh noticed Zarina looking around the room. "Is something wrong?"

Zarina paused and stared at him with her mouth open. "No. We must do as they ask." She nodded to Gino. "Continue."

"The first thing we'll discuss is your need to follow our instructions and abide by the rules we will explain to you." Joe said. "Without your complete cooperation, we cannot keep you alive."

Three hours later, Gino, Joe, and Angelo, in a room outside the apartment, leafed through papers scattered across the table.

"Good," Angelo said.

"Everything is arranged. Witness Security in Italy and the U.S. will make all the decisions," Joe said.

"How many people will know where they are living," Angelo asked.

"Besides us; Aldo, the Chief of WITSEC, and one Case Analyst. Gino shouldn't need to bring in anyone else unless they're moved back to Italy." Joe grinned. "I guess the three of us make the decisions."

Angelo squinted and furrowed his brow. "There's one thing that's bothering me. So far, his friends haven't had a difficult time finding him. They tried to kill him twice in Rome and once at the villa. He's lucky to be alive."

Gino smiled. "It's like he has a GPS implanted in his ass."

XVI
YOU NEED HELP

The next day, Joe walked into Angelo's outer office at five minutes to four and stopped. *What does he have up his sleeve?* He had hoped he would run into Mia, but her chair was empty. The door to Angelo's office stood open. "Angelo?"

"Come in."

Angelo met him halfway across the room, pointed at the chairs near the low table, and both sat. "You need to go back to the embassy today?"

"No. Why all the secrecy?"

Angelo took a deep breath. "I consider you a close friend. We've worked together for ten months and I think of you a member of my family. My wife and Mia both like you."

Joe leaned back and stared at his partner. "Okay. What did I do wrong?"

"Nothing. We've built a great organization together, and we arrested some of Italy's most wanted fugitives."

Angelo doesn't beat around the bush, something's up, and it's important to him. Joe couldn't remember the last time Angelo made such a request. Clearing his late afternoon schedule wasn't surprising, but a little out of the ordinary. Whatever it was, Joe wanted it settled, now.

"Come on, Angelo, I know that. Why are you stalling? Something happened and I want to know about it."

Mia called through the doorway that she had returned.

Angelo raised his voice. "Thank you, Mia." He leaned toward Joe. "You can tell I've been delaying?"

"Of course I can. It's not like you. Get to the point. I can take it."

"Okay. I've decided to bring in another person."

Joe shook his head. *It makes little sense.* Law enforcement agencies in the States didn't like to share information, but the Italians were notorious for interagency rivalry and case secrecy. *Got to be someone from within the Carabinieri.* "This is crazy. You and I have done everything together with no one's help for almost a year... why now? Aren't you satisfied with the job I'm doing?"

"Yes, I'm satisfied. No one could do it better. If your government tries to transfer you back to America, I'll fight them."

"Come on, Angelo. Why the hell do we need help?"

Angelo sighed and filled his lungs. "Well, we don't need help, you do."

"Me! I'm the guy who drew up the organizational structure and presented the plan to Colonel Aldo."

"I know, and Aldo said if he has anything to do with it, you'll spend the rest of your career here in Italy." He called to the open door. "Mia, bring us coffee."

Joe's muscles tensed. "We're leaving for Sicily tomorrow. I don't know if I have enough time to make arrangements for another person on the plane."

"Everything will fall into place. It won't be a problem," Angelo said.

"Listen, it takes time to build trust." Joe shook his head. "You can't just bring someone in. It will take months to learn our procedures and be accepted by the guys working the streets. I don't like this... I'm doing fine and everything is going..."

Angelo held up his hand to stop him. "Please Joe. Soon you'll be doing better."

"Better than what? There's nothing wrong with me."

Mia walked through the doorway empty handed and Angelo stood.

Joe looked at him as if he were crazy. *What the hell is he doing? Since when does he stand for Mia?*

Joe followed suit.

A tall young woman in form-fitting black low cut jeans, red heels and a red silk blouse stepped into the office carrying a tray with four espresso cups. Joe's mouth dropped open. Her long brown hair flowed over her shoulders and down her back. She set the tray on the table and stepped in front of Joe. He stared into her blue-gray eyes and didn't blink until she kissed him on both cheeks.

"Hi, Joe. I'm Nina, Sofia's cousin."

He closed his mouth and smiled. Angelo had told him she was pretty, but stunning was the word he should have used. Rome was known for its beautiful high-fashion women, but until this moment, none had grabbed his attention like the gorgeous lady inches in front of him. For a split second, time stopped and his broad smile lit the room. "Nice to meet you, Nina." He motioned to his partner. "Angelo said you were in London. He's been hiding you from me."

"My transfer to Rome was approved."

Joe looked at his partner and raised his eyebrows. "We're leaving tomorrow. Why didn't you tell me sooner?"

Nina answered before he could speak. "I arrived last night."

"I made reservations for dinner at seven," Angelo said. "Sofia cannot join us so Mia agreed to be my date for the evening."

Joe glanced at Angelo. "I've got nothing planned for the rest of the day or tonight." He looked at the two women.

"Angelo and I may have to fight off the crowd. Every man in Rome will be jealous."

For the next two and a half hours, he seldom took his eyes off Nina, except to grin at the equally beautiful Mia, or glance at Angelo. They discussed Nina's job with Alitalia Airlines, Joe's family in Italy, and the places they both liked and could visit together when he and Angelo returned to Italy. He wanted to grab her and tell her he'd cancel his trip. *Play it cool, be calm, and pray she doesn't meet someone.*

That night, Angelo and Mia left the restaurant at half past ten. Joe and Nina shared another bottle of wine.

XVII
A NEW BEGINNING

At eight PM, the corporate jet pulled into a private hanger at Atlanta's Hartsfield-Jackson International Airport, and shut down its engines beside a black SUV with dark tinted windows. The door opened and stairway deployed.

Joe, in slacks and a sport shirt, carried a suitcase as he descended the steps, and headed to the SUV. *Sicily to Atlanta via Tampa. Thank God twenty one hours traveling from Italy has ended.* He removed the keys from the ignition, opened the rear hatch, and threw his suitcase in the back.

Angelo passed him luggage from the plane and stepped aside, allowing Saleh and Zarina access to the exit.

Joe stretched his back and legs, then loaded their bags into the SUV. He walked to the side of the vehicle, leaned across the steering wheel, and turned on the engine and air conditioner. "Everyone is stiff from small airplane seats," he said to Saleh. "Walk around for a few minutes and then we'll leave."

Angelo bent forward stretching and reaching for his ankles. "Now I know why I didn't join the Air Force." He looked around the hanger. "It would have been nice to stay in Florida."

Joe shrugged. "MacDill Air Force Base was where the plane from Sicily was going. WITSEC headquarters wanted us to come to Atlanta."

The SUV pulled onto the highway near the airport. Joe glanced at Saleh in the rearview mirror. "Tired?"

"Yes."

"Where are we?" Zarina asked.

"Atlanta, Georgia, the southeastern part of the country."

"Where are you taking us?" Saleh asked.

Joe opened the center console and removed a brochure and a key card. "A hotel room, about thirty minutes from here."

"How long will we stay there?" Zarina asked.

"One night, tomorrow you'll move to a furnished apartment."

Saleh leaned between the two front seats. "Will the police guard us?"

Angelo turned to him. "You're safe here... there's no need for guards."

Joe noticed Zarina frown at Saleh. *Culture shock.*

She glanced out the window at the large cars on the highway, the skyscrapers in downtown Atlanta, and then back at Saleh.

"Must we stay in the room... can we go out?" Saleh asked.

"There's no need to hide," Joe said. "But don't go too far. You have no identification."

"How can we leave the room? We need documents," Zarina said.

Angelo looked at her. "America is not like Europe. No one will ask you to identify yourself. The hotels don't even record your personal information and notify the police when you register."

Joe raised a hand from the wheel. "Remember Al Provitti? He's making arrangements for temporary identification documents." He handed Saleh a folded paper. "You're registered as Saleh and Zarina Sania. It's written on the paper. Practice using that name. I wrote my cell phone number on the page. If it's important, call me."

Angelo looked back. "Never use the name al-Filistini again."

"Why have you done this?" Zarina shouted.

"What?" Joe asked.

"Given us the same name. I have my own name, Zarina Gafar Muhammad al-Ansari!"

Joe glared at her in the rearview mirror. "I know it's customary for you to keep your own name. Here, most women take their husbands name after marriage. Someone in Washington picked Sania... it's temporary. When your new legal name is chosen you can pick something different than your husband... so long as it's not associated with the Ansari family or any of their friends."

Zarina focused on Joe's eyes in the mirror. "You should have thought of this."

"Maybe, but we didn't. Try to relax and not make life more difficult."

"You trust us to be alone?" Saleh asked.

"Yes. You signed an agreement. Violate it and you'll be returned to Italy and sent to prison," Angelo said.

Joe glanced over his shoulder. "No one will ask you for identification unless you do something stupid. Since you'll be at the hotel for only one night, it's best if you eat at their restaurant or one nearby. Please don't think about fleeing. If, by chance, you cross into Canada or Mexico, they'll hold you until you're identified. When they do, we'll come to pick you up and as Angelo said, you'll be returned to Italy and sent to prison."

Joe pointed at an exit from the highway. "We're almost there." He pulled into a parking lot in front of a multi-story Embassy Suites, drove to the side entrance and parked.

###

An hour later, Saleh and Zarina sat at a small kitchenette table in a two-room suite. Five, ten, and twenty dollar bills lay in front of them.

Zarina scanned the room, looked at the money and sighed. "How much did he give you?"

"Three hundred dollars."

"How can we live?"

"Three hundred for today, and tomorrow." From the moment he made his decision, he knew Zarina would oppose it. With each new confrontation, his patience diminished. *Stay calm. It'll take time for her to adjust.*

"Are you happy with what you've done?" she said, looking at the money on the table.

"What do you mean?"

"I can never go back to Saudi Arabia."

Saleh shook his head. "There's no reason to return."

"I'll never see my family again."

"Your place is with me. We can build a new life together."

"I love you Saleh, but you ask too much."

"The Americans and Italians will not allow you to return to Riyadh." he said.

"I would go without them knowing. You are the one who thinks the Prophet sent a message."

"You have no documentation. How can you leave?"

Zarina looked at her fingers, picked at one of her nails and did not answer.

"You're my wife, stand beside me. We're here for one day. Tomorrow we'll move into someplace larger."

"I don't like it... but I will." She shoved her chair from the table and stormed to the bedroom.

###

The day after they moved into their new apartment, Saleh noticed Zarina pouting. She spent thirty minutes pacing from the kitchen, past the dining room table, into the living room and on to the two bathrooms. She surveyed each room with the intensity of a woman looking for her lost diamond ring.

He stood near the sliding glass doors to a spacious balcony and watched her curl up on the couch pressing her handbag against her leg and the armrest. "Do you like the apartment?"

"It's okay." She did not look at him.

"It's better than the one in Italy."

She ignored his words. "What time are they taking us shopping?"

"They'll be here in an hour."

She continued to avoid looking in his direction. "How long will we stay here?"

"We have a new life, maybe a long time."

Zarina turned to him. "When will we get our money?"

He sighed and stepped in front of her. "I told you, Mr. Provitti said he would take care of it. It takes time to move that much money from one account to another."

Her face contorted and words hissed from her lips. "The CIA."

Saleh sighed. "The Americans will be honest."

"They're stupid. That's the reason they'll be defeated."

His hands closed to fists, and he exhaled. *Not again Zarina. Will you ever learn?* "Defeated... how? You think we can kill all of them?"

"If it takes a hundred years... our people immigrate, we'll conquer them. All infidels will turn to Islam."

Saleh nodded. "And if they don't?"

"Serve the needs of Islam or die."

He tried to suppress a laugh. "You don't understand America. You've lived in countries that are different... even repressive."

"How?"

"It's called freedom. People here treasure freedom."

She sat erect. "People in Saudi Arabia are free."

Saleh looked at her and rolled his eyes. "Are women allowed to drive cars on the streets of Riyadh?"

"No but..."

"Can they leave their homes alone to go shopping?" He didn't enjoy making his wife look foolish, but she needed to face the truth. In many countries of the Middle East women lived behind closed doors and did what men told them to do. *Is that what she wants?*

Zarina locked her eyes on his and tightened her jaw. "The Koran says..."

"How many Christian churches are in Saudi Arabia?"

She glared at him and pursed her lips. "None."

"In Europe did you have to carry a national identification card?"

"Yes!"

Saleh marched back to the sliding doors and pointed out the glass. "People out there don't carry cards to prove their citizenship." He turned to her. "In the west churches, synagogues and mosques exist on the same street. People of different religions pass each other on their way to pray."

She raised her voice and her nostrils flared. "Their beliefs violate the teachings of the Prophet."

Saleh shook his head and raised both hands. "So, because of beliefs... what they think... we should force them to submit or kill them?"

Zarina's dark eyes burned into him.

"After we kill a thousand, are we to smile at those who remain alive, and ask them to convert to Islam?" he asked. "Our friends kill people and sneak out the back door to slaughter Muslims in the marketplace because their prayers are different... women and children included. Maybe this is what you want Zarina." He slapped his chest. "But not me. I will not stand in the shadows and watch men enrich themselves by picking passages from the Koran and preaching hate to their followers."

Zarina grabbed her handbag and sprang from the couch. "I'm going to bathe."

Later that afternoon, Saleh and Zarina strolled through a mall with Joe and Angelo.

Joe stopped in front of a store. "I'll be back in a second." He headed through the door.

"He said it is going to rain," Angelo said.

Joe returned carrying two golf umbrellas, both with pointed four inch metal tips. He handed them to Saleh. "You'll need these later today. They're the biggest I could find... they'll keep you dry."

"Thank you," he handed one to his wife.

They sauntered past stores, stopping at displays to window shop.

Ahead of the group, a Muslim couple walked out of a store and stopped at the next display. The woman wore an abaya and hijab.

Zarina slowed, glanced at Saleh, raised her eyebrows and stopped. "Let's go the other way."

"Why?"

Her eyes darted to the woman. "Those people are Muslim," she said as the couple entered the store.

"There's many Muslims in America. They don't know you," Angelo said.

"A few months ago I came here with my brother," Joe said. "He bought a table in that store. I think the owner said he was from Damascus. Come."

Saleh took his wife's hand. "It's not a problem," he said.

The group headed toward the store.

"If they ask, tell them you're visiting from England," Joe said.

When they reached the entrance, Angelo stopped. "I'll wait here."

Saleh handed him the two umbrellas, and they walked into the store with Joe.

Joe noticed the Muslim couple speaking with a man he recognized. The man walked to Saleh.

"Hello, I'm Hami. Can I help you find something?"

Zarina slipped behind her husband and lowered her head.

"No, we're just looking," he said.

Hami studied him for a moment. "Are you Syrian?"

"No, English, but my mother is Lebanese. We're visiting from London."

Hami looked at Joe and furrowed his brow. "Have I seen you in my store?"

"Yes, two months ago. I thought I'd show my friends what you sold."

Hami nodded and smiled. He looked at Saleh and swept a hand toward items around the store. "If I can help you, please ask. I import from all over the Middle East."

"Thank you."

Hami returned to the Muslim couple. They glanced at Saleh and Zarina. The man nodded.

Zarina clutched Saleh's hand and lowered her voice. "Please Saleh, let's leave."

She's frightened, Joe thought.

"Okay." Saleh led them out of the store.

As they retraced their path through the mall, she kept glancing over her shoulder. "Joe, I want to leave."

Saleh placed his hand on her shoulder. "Is something wrong?"

"I'm scared."

Joe stepped beside them and nodded. "It takes time to adjust to a new environment. We'll take you back to the apartment."

As they approached Joe's SUV, Angelo turned to Zarina. "Tomorrow morning we'll come by to get Saleh. He needs to sign papers. You can go with us."

"I'll stay at the apartment."

"We won't keep him long," Joe said.

XVIII
THE CONFRONTATION

Gafar and Akram drank coffee at a small table in Akram's office.

"How old is the message?" Akram asked.

"One day. America makes it more difficult."

Akram furrowed his brow. "Saleh is important to them. Do you know where?"

"All I know is Atlanta, Georgia."

Akram pressed his lips together. "Florida is to the south. The sheik has friends there."

Gafar removed a paper from his pocket and unfolded it. "A contact in Rome said Saleh met with an American named Provitti. Someone told him he works at the U. S. Embassy."

Akram nodded and smiled. "This man may know where they are living. We need to search his house."

Don't be a fool, old man, Gafar thought. Akram often spoke before he engaged his brain. If the man worked at the American embassy, he'd be well protected. "More of your men will die, or they will kill innocent Italians, making our job difficult. Do nothing and wait. I'm sure we'll get more information."

Noon, the next day, the black SUV pulled to the entrance of the apartment building. Saleh opened the back door and stepped into a puddle. He looked at the clouds and the wet pavement from the recent rain as he grabbed his umbrella from the seat.

Joe lowered the window. "Tell your wife we said hello. If you need anything call me."

"Will you come tomorrow?"

Angelo leaned over to look at him. "After lunch, about two."

"Call first." He tapped the metal point of the umbrella against the pavement as he strode through the entrance, entered the elevator and pressed a button.

When the elevator door opened, he strolled to his apartment, reached for the doorknob and froze at the sound of a voice. He placed his ear against the door and listened. After ten seconds, he unlocked the door and pushed it open.

Once inside, he heard Zarina speaking Arabic. He leaned the umbrella against the wall and tiptoed toward the sound of her voice. Outside the kitchen doorway, he pressed himself against the wall and strained to eavesdrop on her conversation. *She shouldn't be speaking Arabic to anyone. She can't be on a phone.* The muscles throughout his body tensed and his hands clenched when he stepped into the kitchen.

Zarina, facing away from him, held a red cell phone to her ear. His heart pounded as he glanced at a wooden block holding a set of kitchen knives and then focused on the phone.

"Who are you speaking with?"

Zarina jumped and spun toward him. With a terrified expression and taut lips, she fumbled to end the call.

"You were speaking Arabic!"

"I didn't... no I wasn't." Her gaze bounced around the room, avoiding direct eye contact.

"I remember you telling Angelo that phone didn't work."

She looked at the counter behind her and stepped back, pressing herself against the granite. "I lied."

Saleh glared at her and held out his hand. "Give me the phone."

"No."

He moved toward her.

Zarina threw the phone at him.

It bounced off his chest and clattered to the floor. He picked it up and stepped in front of her. "Who did you call?"

She stared at him in silence, her eyes burning into his.

He slammed his free hand across her cheek. The force of the blow knocked her against the counter. She steadied herself, wiped blood from the corner of her mouth, and pressed her hand against the side of her face.

"Answer me," he screamed.

Tears filled her eyes, and she glanced over her shoulder.

Nowhere to go, Zarina. He struck her face a second time with the back of his hand.

She leaned over the counter and sobbed, touching her split lip. Blood dropped to the granite.

Saleh raised the cell phone, tapped the screen and read the number. "This is your father's number. You've been telling him where we are. You're the one who wants me dead."

Zarina pushed herself up and glared at him. "I won't let you destroy my life!"

"You're a vicious woman, Zarina." He headed to the front door, picked up the umbrella, and looked at her standing in the kitchen doorway with a hand behind her back. "I should have left you in Italy and told the Italian authorities about your family."

"Where are you going?" she yelled.

"I don't want to see you again. I'm finished with you."

"Saleh, I'll find you. I'll kill you!"

The moment the words passed her lips, calmness came over Saleh. He thought about the shooting at the hotel, the explosives in the motorbike, and the rockets that almost killed him in the villa. "You and your father's friends tried three times and I'm still alive. You're nothing but a failure, Zarina."

"I will not fail. You will die!"

"Maybe I will, but I'll be alone and you will not see it happen. Now go back to your home. Go back to your friends who kill Muslim men, woman, and children for no reason except to control those they allow to live."

"No!" Zarina swung a large butcher knife from behind her back and leapt toward him.

With both hands he lifted the umbrella, the only thing he had to protect himself, and thrust the pointed metal tip into her chest.

Her eyes widened, face contorted, and she gasped. The knife dropped from her hand.

Saleh focused on the middle of her chest. He shoved the tip further into her body, leaned in and stared into her large eyes. "You failed again Zarina... your last failure." He loosened his grip as she slumped to the floor.

XIX
SHE IS DEAD

Joe and Angelo took their time driving along the two-lane country road back to his temporary office.

"Did you thank your brother for me?" Angelo asked.

"Yeah. He said he won't be back for two months. The house is ours... if we need it that long."

"If we're lucky, we'll be gone long before he returns." Angelo shook his head. "I feel sorry for Saleh, she's a bitch."

"She can be, but she's upset because she won't see her family again."

"During the trip over here, she kept her finger in his face and the complaining never stopped."

Joe shrugged. On the plane out of Sicily he spent most of his time talking with the crew and pilots. Ten years in WITSEC taught him two important lessons. He looked at Angelo "I learned two things working witnesses. Don't get too friendly with them. They're snitching on their friends and family and would like nothing more than to get something on you. Always remember, most of them are psychopaths. What you and I want doesn't matter, it's all about them. On the plane, I didn't pay them much attention. What's her complaint?"

"Money and family."

Joe nodded. He had heard the same story a hundred times. Everyone wanted the government to hand over the stolen money they squirreled away and then demanded the IRS not be informed. "She signed the agreement... may as well forget about family."

"When Provitti empties the account, maybe she will."

Joe laughed. "Amazing what a million will do."

Angelo nodded. "Have you talked to Nina?"

"Yeah, last night."

"She told me she likes you."

"The feeling is mutual. We're planning to take time off together when you and I get back to Italy." He smiled. "I thought someone that beautiful would be married."

"Nina is choosey and doesn't like to be told what to do."

"The only order I'd ever give her is to kiss me." His cell phone rang. "Hello." As he listened, he sat up in his seat. "Sure, is there a problem?" His muscles tightened. "What is it... are you all right?" The next words out of his phone made him cringe. He slammed on the brakes. "Dead!"

Angelo thrust his arms forward as the seat belt halted his flight into the windshield.

"We'll be there in a few minutes, don't do anything."

"What the hell happened?" Angelo repositioned himself.

Joe threw the SUV into a U-turn and smashed the accelerator to the floor. "Grab the blue light and plug it in here." He pointed to the empty cigarette lighter receptacle. Angelo handed him the flashing strobe light, and he lowered his window and placed it on the roof. "He said Zarina is dead!"

Angelo's mouth dropped open, and he turned sideways. "Dead?"

Joe kept the SUV in the center of the lightly travelled road.

"I can't believe they found him," Angelo yelled. "How the hell are they tracking him and why would they kill her and not him?"

Joe looked at him. "You think he's calling them and trying to talk his way back into the organization? Even here, with the right contacts and a few hundred dollars, they'd be able to trace the phone calls."

Angelo focused on the dashboard before he replied. "Al Qaeda tried to kill him three times. I don't think he's that stupid."

"I don't know, but the first witness killed will not be on my watch."

He stopped along the curb in front of the apartment building and pulled the light from the roof. "Unplug it."

Joe looked at the building entrance and saw Saleh through the glass door. Both men jumped out and raced to him.

Joe looked at Saleh, then to Angelo and back at Selah. *How can this guy be so calm?*

"She's upstairs," Saleh said. He stepped into a stairway and took two steps at a time. Joe and Angelo scrambled to follow.

The three men entered a hallway, and Saleh led them to his apartment. He reached for the doorknob.

"Saleh!" Joe said stopping him from turning the knob. "We'll go in first. Is the door locked?"

"No."

Joe removed a Glock 27 from under his shirt and Angelo slid a Beretta PX4 Storm from his back waistband.

Joe's eyes widened. "What the hell! You're not supposed to have that."

Angelo shrugged. "I know, but I don't want to send you in there alone."

The day they departed Italy, a request went to the Department of Justice to get Angelo sworn in as a Special Deputy U. S. Marshal so he could carry a weapon. Joe hadn't received a reply and didn't know Angelo brought his weapon with him. *Screw it. One gun may not be enough.*

Saleh raised a hand. "You won't need those. No one is here."

Joe listened to his words, but it took a second for them to sink into his brain. *Better safe than sorry.* He cracked open the door, cradled the pistol with two hands, and shoved the door open with his foot. He and Angelo slipped into the apartment.

Zarina's crumpled body lay in a pool of blood, the long point of the umbrella buried in her chest.

Angelo raised his pistol to cover the inside of the apartment as Joe leaned over Zarina and checked for a pulse.

"She's dead, don't move anything," Joe said.

"Christ. How did this happen?" Angelo asked.

Saleh walked in and pointed at the knife lying on the floor beside her body. "I killed her because she tried to kill me."

Joe sucked air into his lungs and swung his head toward him. "You what?"

XX
THE TERRORIST FAMILY

Saleh sat on the couch and watched Joe and Angelo, both seemingly in a daze as they dropped into chairs. *There's no reason to continue protecting her.* He removed Zarina's cellular telephone from his pocket and handed it to Joe. "She told Angelo it didn't have a SIM card but it does. She's been calling her father and telling him where we were."

Angelo nodded. "I checked the phone when we first met. I should have done more, but she convinced me she threw it away."

Joe cocked his head, looked at Saleh and frowned. "Why haven't you told us anything about her father?"

"I loved her and didn't want to hurt her by telling you about him and his family."

Joe took his cell phone from his pocket and headed across the room. "I need to call Washington."

"We're not getting any sleep tonight," Angelo said. "Why would her father try to kill both of you?"

"He wouldn't. It's me he wants dead."

"Why?"

"The photos you have, don't tell the whole story. Zarina was a terrorist, everyone in her family is a terrorist." He rubbed his temple. "Do you know of Saudi Prince Mohammed bin Naif?"

"Sure," Angelo said. "The prince that's been a thorn in Al Qaeda's side for many years."

"We tried to assassinate him in 2009."

Angelo sat up and raised his eyebrows. "The body cavity bomber?"

"Yes, Abdullah Hassan al-Asiri. That was Zarina's idea... her plan."

Angelo swallowed hard and shook his head. "The only thing that saved the prince, was the short wall in front of him, and the fact that the bomb exploded inside Abdullah's body."

Joe ended his call and joined them. "An Assistant U.S. Attorney and someone from the U.S. Marshals office will be here soon."

Angelo bit his lower lip and scanned the room. "You need to call the local police?"

"Yeah, but not yet," Joe said.

Saleh glanced around the room. He had avoided jail up to now, but realized it may not be for long. *Surely they will understand, it was self-defense. I'm the one who can tell them everything.* "What will happen to me?"

Joe shrugged. "I can't answer that, but you'll remain protected."

"Will the police arrest him?" Angelo asked.

"It's up to them. The Associate Director told me he would ask the Attorney General's office to get involved."

"What about the press?" Angelo asked.

"A local Marshal will notify the police in person... too many people monitor their frequency."

Angelo leaned forward. "Saleh said Zarina's father is the one who's been trying to kill him."

Joe stared at Saleh for five full seconds. "Why the hell would he do that?"

Saleh hesitated, wondering how to word his next statement. With Zarina gone, he had no reason to continue hiding who she was. *Time to be honest.* "His daughter, Zarina's sister, was one of bin Laden's wives."

Joe pressed his fingers against his forehead. "Jesus, I better make another call." He walked to the kitchen.

Angelo scrambled to pull his cell phone from his pocket. "I'm calling Rome. After they find out bin-Laden was her brother-in-law, no one's ass will get much sleep."

###

Two hours later, Joe and Angelo had no more calls to make. Both sat with Saleh in the living room.

"All we can do now is wait for the big guns to arrive," Joe said. *What's taking them so long?*

There was a knock on the door and Joe checked the credentials of Chief Deputy Larry Gunn, from the local U.S. Marshals office, and Chief Assistant U.S. Attorney Maggie Hanover. He let them into the apartment.

Larry did not react when he stepped around Zarina's body but Maggie's eyes widened and she cringed.

"The Deputy Attorney General asked me to keep him apprised of the situation," Maggie said.

Joe nodded. "This is my partner, Italian Carabinieri Captain Angelo Randi, and Mr. Saleh Al-Sania, the dead woman's husband." He looked at Angelo. "This is Chief Larry Gunn and U. S. Attorney Maggie Hanover."

Maggie nodded, dragged a chair from the dining room and sat. Everyone stared at each other for a moment.

"WITSEC Chief Inspector Ralph Newberry should be here in a few minutes," Joe said.

"I heard you're not WITSEC," Larry said.

"No, fugitive investigations... assigned to the embassy in Rome."

"I guess that's why Newberry is on his way?"

"Everyone's got an ass to cover," Joe said.

Larry shook his head and looked at Joe. "Talking about ass cover, the Marshal is pissed. He wants to know why you chose his district as the relocation area."

"We'd rather keep politics out of this, Chief. I'm sure he wants to be reappointed... best if he gets his questions answered by headquarters." Joe glanced at Maggie and then back to Larry. "Were both of you told this case has national security ramifications?"

"Yeah, but that's about it," Maggie said.

"Did you call the locals?" Joe asked Larry.

"I contacted the Deputy Director at GBI, he's a friend. He sent one of his men to pick the Atlanta Deputy Chief of Criminal Investigations... they're friends. I didn't dare call anyone I couldn't trust."

"GBI?" Angelo asked.

"Georgia Bureau of Investigation," Joe said.

Maggie looked at Saleh. "Mr. Al-Sania, would you mind waiting in the bedroom? I don't want you to worry. The Attorney General of the United States assured me you'll be protected."

Saleh pushed himself from the couch. "Thank you." He left the room.

Maggie waited for the door to close and turned to Joe. "I don't know what this guy did. But based on his Arabic name, and the fact that I'm sitting here with an American investigator who works in Rome, and Carabinieri Captain Randi, it doesn't take a Rhodes Scholar to figure it out. In my twenty-two years with the U.S. Attorney's office, I never received a call from the number two at Justice. When he said the President wants this kept quiet, I almost fell out of my chair."

"We better come up with a good story about who this guy is, and what happened." Larry said.

Joe leaned forward. "I've got an idea that retains part of the truth, but someone will need to convince the locals."

"We'll leave that to the Attorney General's office," Maggie said. "When the locals arrive, I'll get him or an assistant on the phone. It's best if one person does the lying."

XXI
THE RAIDS

Five days after Zarina's death, Joe, Angelo, Saleh and FBI Terrorist Task Force Agent Zeller, sat at a conference table stacked with files and papers. Saleh had not held back any information. He answered every question Zeller asked.

On their way to the meeting, Joe agonized over how productive the interview would be. Now, he sat across from the middle-aged agent and thanked God he wasn't at a table with Duffy or even worse, his bigger than life uncle. *Zeller's professional and attentive to every detail.*

Zeller shoved a stack of folders aside. "That's it. Not including the Middle East, we've covered seven countries. We'll take up the Arab countries the next time we meet."

Saleh nodded. "I already talked to Mr. Alfano and Mr. Provitti about them."

"I know," Zeller said. "We'll want to get more specific information... addresses, places they travel to and family member's locations."

Saleh cocked his head and paused. "Will you be able to arrest them in their countries?"

Zeller smiled. "No, but we can make their lives difficult. Let's see what we can do in the next few days, with the information you gave us."

Joe, Angelo, and Saleh stood.

Saleh extended his hand to Zeller. "Thank you... tell them to be careful. Al Qaeda is prepared."

Zeller nodded. "Joe, can I have a word with you?"

"Sure."

Angelo and Saleh left the room.

Zeller cocked his head. "His information damn well better check out. Do you trust him?"

Joe paused and stared at the FBI agent He trusted his mother. Others followed in a specific order, starting with Angelo and the Pope. He raised his head and rubbed his chin, but could not think of anyone else to add to the list. "Trust leads to betrayal. Betrayal leads to murder, or at least a good ass whipping out at the woodshed. I'm cautious. This guy has lost everything, including his wife. What would he gain by lying at this point?"

"Do me a favor," Zeller said. "Watch him until I let you know the operations in the next few days are completed. I don't want him making any phone calls."

Joe smiled. "I think his heart is in the right place. What's in his head? Self-preservation, rules. Don't worry, I've got it covered."

Special Agent King had spent three hours briefing his men. He now led five other FBI SWAT team members to a door on the fifth floor of a New York City apartment building on East 131st Street, in Harlem. A day earlier, he received information about two men, who crossed into Europe as refugees from Syria, and rented the apartment when they arrived six months ago from Munich, Germany. Intelligence officials identified them as members of a radical group operating in Iraq.

Each of King's man wore black tactical gear and held an MP5, 9mm submachine gun. Three men slipped to each side of the entrance. *No knocking to announce ourselves on this one.* One man held a door ram.

King nodded and whispered. "Now."

The agent stepped in front of the door, slammed the blunt end of the ram into the metal near the deadbolt and stepped out of the way.

A man from the other side of the entrance threw his shoulder against the door near the bent lock, and burst into the apartment screaming. "FBI! Everyone on the floor! Down now!"

Four men followed their supervisor into the apartment, leaving the agent who held the ram to block the doorway.

It took less than a second for King to focus on two targets as they dropped to the floor. A short fat man, on his back, froze after spreading his legs and arms. A young man lay face down with his right arm under his body.

"Show me your hands," the agent next to King yelled as three of his partners ran to check the bathroom and bedroom.

The young man did not respond.

"Your hands! Now!" King shouted.

The young man jerked a small semiautomatic pistol from under his body. King fired a three round burst.

Across the Atlantic, a Renault Fourgon windowless delivery truck, with the name of a fictitious bakery painted on the side, pulled to the curb. It parked at the corner of a side street in the Saint-Denis section of north Paris. It was seven in the morning and the driver, in a white uniform, watched the rear view mirror outside his window and held a cell phone in his lap. Behind him, a dark screen obscured the back of the truck.

He was the only man in the truck not wearing the dark blue uniform of the French National Police Intervention

Group, and not armed with the futuristic looking, twenty inch long, FN P90 Personal Defense Weapon.

His eyes widened when he saw the car approaching. He lifted the phone, ensuring it remained below the window and cocked his head so the men in the back could hear him. "I see the white car, they're coming. Ten more seconds. I'll tell you when they're beside us."

When the car was ten feet behind the truck, he lowered his head and shouted at the phone. "Block now."

A Mercedes sedan pulled from the side street and blocked the roadway in front of the van. The white car stopped.

"Three bearded men... out now!" the van driver shouted.

The back of the delivery truck opened. Four officers jumped out, surrounded the car and leveled their weapons at the occupants.

National Crime Squad Inspector Ugo Claasen watched his driver turn the unmarked Volvo XC70 onto a dirt road ten miles west of Rotterdam. He glanced over his shoulder. Two constables in a marked white VW Polo patrol car followed, a car-length back. He had waited until the fog lifted but the sun had not yet penetrated the overhanging haze. Ugo had no reservations with his decision to use a small force to take custody of a single old man the surveillance team said was the only one at the farmhouse. Four men would be enough if they were cautious.

Ugo turned to his driver. "Jos?"

He replied without taking his eyes off the road. "Yes?"

"When we get to the house, stop ten or fifteen meters from the front door."

Jos nodded as he stared at the wet dirt and gravel road.

They passed through an open gate at a hedgerow and saw the timeworn, unkempt house. Jos stopped the car well away from the front of the residence and the marked police car pulled alongside the Volvo.

Ugo spotted a bearded old man take a look out a smudged window. He opened the car door, got out and stood behind it. Jos and the two constables followed his lead. One officer ran to the side of the house to observe the back yard.

The front door swung open and the old man, wearing a heavy jacket and baggy pants, stepped into the doorway.

Ugo moved to the leading edge of the car door and glanced at Jos and the officer beside the marked patrol car. "Do not expose yourselves," he said in a low voice.

"Are you Amal?" Ugo called.

"Yes."

"I am Inspector Ugo Claasen of the National Police. You must come with us."

The man stared at him and did not respond.

Ugo paused and glared at the man. "Did you hear what I said?"

"Yes." He raised both his arms above his head and touched his hands together.

Ugo had no time to react when he saw the spark as the man's hands came together. A bright flash and thundering explosion propelled flesh and bone toward the cars.

###

Carabinieri Lieutenant Vicario, and three of his men, in uniforms with a red stripe down the leg, waited in the secure area past the magnetometers at Rome's Leonardo da Vinci airport.

Plain-clothes officers had followed two Middle Eastern men into the terminal and notified Vicario when they started through security. Taking them into custody outside the airport would have been dangerous. Anti-terrorism investigators from the Special Operations Group told him both men were Al Qaeda operatives. They waited to question them in a nearby room.

Vicario smiled. If he had his way, he'd volunteer for more comfortable assignments like this one. Waiting to confront them behind the security checkpoint, assured the safety of his men.

The Carabinieri stood in a tight group, as if talking, while they watched the two men grab their carry-on luggage and laptop computers. When the men strolled from the secure area, Vicario and his officers approached and took up positions around their targets. "Excuse me. Are you travelling together?" Vicario asked.

"Yes," the one in a gray suit answered.

"What is your name?"

"Fardeen. This is my associate Dahi."

Vicario nodded. "Thank you. I'm Lieutenant Vicario. Both of you are to come with me."

"Is there a problem?" Dahi asked.

"No. Follow me please." He looked at his men. "Take their bags."

Fardeen held up his hand. "Wait!"

Vicario stepped next to him. "At the moment there's no problem, please do as I ask." He began walking. One of his men pointed in the direction Fardeen and Dahi were to take.

"Why are you doing this? I want to talk to your commander," Fardeen said.

Vicario stopped and looked at both men. "I suggest you do not make this difficult for me and my men." He turned and took one-step before Dahi opened his mouth.

"Did you hear him? Where are you taking us?"

Vicario's muscles tightened. He took a deep breath to calm himself. *Is he ignorant or stupid?* "Gentlemen, you can walk with me or I can arrange for stretchers to carry you."

"What's your commander's name?" Fardeen asked.

Vicario smiled. "Follow me. I plan to introduce you to him." The Carabinieri forced them forward.

XXII
THE CHILDREN

A week after the New York and international arrests, Joe and Saleh approached a door in the U. S. District Court building not far from the United States Capitol. Above the frame hung a brass plate with the engraved words 'Grand Jury Waiting Room'. Inside were two coffee tables, two couches and four padded chairs. Styrofoam cups, sugar and creamer sat on a table next to a Keurig coffee maker and a K-Cup carousel.

Saleh crinkled his nose and pointed at the coffee machine. "Black water."

"Americans drink little espresso and Turkish coffee is out of the question."

They unbuttoned their suit jackets and dropped into chairs.

It had been two months since Joe met Saleh in Italy, and most of that time they spent together in the United States. He missed Rome and looked forward to returning in a week. The few people he had to deal with in WITSEC had been friendly and helpful, but he longed for the slow-paced life in Italy and the sight of Nina's face.

"I've seen nothing on the news," Saleh said.

"They're trying to keep it quiet."

Saleh lifted his eyebrows and shook his head. "They won't be able to hide it for long. Akram will know the information is coming from me."

"I'm sure he does."

"You know where they arrested people?"

Joe shrugged. "Agent Zeller said they contacted Italy, England, the Netherlands, Canada, Germany, France and a few more countries."

"What about Saudi Arabia and Iran?"

"The Iranians won't do anything to help. The Saudis said they'd handle their own problems without our help."

Saleh stared at the wall across the room. "I'm sure my old friends already called each other."

"That's good. They can't wait to tell people to protect themselves. Messengers are too slow, and the more phone calls they make, the more information we get. We'll see what happens." Joe pointed to a door with 'Grand Jury Room' printed on it at eye level. "You ready for this?"

Saleh nodded.

"Leonard will ask the questions. Just be honest. The jurors have already heard your name so they shouldn't be surprised when they see you."

"I will."

The Grand Jury room door opened and Angelo, in a dark suit, stepped out and beckoned Saleh. "They want you."

Saleh buttoned his jacket and left Joe and Angelo in the waiting room.

"It's almost over," Joe said after Saleh left the room.

Angelo nodded and sighed. "Good. America is nice but everyone is in a hurry. I'm ready to go home, I miss my family."

"I miss your family too."

Angelo smiled. "We both know why."

The moment Saleh entered the Grand Jury room, every person turned to look at him. Twelve evenly spaced tables stood before him. Most of them occupied by two people with women outnumbering the men.

Assistant U. S. Attorney Leonard Harrison, standing at the front of the room, leaned on a conference table covered with cardboard boxes and file folders. A court reporter sat to his side.

"Come in Mr. al-Filistini." Leonard pointed at the witness box and a high-backed leather chair. "Please stand next to that chair."

From the moment they heard his name, he noticed the jurors watched his every move.

Leonard pointed to a Koran on the corner of the witness box. "Please place your right hand on the Koran."

Saleh complied.

"Please repeat my words. By the right of this, I solemnly swear the testimony I will give is the truth."

Saleh repeated the words.

Earlier that morning, Leonard explained what would happen in the room and had discussed the questions he would ask. Their talk did little to settle the emptiness invading Saleh's stomach.

"Take a seat. I'm Leonard Harrison from the U. S. Attorney's Office."

"Yes, we've met."

Leonard stepped to the large table and leaned against it. "Are you familiar with the American Grand Jury process?"

Saleh shook his head. "Only what you told me."

"Do you recall me explaining the American justice system and the purpose of the grand jury?"

"Yes."

"I told you our sole purpose here was to determine the crimes committed and to discover who should be charged with those crimes, correct?"

"Yes, I understand."

"And I explained that the grand jurors do not convict people... they formalize the charges to be brought against those they think have committed an offense."

"Yes."

"Good. Let's begin." Leonard walked behind the table and opened a file folder. "Please state your name."

Saleh directed his answer to the jurors. "Al-Filistini, Saleh."

"Is that your real name?"

"Yes."

"Are you known by any other names?"

"Yes, Mohammad Halabi."

"Is that all?"

"No. I have passports in two more names. One German and one British."

"And those names are?"

"Omar Jager, and Omar Harrington."

"The first name Omar is on both passports?"

"It's easier to remember."

"During the last seven years were you employed?"

"I have had a job."

"Who did you work for and what position did you hold?"

Saleh hesitated and scanned the jurors. "I worked for Al Qaeda. I planned and organized bombings and murders for them in Europe." Saying those words in front of a group of people felt like admitting he was a barbarian. His heart pounded as he watched the jurors stir, exchange glances and stare at him as if they were eyeball to eyeball with a monster.

"Did you plan and organize terrorist attacks and murders in the United States?"

"I assisted with the plans but didn't organize them."

"Do you recall the terrorist bombing of a bus carrying school children, forty miles outside Vicenza, Italy?"

Saleh looked at the floor. He realized talking about the bombing would not be easy, but didn't expect the question to hit him with the force of a fist smashing into his chest. After taking a deep breath, he raised his head and looked at the jurors. "Yes."

"Do you know if that act of terrorism was an accident?"

"I do." With each response, his heart beat faster.

Leonard hesitated, passing his eyes across the men and women in the room. His speech slowed. "How do you know this?"

"Because I planned it, organized it and watched it happen."

A female juror gasped and covered her mouth.

"Who was the target? Who was supposed to be killed in that attack?"

"American soldiers."

"The children killed, do you know where they were from?"

Saleh exhaled, took a deep breath, and paused. "The Islamic Center School in Milan."

"Milan, Italy?"

"Yes."

"If you planned to kill American soldiers, how did it happen that Muslim children and three adults died?"

"Two buses looked the same. The American bus had a flat tire and stopped. The bus full of children passed the car bomb."

"Your car bomb?"

"No. A man named Pasha put the bomb in the car."

"And who asked him to do that?"

A sinking feeling came over him and he lowered his head. "I did."

"What were the ages of the children on the bus?"

"Eight... ten years old."

A female juror dropped her pencil and covered her mouth with both hands. Leonard waited for her to recover.

"Have you killed or known of other Muslims that were killed by Al Qaeda?"

"Yes. In the Middle East and in Europe."

"Mr. al-Filistini. Were you charged with a crime in Italy, or the United States, for killing forty Muslim children, or attempting to kill thirty-five American soldiers?"

"No."

"Were you told why charges were not brought against you?"

"I agreed to testify and tell Italian and American authorities about the structure and activities of Al Qaeda." Saleh looked at the jurors. Every eye in the room remained locked on him.

"Do you believe you won't be charged with a crime because you agreed to testify?"

Saleh sat erect in the chair. "No. I will be, at a later date."

"If you will be charged with the children's murder, there must be another reason you agreed to testify."

"There is."

"Please explain to the jurors what that reason is."

Saleh slowed his breathing and spoke to the men and women in front of him. "I no longer want to see children killed for a cause that is unattainable."

Leonard stepped closer to the witness box. "What made you reach this decision?"

"Watching Muslim children in Italy die. There can only be one explanation for their bus traveling along that road."

"What is that explanation?"

"A message from the Prophet was sent to me and to all Muslims."

"A message that their cause is unattainable?"

"No, that's not it."

"But you said it was unattainable."

"In a way it is. Non-Muslims around the world will never accept a religion violently forced upon them."

"So you think more people around the world will join in the fight against terrorism?"

Saleh looked at the ceiling and shook his head. *He doesn't understand, no one understands.* "No. They will join in a fight against Islam and the world will suffer."

"How did the death of the forty Muslim children convince you of this?"

"Muslim, Christian, Jewish or even Buddhist... it doesn't matter."

Leonard looked around the room, raised his shoulders and took a deep breath. "What doesn't matter?"

"Their religion doesn't." *Don't you understand?*

"Excuse me, but the jurors may be confused. If al Qaeda's goal is unattainable and their religion doesn't matter, then what does?"

Saleh made eye contact with each juror and lowered his voice. "The children are the ones who matter. They are the world's future."

THE END

OUT OF TUNIS

People seldom do what they believe in. They do what is convenient, then repent.

–Bob Dylan

Chapter I
CLOSE TO HEAVEN

Chasing fugitives across Italy with Carabinieri Captain Angelo Randi provided U.S. Marshals Service Inspector Joe Costa with all the intrigue he needed. A short vacation with his girlfriend, Nina Belsogno, furnished the excitement and the fun.

Seven months had passed since he met Angelo's wife's cousin, Nina. Every detail of their afternoon and evening together that day remained fresh in his mind as if it were yesterday. When the tall blue-gray eyed flight attendant walked into Angelo's office, and pulled her long chestnut hair over her red silk blouse, her beauty caught him by surprise. Angelo said she was pretty, but that understated the facts. Gorgeous, stunning and ravishing didn't seem enough to describe the woman now walking beside him and holding his hand.

A mini vacation with Nina had been hell to plan because of their crazy schedules. The embassy in Rome took four months to give him enough time off and Alitalia Airlines kept her busy flying routes throughout Europe. On top of their scheduling conflicts, the Carabinieri Fugitive Task Force opened five new cases. They kept him and Angelo hustling from Bolzano in the north, to Messina in the south.

"It's amazing you and Angelo went so long without two days off in a row," Nina said.

Joe also could not believe the increased workload. Once he and Angelo had completed testifying before the grand jury in Washington D.C. he figured he'd get a break.

Saleh al-Finistini, now in the safe hands of the Witness Security Program, would spend a few years testifying against his former Al Qaeda bosses. He raised his eyebrows and nodded. "If Angelo hadn't convinced Colonel Aldo that he and I needed a break, we'd still be working six days a week."

"How did the colonel know to call Alitalia so I could get a week off from work?"

"He didn't." Joe smiled. "Angelo has a few connections of his own."

Nina furrowed her brow. "What connections?"

"I don't have a clue, but a free week appeared on your schedule at the same time one appeared on mine."

Joe loved two places in Italy. Positano, along the Amalfi coast and the small town of Anacapri at the top of the island of Capri. Nina picked Capri, the closest place to heaven on earth, she called it.

High atop the island, they walked along the sidewalk in front of the Church of San Michele and turned onto Giuseppe Orlandi Street. Joe squeezed Nina's hand, and they headed toward the Galleria della'Arte ceramic shop. *How did I get so lucky? A flight attendant who looks like a movie star, and a member of my partner's family.*

Nina stopped, tilted her head and raised her eyebrows. "I've been meaning to ask you what happened to the terrorist the Carabinieri arrested. Is that why you and Angelo went to America?"

"Yeah, we took him there, but back then I couldn't say anything to you. Italian and American authorities are now hauling him around the world to be interviewed by terrorism investigators."

"He didn't go to jail?"

Joe smiled and winked. "Not yet, but he will."

Nina pursed her lips. "Hope it's for the rest of his life."

"Not likely, even though he killed forty children. That guy provided more information on Al Qaeda than anyone else ever has. He'll spend time in prison, but it won't be hard time." Joe raised her hand and kissed it. "Let's not talk about work. Tell me about your new apartment."

"It's a two bedroom. You'll like it."

"How do you know?"

"The embassy is a twenty-minute walk."

"Love it already, but that's an expensive area of town."

"We have a new flight attendant, Monique LaCroix. She's Algerian... French father. We'll share it."

"Is she new on the job?"

"New to Alitalia. She flew for Air Arabia out of Alexandria, Egypt, but wanted to work in the EU. Someone told me they hired her because she speaks five languages."

"Are you sure she'll be a good roommate?"

"Yes, but I don't plan to introduce you to her for a while." She poked him in the rips. "She's exceedingly beautiful."

Joe wrapped his arms around her. "There is only one exceedingly beautiful woman on earth. I'm holding her in my arms." He stepped back. "Come, it's our last night here. The day after tomorrow we'll both be back to work, and busy as hell."

"I don't think it's possible to work more than you did for the past few months."

"Tracking fugitives is not an eight-to-five job."

Chapter II
THE IRAN IRIS

The rusted 270 foot cargo ship, MV *Iran Iris*, had plied the ports along the Mediterranean coast for the past ten years. *Busy cargo vessels don't look like cruise ships, but this rust bucket is long overdue a new paint-job,* Omar Hassan thought.

He felt out of place standing on the bridge scanning the horizon with field glasses. His black dress pants and dark blue silk shirt identified him as an outsider. He wasn't fond of ships and had never thought of working on one. The three-man bridge crew wore white. *Moving cargo... a dirty job. Why white uniforms?*

He lowered the binoculars and looked at Captain Jamal Jalili, his soiled white shirt a size too small for his large frame, and protruding belly. The man barely fit in the captain's chair and looked to be a physical wreck, but he had never missed a voyage. *Why would he? His cut from the delivery of twenty-five kilos of heroin exceeded most Tunisian's yearly pay.*

Omar looked through the field glasses and contemplated the last year. This was his fifth trip on the rusted freighter and the one voyage that bothered him the most. Transferring heroin to the mafia and collecting the payment was easy. Murder wasn't.

Thirty minutes earlier, Omar positioned four men along the side of the cargo deck. They taped dark plastic on the open steel railing to conceal themselves from any vessel pulling alongside the ship. Two of them held AK47 rifles, the other two held RPG-7 Rocket-Propelled Grenade Launchers.

A black backpack, containing a kilo of C4 plastic explosive, lay at their feet.

A young woman in a torn, food-stained sundress, slouched as she carried bottles of water through the door near the captain's chair. The girl lowered her gaze when Omar looked at her black eye and bruised cheek.

Jamal spun his chair toward her. "What are you doing here? I told you to stay in the galley."

She set the bottles on the floor and scurried out the door.

The women back in Tunisia won't come near this bastard. He recalled the girl was brought aboard the *Iran Iris* almost a year ago. She had kept him company a few times, but after the captain had his way with her, there wasn't much left to look at. "You treat her too nice," Omar said.

Captain Jalili stood and kicked the plastic water bottles across the deck. He turned piercing eyes to Omar indicating the remark didn't sit well with him. "This is my vessel, I do what I want." He pointed at Omar. "Worry about what you must do. How did Majid find out his new customer was the Italian police?"

Careful. He's worked for Majid longer than I have. If he throws me overboard, it will take one day for Majid to hire my replacement. "We don't know. He has an informant in Rome. The guy must be a police officer or someone who works for them. He told Majid everything about their plan, even the name of the fishing boat."

"Be with your men when they come alongside and do it quickly. I want to be on the other side of Crete when the Italians come looking for revenge."

Omar nodded and raised the binoculars. "They're coming." He bolted from the bridge.

###

Five undercover officers, dressed in old clothes purchased on the docks of Naples, manned the fishing boat. Italian Narcotics Officer Paolo Borelli and DEA Agent Ralph Marino led the deck crew of three other agents, one American and two Italian. They had worked the case together for the past six months. *Three million dollars' worth of heroin will never make it to the streets of New York City,* thought Ralph.

The forty-foot trawler, San Giovanni, out of the port of Naples, appeared to be a fishing vessel. The boat's one oddity was the twin marine radar domes above the wheelhouse. One, a compact global maritime terminal, provided simultaneous data and voice communication with the Carabinieri Counter-Narcotics Group, monitoring from Naples.

Paolo kept his eyes on the cargo ship a quarter mile in front of the trawler and leaned out a window. "Get ready!"

One of the Italian officers moved to the bow and the other two men ran to the stern.

During the briefing on the dock in Naples, Paolo stressed to his men they needed to get a good look at everyone lowering the drugs from the ship. He wanted each officer to identify them when they were arrested and taken to court. He took one hand off the wheel and reached for a toggle switch. "I'm turning on the microphones, they'll hear everything at headquarters."

Ralph raised a set of binoculars and focused on the railing of the MV *Iran Iris'* cargo deck. "The informant was right. Hassan is standing next to the railing." He lowered the field glasses. "How long will the transfer take?"

"Once alongside, ten minutes. I want to get the drugs and give them the money as fast as possible." Paolo pointed at a hand-held spotlight. "Signal them now."

###

Omar leaned on the cargo deck railing. His four men squatted behind the plastic, their weapons ready. "I'll tell you when to shoot."

The trawler slowed and began its turn to position itself parallel with the ship.

"Not yet. Wait... wait," Omar said.

The smaller vessel pull alongside and bounce off the hull of *Iran Iris*. "Now!" he said.

The four men stood and the two with AK-47's opened fire. The other two leaned over the railing and aimed their RPG-7's at the wheelhouse and the aft deck.

Bullets raked across the deck and into the roof of the trawler's wheelhouse. The Italian officer at the bow dove to a folded canvas tarp lying on the deck and pulled a Spectre M4 submachine gun from beneath it. He raised the weapon as bullets slammed into his body.

Omar clamped both his hands over his ears and ducked to the deck as one man fired his RPG-7 into the trawler. The second rocket exploded an instant later.

He picked up the backpack, cradled it under his arm and yanked the cap from the pull-wire fuse lighter. He threw it over the side and watched it bounce on the deck below the fishing boats wheelhouse. From his pocket he yanked a hand-held radio. "Get away from them, fast."

The deck vibrated as the propeller turned and the ship pulled away from the trawler. When they were a hundred meters from the small vessel, the charge exploded sending parts of the boat into the air.

Omar cringed as the burning boat listed to one side and disappear below the surface. *Murder isn't easy, even when it's necessary.*

Chapter III
FIND HIM

The evening of their last day on island of Capri, Joe and Nina had caught the tail end of a news broadcast about the deaths of the five narcotics officers. He held back his eagerness to call Angelo, knowing a more detailed account of what happened would mar their vacation with bad news.

For the next week back in Rome, Joe kept up with the Italian press stories of the murders. Every newspaper in Italy ran daily updates on their front page. Higher-ups at the Carabinieri Counter-Narcotics Group struggled to answer questions from the press without releasing sensitive case information. The Drug Enforcement Administration sent the Special Agent-In-Charge of the Washington D.C. office to Rome to coordinate the investigation with the Department of Justice.

Joe realized the Fugitive Task Force would get a call, and he waited for his partner, to notify him when it did. It came on a Friday morning and by ten o'clock he sat at a table in a conference room next to Carabinieri Colonel Aldo's large office. He hadn't seen the colonel since he and Angelo returned from Washington.

Seated next to him were Angelo, and Lieutenant Sergio Lacona. Joe wore a dark suit and the Carabinieri officers wore their distinctive dark uniforms. A leather briefcase sat on the floor beside Sergio.

Colonel Aldo stepped into the room and closed the door. All three men stood. Aldo motioned them to sit and lowered his imposing frame into the chair at the head of the table. He looked at Lieutenant Lacona. "Did you bring the reports, Sergio?"

"Yes, sir." He raised his briefcase and slid it onto the table.

Angelo glanced at the colonel and looked at Joe. He pressed his lips together and raised his eyebrows.

Joe eyed Sergio as he opened the briefcase. It was the first time the young lieutenant had carried it to one of Aldo's meetings. *Scratch the colonel's table, and he'll chew you a new asshole.*

Sergio looked at Colonel Aldo the instant he pointed at the briefcase and frowned. He lifted it, placed it on his lap, and removed two thick folders. Before he set them on the table he glanced at Aldo, who was now smiling. "This is all the information in our files on Omar Hassan and his boss Majid Ziyad. Six months ago our informant identified Hassan. A Rome judge issued the warrant for his arrest. We haven't been able to find him, but if the ship stops in a European Union port, we'll get him."

"Is there an open fugitive case on Hassan?" Aldo asked Angelo.

"Yes, sir, but we haven't been working it. We didn't want to interfere with the Narcotics Group and the American DEA undercover operation."

Sergio leaned forward and looked at the colonel. "Hassan is not his real name."

Aldo nodded. "Where is he now?"

Angelo shrugged. "We know he was on the ship. After Agent Borelli turned on the microphones, we heard DEA Agent Marino say Omar was standing on deck. After that, little except for automatic weapons fire and an explosion is heard. If he's not still there, then he's back in Tunisia."

"How is Ziyad involved?"

Sergio pointed at the folders in front of Aldo. "It's explained in the case file, sir. Majid Ziyad owns and operates MZ Shipping and Export. He supplies cheap products to thousands of small stores throughout the Mediterranean and Europe. During the past five years, he's been bringing in heroin from Afghanistan. The men who work for him moving the drugs have been hard to identify. They don't use their real names."

Aldo furrowed his brow and bit his lower lip. "Is there's an arrest warrant for Ziyad?"

"No, Sir. There isn't enough information to satisfy a judge."

Aldo nodded and looked at Angelo. "Were you told about the trawler operation?"

"Yes, sir. Because of the Fugitive Task Force case on Omar."

"Did your DEA tell you about it, Inspector Costa?"

"Yes, sir, but it was only a passing comment, no specific details."

Aldo paused, pressed his palms together, and placed his fingertips against his chin. "How did Ziyad and Hassan find out police were on the trawler?" he asked Lieutenant Lacona.

Sergio shook his head. "We're not sure. Only ten people had knowledge of the operation. Someone here in Rome is giving them information."

Aldo pointed at Captain Randi. "Start today Angelo. Interview the other nine people. Since two of the men killed were American, have Inspector Costa hand carry my official request to the ambassador. My secretary will have it ready for you in an hour. Where's the ship?"

Joe answered when the others remained silent. "Somewhere in the Med, sir. The U.S. Navy has offered to help find it."

Aldo paused and rubbed the stubble on his cheek. "Good, ask them to start." He looked at Angelo. "It's been many years since three Carabinieri were killed on the same day, and the first time American agents died while assisting Italy. Find Hassan. Make it your top priority. I want the bastard brought to Rome."

Chapter IV
MONIQUE

Monique LaCroix had met Omar Hassan while on vacation at Sharm el-Sheikh on the southern tip of the Sinai Peninsula.

During that evening she glanced at him twice and he slipped her a business card while she sat at the nightclub bar in the five star Cleopatra Luxury Resort. From that night on, their relationship flourished.

Six months later, she and Omar finished their lunch in a restaurant overlooking the water along Rue du Lac Biwa in Tunis. "Do you think the Italians will find out who did it?" she asked.

Omar shook his head. "No, they had no idea we knew the police were on the fishing boat."

She toyed with an intricate gold bracelet, spinning it around her wrist. "This is beautiful. Where did you get it?"

"At the souk el Birka... the former slave market which closed four hundred years ago. The best gold shops in Tunis are there."

"Thank you." She kissed him. "Your boss must be rich and pay well."

"I'm Majid's most trusted man."

Monique furrowed her brow. "Majid? Didn't you tell me you worked for a man named Ziyad?"

He pressed his lips together and raised his eyebrows. "His first name is Majid, but tell no one I work for his company at the port. It's best not to talk about my employment."

"I won't." She held a hand in front of a passing waiter. "Excuse me. Please take our photo," she said handing him her cell phone. As she leaned against Omar, she raised the bracelet.

The waiter snapped the picture, smiled at Omar and returned the phone.

Omar's cell phone rang, and he tapped the screen to end the call.

"Was that your wife?"

He nodded.

"Will you stay with me tonight?" she asked.

"I would if it was possible. Your overnight flights give me little time to plan. We'll be together for a while but she expects me to return."

Monique never had a boyfriend as generous as Omar. She hated sharing him with a wife. *I wish he'd end that marriage.* "When are you going to leave her?"

"You and I have been together only six months. I need to plan everything. You want to be happy don't you?"

"Yes, but I don't want to be number two."

He placed a hand over hers. "Don't worry, we'll be together soon and I'll have enough money to start a new life. How do you like working for Alitalia?"

Monique shrugged. "Most of the large airlines are the same. There's less turmoil in Italy than in Egypt."

Omar smiled. "And the food is much better." He removed an envelope from a pocket and handed it to her. "When you get back to Rome, buy a stamp and mail this for me. Don't open it."

The next day Nina, wearing a bathrobe, relaxed on the couch in her apartment and watched television. Packed and half-full boxes lay near a hallway leading to the bedrooms.

The deadbolt clicked open and Monique entered dragging her overnight bag.

Nina sat up. "How was your trip?"

Monique sashayed across the room and extended her arm, showing off the bracelet. "Wonderful. Did you get the picture I sent?"

"Yes, let me see."

Monique raised her wrist. "Omar bought it before I arrived."

Nina rubbed a finger across the chain. Her eyes widened. "Beautiful."

"Next time come with me, you'll like him."

She sighed. "If we ever get on the same schedule I might. My flight leaves tonight."

Monique pulled her bag to her bedroom and returned. "I'm hungry, want to get something to eat?"

Nina slid from the couch. "Wish I could but I need to get ready, maybe tomorrow," she said heading to her bedroom.

"I'm going to get a pizza, I'll see you when you get back," Monique yelled from the living room.

Five minutes later Nina walked out of the bedroom in her bra and uniform skirt. *Damn, I hope she has a clean work blouse I can borrow.* She went into Monique's room, stepped to the closet and removed a white shirt from a hanger. As she turned, she knocked a book off the nightstand and a folded newspaper article fell to the floor. When she picked them up, she read the headline 'Murdered Police' at the top of the article, and 'Diary' embossed on the front of the book. She set the book on the night stand and slid the article back into the diary. *Why does she keep an article about that?*

###

The next afternoon, Nina sat in an empty car on the Leonardo Express train heading from the airport to the train terminal in central Rome. *Joe won't mind if I call him at work.* She pulled out her cell phone and hit the speaker icon.

"How is my Roman lover today... you back?" Joe asked.

"Yes and she better be your only lover."

"No one else stands a chance."

"Will you take me to dinner tonight?"

"I'd love to, what time?"

"Nine. I'm still unpacking boxes."

"Your roommate home?"

"No."

"Good. I'll be there at eight-thirty for a few kisses before we leave."

She laughed. "Come at eight and I'll show you how I'm decorating my bedroom."

Later that evening Joe and Nina sat in the back of the Ciao Bella restaurant, not far from the U.S. Embassy. The waiter cleared their empty plates and filled their wine glasses from a bottle on the table.

"When do you want me to help move the old couch and chair out of your apartment?" Joe asked.

"Oh, I forgot to tell you about the new furniture. I took pictures." She slid her phone across the table. "The photos are on the phone... it's the tan leather couch and chair." Nina stood. "I'm going to the bathroom. I'll only be a minute."

Joe picked up her phone and smiled as she scooted between tables and disappear down a hallway. He tapped the screen and scanned the pictures until he came to a photo of the couch. Next were two pictures from different angles followed by a close-up of an oversized chair. He went to the next picture and stopped breathing when the image appeared. *What the hell is this?* An attractive woman, holding her arm up and pointing at a large gold bracelet, sat beside a fugitive he and Angelo wanted to arrest.

He frowned, put the phone on table and looked to the hallway just as Nina stepped into the room. As she drew near, he tapped the chair beside him. "Sit next to me."

She took a seat and edged the chair closer to his. "Did you like the furniture?"

Joe stared into her eyes. "Yes."

Nina raised her eyebrows. "What's wrong? You look mad."

"No, not mad, worried." He picked up her cell phone, swiped a finger across the screen and turned it toward her. "Where did you get this photo?"

Nina grabbed the phone. "What's the matter with you? That's my roommate Monique and her boyfriend."

Joe's heart pounded as he took her hand. "Please listen. This is important. Did you take the picture?"

Nina pulled her hand from his. "What's wrong? Why are you staring at me? Monique emailed it from Tunisia."

"I'm sorry if I scared you." He looked away and paused. "Have you met him?"

Nina turned her chair toward him. "Quit acting like a cop interrogating a criminal. You're frightening me. Tell me why you're concerned."

Joe raised his hand and touched her cheek. "There's a possibility you could be in danger."

Nina stiffened. "Me?"

Joe looked into her eyes and nodded. "Remember on Capri we heard about the drug agents killed during the undercover operation?"

"Yes."

"I recognize the man in the photo. He's the one who killed them."

Nina's eyes widened and her mouth dropped open. Her eyes darted from side to side. "That can't be. Monique told me she's been going out with him for six months."

"Omar. That's his name, isn't it?"

Nina took a deep breath. "How did you know?"

Joe took both her hands in his. "Angelo and I are looking for him, he's a fugitive. Email me the photo. Let's go back to my apartment. We need to talk before I see Angelo."

Chapter V
THE NOTES

Angelo faced a two-drawer safe against the wall behind his desk. He slid the top drawer shut and turned the combination dial.

Mia, not only his secretary, but his wife Sofia's cousin, tapped on the doorframe. "Joe is here to see you."

"Send him in."

Joe strode into the room, pulled a chair to the front of the desk and took a seat. "You busy?"

"No." He raised a finger and looked toward the door. "Mia bring us coffee!"

Joe took a deep breath and exhaled. "Something came up... you need to hear this."

"Are you and Nina okay?"

"Couldn't be better."

"What is it?"

Joe opened the photo of Monique and Omar on his phone. "Take a look at this." He handed it to Angelo.

Angelo's mouth fell open. "Jesus, that's Hassan!" He didn't blink as he stared at the picture for five seconds. "Where the hell did you get this?"

Joe raised his eyebrows and cocked his head. "I had dinner with Nina last night." He pointed at his phone. "That photo is on her phone."

Angelo leaned over his desk. "What the hell... Nina's phone?"

"The girl next to Omar is Monique LaCroix. She's Nina's new roommate and Hassan's girlfriend."

Angelo paused and stared at him. "Monique who? Roommate? Nina knows Omar Hassan?"

"Thank God, no. They've never met. In the photo the roommate is having lunch with him in Tunis, and he gave her the bracelet. She sent Nina the photo."

"Did Nina know we're looking for him?"

"Come on Angelo. Until last night she didn't. When I saw the picture, I almost fell out of my chair. I explained everything to her but that's not all of it. Nina found a newspaper article about the murdered drug agents in Monique's room."

Angelo shook his head and pulled a notepad from his desk drawer. "Let's go back over everything you said."

An hour later, Angelo shoved the pad aside and rubbed his temple. "Did you tell anyone else?"

"No. Once I explained to Nina about Omar, she said she'd try to find more information. She mentioned a diary in the room, but when I suggested she read it, she refused. You and I would read it but I guess women take their diaries serious. I told her to stay out of Monique's belongings for the moment."

"Were you introduced to her roommate?"

"Hell, no. Ever since the Milan court convicted the CIA agents, most Italians are cautious with people working at the U.S. Embassy. An American cop working in Italy may raise a few questions. Nina even told me no one at Alitalia knows there's a Carabinieri Captain in the family. I want her name kept out of it."

Angelo tapped his notes. "I must tell Colonel Aldo."

"I want her identity protected, Angelo. She's a member of your family and she's important to me."

Angelo pressed his palms together and placed his fingertips against his lips. He did not move for ten seconds, lowered his hands and lifted his head. "Her name can be kept secret. We need to put this information in a report and bury these pages and the photo. We'll give her a code name. What are you doing for the rest of the day?"

Joe sat up in the chair. "Drinking a lot of coffee and helping you write the perfect report."

After Angelo and Joe left the office, a man in gray work clothes shuffled into Angelo's office. He walked to the desk, removed papers from the center drawer, and grinned. *Keep leaving it open for me.* He took less than two minutes to make notes and replace the pages in the drawer.

Early the next morning, Joe and Angelo rushed into Colonel Aldo's conference room. Sergio, Paul Sacca, the embassy's resident DEA Special Agent, and the Colonel sat at the table. Aldo occupied his customary position at one end.

They both sat and Joe set a file folder on the table.

Angelo took a deep breath and looked at his boss. "Sorry we requested this quick meeting and were late. It concerns the agents murdered on the trawler."

Joe placed a hand on the file. "We have an informant who has asked to remain confidential... we gave him the code name Miami." He handed a copy of their investigative report to Aldo and slid copies to the others. He and Angelo waited for everyone to read the report.

"Sir. We need your permission to keep this person's name secret," Angelo said. "For now, only Joe and I will know the true identity."

Aldo cocked his head to the side. "Odd request, Captain Randi."

Angelo nodded and his eyes pled his case.

"Tell us more."

"Our informant, Miami, knows Omar Hassan's girlfriend... who happens to live in Rome."

"How's that? Are they friends?" Paul asked.

Joe glanced at Angelo. The report they wrote provided no information about their informant and they hadn't planned on answering questions. "They've gone out together," Joe said.

Sergio raised his eyebrows. "Does Hassan realize his girlfriend is cheating on him?"

"No," Joe said.

The colonel furrowed his brow. "What is the girlfriend's name?"

Angelo turned a sheepish look to him. "If possible, we also want to keep her name secret."

Joe held his breath. *He may not want to approve it.* He needed to convince him to agree with their out of the ordinary appeal. Nina's life depended on it. Joe interrupted. "Sir, Miami refuses to talk to us if the girlfriend is followed or questioned. Lives depend on this."

Aldo studied Joe for a second. "If I agree Inspector Costa, understand, the Italian government will one day demand a name."

"If this helps us capture Hassan, once we get our hands on him, we'll release the name," Angelo said. "I talked to everyone briefed on the operation and still have no idea how Omar and Majid are getting information. If we name the informant and girlfriend now, there's a chance someone will get killed."

Aldo leaned back in his chair, scanned the walls and turned to Angelo. "No leads at all?"

"Not yet, sir, but I'm working on it."

Joe could almost see the wheels turning inside Aldo's head as he took a minute to reread the two-page report.

He dropped the pages in front of him, leaned on the table and looked at Angelo. "Let me think about your request. I'll call you in two hours. What is being done about Hassan's Sicilian drug connection, Nari Saladino?"

Sergio smiled. "He's in Rome, we're picking him up tomorrow night."

###

When Joe left the meeting he returned to the embassy. As he walked toward the entrance, FBI Agent Robert Duffy called his name and ran up to him. "I heard you went to a meeting about the trawler case."

"Yeah, with Colonel Aldo."

Duffy shuffled his feet. "No one told me about it."

Joe tilted his head to the side. "Damn, didn't someone on Aldo's staff call you?"

"No, and FBI headquarters won't like being shoved aside. They may have the Justice Department put pressure on people."

Joe raised his eyebrows. "Reconsider before you start something. Colonel Aldo is not someone you want to give agita... you know what that means?"

"No."

"Heartburn. If people make demands, he'll go to the Minister. The Italians will cut the FBI out of the case, and you'll watch this investigation through a telescope."

"Two Americans died on that trawler," Duffy said.

"And three Italians. The Italian government will not roll over because the Bureau throws a tantrum. Play it cool. I'll talk to Captain Randi and see if I can get the ball rolling. I'm sure it's an oversight. DEA is already involved." Joe tapped Duffy on the shoulder. "I'll mention it to the colonel." He headed to his office.

The colonel and Angelo considered Duffy too inexperienced for the position he held at the embassy. The last thing Joe wanted to do was to voice his opinion. *No dog in that fight.*

Chapter VI
MAJID

Majid Ziyad smiled. He had done well for himself. At forty-five, he owned an export business in Tunis that sent goods to stores throughout the Mediterranean and Europe. Shipments went out once a month on the MV *Iran Iris*. He sat behind the executive desk in a large office furnished with a leather couch, chairs and a carved wooden coffee table. When Omar walked into the office, he closed the folder on the desk and motioned to a chair.

Omar took a seat and Majid moved to the couch.

"Did you give her the letter?" Majid asked.

Omar nodded. "She'll mail it from Rome."

"We'll see if it arrives."

"It will. I told you she's trustworthy."

Majid smiled. "Will she agree to move half-kilo size shipments when she flies to Italy?"

"I didn't bring it up yet. She didn't ask any questions about the letter. I don't think there will be a problem."

"Are you paying her?"

"Just expensive gifts."

"Be careful what you say. While she's in Italy we have no control. The more she knows the more dangerous it is to our operation. I wouldn't want to ask you to kill her."

"She'll say nothing, she likes what I give her."

Majid shook his head. "What about your wife?"

Omar raised his eyebrows. "She better never find out."

Majid stood, indicating the end of their conversation. "Call Nari. Tell him the next shipment is on time."

Omar left and closed the door.

He returned to the desk and tapped the screen of his cell phone.

"How is your mother?" Majid asked. He nodded and smiled. "Good. The more information you get, the more money you'll make."

As he listened to the man, his eyes widened. "Nari? When?"

He pushed the chair back and stood. "Tomorrow night?" He furrowed his brow and glanced across the room. "Thank you. I'll send an extra payment... double the money."

Majid ended the call and stared at his desktop. He tapped the cell phone and dropped into the chair.

Nari answered. "Hello."

"How are you today?"

"Good. Is there a problem?"

The last thing Majid wanted to do was make his Italian drug connection nervous. "No. I want to be sure your distributors are ready."

"They are. I talked to each of them."

"Fine. Did the letter arrive?"

"Yes."

Good, she passed the test. "Okay. I'll call before the shipment leaves." Majid hung up, made another call and waited for an answer. "Yassine, it's me. I have a job for you."

Chapter VII
THE ARREST

At ten the next night a police car and a van occupied the corner of a secured parking area outside the Carabinieri Counter-Narcotics Group. Angelo and Joe stood beside an Alfa Romeo parked ten meters away from Lieutenant Sergio Lacona, and four of his men dressed in dark tactical uniforms.

"We'll follow them," Angelo said. "It's their case and they don't want us getting in the way. When we get to the club, stay in the car until they grab him."

"No problem. You think he knows about the freighter?"

"He's getting most of his heroin from Majid. I'm sure he does and I plan to squeeze the information out of him."

###

Two miles from Vatican City, a crowd and a fifty foot long line formed along the sidewalk outside a nightclub. Classic rock blasted from a speaker above the closed double doors. Motorcycles and scooters lined the opposite curb along the narrow street.

Yassine, a dark-skinned man in his twenties, with a close-cropped beard, stood in line ten people behind Nari Saladino, and his much too young date. Yassine smiled at her high heels, skin-tight low-cut jeans and an undersized vest battling to retain her ample breasts. He glanced at a kid sitting on his scooter across the street and nodded.

Nari's cell phone rang. He lifted a hand to his date and stepped into the street to answer it.

The boy on the scooter raised his eyebrows and nodded to Yassine as he started the engine, pulled away from the curb, and stopped. "Hi Nari," he yelled.

Nari looked up, squinted at him and half waved as the scooter headed up the street.

Yassine glanced in both directions. He wiped his perspiring right hand against his pants leg. Prior to stepping into the street, he turned to the girls behind him, held up a finger, and nodded. As he walked up behind Nari, he pulled a pistol from his pocket, and fired one shot into the back of the drug dealer's head.

The crowd panicked, women screamed and people shoved each other to back away from the curb. The girls he had motioned to shrieked, spun around and raced down the street. Yassine took off in the same direction, jumping over a couple who had fallen in the street. He fled with the crowd and bolted down an intersecting alley.

Angelo's Alfa Romeo followed the speeding van and marked police car to the front of the nightclub. He slammed on the brakes, skidded to a stop and jumped out.

What the hell happened? Joe threw open the passenger side door and ran to Angelo's side. "No sense in sitting in the car. It ended before we arrived."

Sergio and his men, carrying Spectre M4 submachine guns, secured the area near the body, and in front of the club.

Angelo and Joe stepped beside Sergio, standing next to Saladino's body.

"Looks as if he pissed off the wrong people, or someone found out you were coming." Joe said to Sergio.

The next morning, Angelo, with an empty feeling in the pit of his stomach, walked to Colonel Aldo's office. Joe called earlier and said he didn't want to stick his nose into Carabinieri affairs. He would have been more comfortable with Joe at his side.

Angelo marched to the front of Aldo's desk and came to attention.

"Sit down Captain Randi."

Normally it's Angelo... not good. "Good morning, sir."

"Sit."

He dropped into a straight-back chair in front of the desk and pressed himself against the thin wood slats.

"It wasn't your operation, but what happened last night?"

"We were two blocks away when we heard the call. He was dead before we arrived."

Aldo shook his head. "The Commanding General wants answers. He's been on the phone with the Minister who is mad as hell. He's ready to replace people in the Narcotics Group, and we're not far down the line."

Angelo held his breath a moment. "Sir, somebody is getting information, and whoever it is, they're related to the trawler case. As far as I know the Narcotics Group decided to pick up Saladino weeks ago. After he arrived in Rome, they chose the day."

"I assume the same people briefed on the trawler case knew of Saladino's imminent arrest?"

"I believe so."

"And you interviewed each of them?"

Angelo nodded. "Yes, sir."

"The Americans?"

"The Ambassador allowed Joe and me to speak with them. Their embassy has security standards that meet or exceed ours."

Aldo leaned over his desk. "Two outside investigators will look into the matter. Prepare yourself for questions. I suggest you have the right answers." He picked up a folder on his desk.

The colonel had finished. Angelo headed to the door, and when Aldo called his name he stopped and turned. "Yes, sir?"

"Miami's name stays secret. If I were you I wouldn't bring up your informant. Answer their questions, but get them off our asses."

Chapter VIII
THE INVITATION

Nina shook her head as she pulled her suitcase down the passageway leading from the plane. She looked at her white tennis shoes, "Damn it". Nothing went right since she met with the other flight attendants at the Munich airport. The heel of a shoe broke off getting on the plane and the flight into Rome had no vacant seats. Rowdy passengers returning from a Roma and Bayern Munich soccer game filled the cabin. Roma won the game and their followers continued to party on the flight home. When she stepped into the gate waiting area, Joe and Angelo waved to her.

"Hi beautiful," Joe said as he kissed her.

Angelo kissed her cheeks. "Tired?"

"I am."

"Sneakers? Where are your heels?" Joe asked.

"Don't ask, it's been a bad day."

Joe took her bag and hand. "Angelo thought it would be nice to pick you up in the Alfa."

Joe met her at the airport whenever he had time, but she hadn't told him which flight she planned to take. It seemed odd Angelo was with him. "Is everything all right? How did you know my flight number?"

"A family member, who works in the tower, made a few calls," Angelo said.

Nina grinned. *Got more connections than a hooker with a little black book.* "Your cousin, or my cousin on your wife's side?"

He smiled. "A Randi."

Angelo and Joe sat in the two large chairs near the coffee table. Nina, who had been talking to her cousin, walked into the office.

Angelo gave her his seat and dropped onto the couch. "Joe said you don't have a telephone in the apartment."

"Just cell phones."

"What's Monique's number?" Joe asked.

"336, 811, 2114."

Angelo wrote the number on a note pad. "Does she use email?"

"Yes, tiscali... LaCroix, a period, and Monique."

"Does she email Omar?" Joe asked.

"I don't know."

Joe slid to the edge of his chair and leaned toward her. "If you don't want to, you don't have to do this. Try to get her to talk... tell her something made you angry."

"It won't be difficult, I'm already mad at her."

"We may want to put a microphone in her room. For now, talk to her and keep good notes. Don't hunt for more information in her room. She may notice things misplaced and I don't want her to get suspicious." Angelo said.

"Okay, anything else?"

"Yeah," Joe said. "Keep it simple. The more complicated the story you make up, the harder it will be remembering it. Let's get coffee and I'll get a taxi for you."

"I have a call to make. Meet you at the bakery down the street," Angelo said.

Joe, drinking espresso, sat alone in the bakery when Angelo arrived. "She left a few minutes ago."

Angelo walked to the counter, got a coffee and returned. "I'm sure the informant is inside the Narcotics Group Headquarters."

"Thank Jesus we didn't give anyone Nina's name," Joe said.

Angelo downed his espresso and slid away from the table. "Let's go back to my office and develop a plan."

Nina walked into her apartment and saw Monique on the couch half asleep. She left her bag by the door. "Hi."

"I thought you'd be home earlier."

"The police were on the train from the airport Nina said. "A woman stole a purse, and they said I looked like her." She dropped onto the couch.

Monique shook her head and frowned. "Don't they have better things to do? They could chase politicians who steal millions of Euros."

Nina took advantage of the opportunity, raised her head and smiled. "Chase politicians? Why? No one wants to lose their job or the money that changes hands."

"They're useless. When's your next flight?"

"I'm off for three days. You?"

"Me too. Want to meet Omar? We can fly to Tunis tomorrow."

Meet a killer? "I don't know. He'll want to be alone with you."

"I'll call him and ask." She leapt from the couch and dashed to her bedroom.

Nina sat on the couch and gazed around the room. *It might help Joe if I go.* She pressed her lips together and frowned. Concerned with her safety whenever she traveled, he always reminded her to lock her door, watch her bags, and guard her purse. Going to Tunis wouldn't set well with him and once she told him she planned to meet Omar, he'd go crazy. *Better find an excuse.* She lifted the television remote and clicked through channels.

Monique ran from the hallway. "He wants us to come and said we can stay in the villa."

"What villa?"

"His boss Majid owns it. It's on the outskirts of Tunis."

"I don't know. You sure it's no problem if I go?"

"Of course not. You'll have fun... we'll stay one night."

She answered without thinking of the ramifications. "Okay, make the flight arrangements."

"Great, I'll shower... let's go shopping."

"I'll take one when you're finished," Nina said as Monique headed down the hall.

She walked to her bedroom, closed the door and called Joe's cell phone. Two taps on the screen lowered the speaker volume. *Why did I say yes?*

"Embassy, Costa."

"Hi Joe." There was a pause.

"You home?"

"Yes."

"Is something wrong?"

"No but I need to tell you something. Don't be mad."

"There's nothing you can do to make me angry."

"Good. I'm going to Tunis with Monique."

"You're what?"

"It's a chance to meet Omar... just for one night." She looked at the phone waiting for a response.

"No. You can't."

"Monique came up with the idea. I'll get more information. It will help you capture him."

"It's too dangerous."

"Why?"

"It just is."

"I've decided to go!"

"Nina, please."

"No." She heard him sigh.

"When do you leave?"

"Tomorrow morning."

"I want to see you before you go."

So he can change my mind. "I won't have time... it's only for one night."

"Okay. Keep your cell phone with you and call as soon as you get back."

"I will, don't worry."

"Worry? I'll go nuts while you're gone."

"I'll make it up to you when I get home. I love you."

"I love you more."

Joe wasted no time. He called Angelo and asked him not to leave his office until they spoke.

Outside the door in front of Mia's office, he stopped. *Why won't Nina listen?* Trying to change her mind was fruitless. Although it wouldn't make him feel much better, he knew she'd be cautious. She often told him her degree in psychology taught her to spend more time listening and less talking. *Love her attitude but getting involved in a major international investigation isn't a smart decision. Angelo won't like this.*

Before Mia looked up from her keyboard he stepped past her and marched into Angelo's office.

Angelo, flipping through a file on his desk, didn't see him enter.

"Glad you're sitting. You don't want to be standing when you hear this."

Angelo smiled. "Relax. Whatever you say can't be any more of a surprise than the photo on Nina's phone." He shoved a stack of papers aside, looked at Joe and furrowed his brow. "Something bothering you?"

"That word isn't strong enough and angry only approaches the way I feel." He dragged a chair in front of the desk and dropped into it. "You will not believe this. Your wife's cousin... my girlfriend... is going to Tunis with her roommate."

Angelo took a deep breath, his eyes widened. "Tell me they're only going shopping."

Joe glanced at the floor. "Monique's going to introduce her to Omar."

Angelo bolted upright in his chair. "Is she crazy?"

"I asked, and she wasn't happy about it."

"Tell her not to go."

Joe took a deep breath and shook his head. "You've known her longer than I. Ever been able to tell her what to do?"

Angelo held a finger in front of his lips, lowered his hand and looked toward the office door. "Mia! Shut my door and don't disturb us." He waited until it closed and lowered his voice. "Once she makes a decision, that's it. If Mia or my wife find out they'll blame us, no matter what Nina says. When is she supposed to leave?"

"Tomorrow... for one night."

"Stop her from going."

Joe raised both his hands. "How? Got any ideas?"

Angelo shook his head and rolled his eyes. "Sofia said Nina's the stubborn one in the family. I'll get someone to follow her."

Joe pondered the proposal. "Not the police."

"When the new Tunisian government disbanded the secret police, many of them went into what you call private practice."

Joe stared at him for five seconds. "No. They'll be spotted. I'm always telling her to be careful. If she doesn't see them, Omar's men might."

"At least get her flight numbers."

"She's already mad at me. Call your relative at the airport. Maybe he can find out. Before she leaves she'll call, and if I ask which flight she's taking she'll think I'm planning something. I don't want to make her nervous."

Nina and Monique walked along Via dei Condotti, two blocks from the Spanish Steps.

They stopped in front of a display window at the Gucci store. Nina had wandered the street many times but bought nothing. The fashions and accessories of Prada, Louis Vuitton and Stuart Weitzman, didn't fit into her budget. Monique's wallet produced a constant supply of hundred euro bills. *She's getting more than a sex and bracelets from Omar.*

"Where does Omar work," Nina asked.

"An international shipping company."

Nina nodded. "What does he do?"

"I don't know... must be important, he's paid well."

"Does he ever come to Rome?"

"The job keeps him busy."

They left Gucci, stepped into the crowded street and walked past the Bulgari and Prada stores, stopping at the window of a small boutique.

Nina looked at the prices of the women's clothing on display. *Even the small shops think we should pay extra for their name.*

"Wait until you see the villa. It has big pool and a hot tub."

"Is it nice?"

"I stayed there once, it's beautiful."

"Will he meet us at the airport?"

"No. He'll send a car to get us. The last time I went a new Range Rover picked me up outside baggage claim." Monique headed to the store's door. "Come on, I need a new dress."

Wish she'd talk more about him. I can't keep asking questions.

Majid sat at his desk while Omar finish counting a stack of five hundred euro notes. "Fifteen thousand, correct?"

"Yes."

"Tell Jamal to get rid of his galley girl, she's seen enough."

"He did... last week." He grinned. "She was fun while she lasted."

Majid raised his eyebrows. "Be careful. I can't protect you if Jamal catches you playing with one of his personal toys."

"Five trips and five pleasurable late night meetings. I'm still here, he hasn't caught me yet."

Majid shook his head. "You're crazier than I thought."

Omar smiled and raised his eyebrows. "Monique is coming tomorrow, she's bringing a friend. Can they stay at the villa?"

"Sure, call Ayisha. What's her friend's name?"

"Nina, you want to meet her?"

Majid shook his head. "I'm leaving tonight, I'll be in Tehran."

"The next shipment?"

"Yes."

"Can I use your car and driver to pick them up at the airport?"

Majid nodded. "Tell Kojo, he'll set it up for you."

"I guess I must take care of both women," Omar said tapping his chest.

"Be careful. You play more than you work."

"I'm here when you need me."

"Watch what you say to them."

Chapter IX
THE VILLA

The chauffeured Mercedes pulled up to the iron gate in the ten-foot high concrete wall. It swung open, and the car drove to the front entrance of a sprawling two-story villa.

Nina's eyes opened wide as she surveyed the exterior of the house. The large windows reflected the cloudless sky as if they were mirrors. Except for creamy beige accents around the windows and doors, the white stucco walls reminded her of Santorini, Greece. *The only thing missing is a deep blue domed roof, centered with a simple cross.*

The driver stopped near five half-circle steps leading to a landing and the entrance. A short middle-aged woman, wearing a hijab, stepped from the house. She walked to the edge of the steps and watched as the chauffeur opened the car door.

"See what I mean?" Monique asked.

Nina examined the massive double wooden doors. "We're staying here?"

"Wait until you look inside," Monique said as she stepped from the car.

Nina slid across the seat and got out.

"Good afternoon, madam," the woman said to Monique.

Monique ignored the greeting. "Her name is Ayisha. She'll take care of everything we need."

Nina smiled and nodded. "Hello Ayisha, nice to meet you. My name is Nina."

The driver opened the trunk and Nina stepped beside him to get her bag.

"Don't worry, he'll bring them inside," Monique said. As she walked up the steps and entered the house, she turned to Ayisha. "Hold the door for Nina!"

Nina frowned on her way up the steps. *That wasn't nice.* "I'll follow you, Ayisha." When she passed through the doorway she stopped and gasped at the surrounding beauty.

Monique waited for her in a foyer with a marble floor and white walls accented in the color gold. At the end of the hall stood a three-tier gilded fountain on blue tile.

Monique led her to a corridor off the foyer. "I'll stay in the same bedroom I used last time," she said.

"Please follow me madam," Ayisha said, turning to Nina "I'll show you to your bedroom. I'm sure you'll be comfortable."

"You don't need to call me madam. Nina is fine."

"Thank you, this way." She reached a door and stepped into a bedroom.

As Nina crossed the threshold, she hesitated. A canopied bed with a carved wooden headboard, and two night tables accented in reddish gold caught her eye. Through the door to the bath, black tiles surrounded a large marble tub. "This place is beautiful. Who lives here?"

Ayisha stared at her for a moment. "No one. The villa is used to entertain guests."

"Omar's friends?"

She smiled. "No. Majid Ziyad, Omar's employer owns the house. Business associates and important customers meet here." Ayisha slipped out the door.

Nina sat on the bed and surveyed the room. "Someone named Majid has a lot of money." She furrowed her brow. *Joe didn't mention his name. Wonder who he is?* There was a tap on the door. She opened it, looked down and pulled her overnight bag into the room.

As she dropped the bag on the bed and unzipped it, Monique walked in wearing a tiny white bikini. "You like it?"

Nina smiled and raised her eyebrows. "Doesn't hide much, but it looks great on you."

"No, I mean the villa."

Both women laughed.

"Oh, yes, it's beautiful,"

"Wait until you see the rest of the house." Monique headed to the door. "I'll be at the pool, it's at the back, past the portico. Put on your bathing suit and join me."

A dip in the pool sounds great. I need to keep her talking. Nina dug out her emerald bikini, changed into it, and removed a sheer wrap from her bag. In the bathroom, she turned in a circle in front of the mirror. *This one is small enough. How does she dare walk around in that tiny thing?* She shrugged at the mirror and left the room.

Not knowing which way to go, she returned to the foyer, turned and passed between a living and dining room. *Gaudy. Way too much white and gold.*

When she came to an open area where marble columns supported a stucco ceiling painted with intricate flowers and vines, she stopped. *She's right. It's a portico, not a patio.*

She spotted Monique waving to her from an umbrella covered table near the pool. Out of the corner of her eye, she noticed Ayisha watching from a doorway. As she reached the table and pulled out a chair, Ayisha stepped beside her.

"Would you like something to eat and drink... wine?" the housekeeper asked.

Nina nodded, "Red, please?"

"Red for both of us," Monique ordered.

"Yes, madam." She scurried away.

"Why don't you like her?" Nina asked.

"Ayisha? She's all right, but she's only a servant."

Surprised at her friend's callousness, Nina changed the subject. "I thought Omar would be here."

Monique stood. "He'll come soon. Let's sit by the pool."

They sat at the edge and dangled their feet in the water.

"Ayisha said a man named Majid owns this house. Omar's lucky to have such good friends," Nina said.

Monique pursed her lips. "I've never met him." She raised a finger to her mouth. "It's best if you don't mention his name."

"Why?"

"I'll tell you later, just don't. Omar will be angry. He's doesn't want people to know about his private life."

"Why?"

"He doesn't want the authorities to know how much money he makes."

Omar arrived at eight and went into the house to change into a bathing suit. He returned to the poolside table where Ayisha cleared away half-full plates of food. She had placed a bottle of scotch beside the bottle of wine in front of the two women.

"When did you and Monique meet?" Omar asked.

"Two months ago, at work." She didn't take her eyes off him. *Good looking. His dark hair and complexion make his green eyes glow against his olive skin.*

Monique interrupted. "Nina found a wonderful apartment and needed a roommate."

When she didn't continue speaking, Nina did. "How long have you and Monique been together?"

"A little over six months. We met in Egypt."

Omar lifted the wine bottle and half-filled their glasses. He poured himself scotch.

Monique held out her glass. "Fill it to the top."

Aware Omar was staring at her, Nina covered her glass with her hand. "No thank you."

"Do you enjoy being a flight attendant?" he asked.

"Yes, I love to travel. What type of work do you do?"

"International shipping... at the port."

Monique downed half the wine in her glass. She held it to Omar, and he refilled it.

"Sounds interesting," Nina said. "I'll bet owning a company keeps you busy."

"It does, but it's not my company. I work for MZ Shipping and Export. One day I'll start a business."

"That will be nice... lots of travel."

"Yes."

Monique emptied what remained in the wine bottle into her glass. "Enough talk about work." She turned to Omar. "You should come to visit Rome and stay with us."

"The next month will be busy. One day I'll plan a trip."

Ayisha walked to the table and replaced the empty wine bottle with a full one.

Nina waited until she stepped away and smiled at Omar. "When you come we'll show you Rome." She stood. "Excuse me, I'll be back in a minute." She walked away from the pool.

Tall... and beautiful, Omar thought as Nina walked into the house. He smiled at Monique. "I'm glad you found a good friend when you moved to Rome."

Unsteady in her chair, she sipped more wine. "Me too."

He took her hand, lifted the bottle of wine and led her to the nearby hot tub. She held his arm and leaned against his side as he helped her into the water and refilled her glass.

"You look wonderful but you don't need this." He unhooked her top, slid the bottom from her legs and pulled her to him pressing her back against his chest.

She leaned her head against his shoulder and slurred her words. "We shouldn't do it here, Nina will be back soon."

Omar kissed her neck. "Good, the tub is big enough for the three of us."

Nina, now wearing a floral sun dress, strolled to the tub and looked at them. She bit the inside of her cheek trying not to show her surprise. *Should have taken longer to change.*

"Are we embarrassing you?" Omar asked.

"Of course not." She stepped to the table and took a seat.

"Join us," he said. "The water feels good. Leave your dress on the chair."

Here we go. I know your culture. Don't raise your hopes. "Love to, but tonight, I can't."

"Why?" Monique asked.

"It's the wrong time of the month."

Omar's eyes widened. "Best if you don't. Another time."

She picked up her glass of wine and pushed away from the table. "I'm tired. You have fun. We'll talk in the morning."

"I'm leaving early," Omar said. "See you next time you visit."

"Yes, next time, or in Rome when you come. Good night."

###

Glad to be alone in her room and away from the awkward scene at the pool, Nina folded her dress and laid it on the bed. She removed the robe from a hook on the bathroom door and slipped into it when there was a soft knock on the door. "Who is it?"

"Ayisha."

She opened the door. "Please, come in."

Nina studied the woman. A white work tunic over black pants hid her small frame. A colorful hijab covered her hair. Nina focused on thin lines etched into Ayisha's tanned face. *Hard to tell her age. Fifty?*

"Is something wrong, madam?"

"No, Ayisha. I'm tired."

"Please do not take offense. Why are you here?"

Surprised at the woman's question, Nina stared at her. "I don't understand."

"I've watched you since you arrived. You are courteous, and like a lady, you are careful what you say and do. You're not like the people who come here."

"What do you mean, Ayisha? I'm no different from others."

"You don't act like the women who are brought here. Most have no honor and, sometimes bad things happen."

"What bad things? Monique and I aren't in danger, are we?"

"No, but you must be careful."

Nina paused and stared at her. "What about you?"

"I'm fine. When I meet good people, it makes me realize my grandchildren will one day live a good life."

"Where do they live?"

"Here in Tunis, with me. I'm from Iraq. My daughter and her husband are dead. Most of my family died in the war."

Nina shook her head. "I'm sorry."

"One day we will leave here."

"Where will you go?"

Ayisha smiled. "I've saved most of the money I'm paid. We'll go to Europe and get away from people in the business of destroying lives."

"I don't understand."

Ayisha looked over her shoulder, turned, and closed the door.

"I can tell you are different. You care how you treat people. Be careful. It's best if you don't come here again. Omar is not a person you want as your friend."

Nina took a deep breath. "What's wrong? Tell me, I won't say anything to Monique."

Ayisha lowered her voice to a whisper. "Listen to what I say. I'm here because I need this job."

Chapter X
WORRIED MEN

Joe, Angelo, Sergio and DEA Agent Paul Sacca sat at the table in Colonel Aldo's conference room.

Paul looked at Joe. "Did Duffy say anything to you about the last meeting?"

"Yeah."

"He told me the FBI wanted to be part of the investigation."

Out of the corner of his eye, Joe watched Angelo leaf through papers in front of him. *Guess I'm stuck with this one.* He nodded. "They do, but I don't know what happened. I'll ask the boss."

Colonel Aldo entered and the four men stood. Everyone waited until he took a seat.

"You have news for us, Angelo?" Aldo asked.

Joe raised a finger. "Sir, before we start, did you receive an inquiry from the FBI?"

Aldo smiled and stared at him for a moment. "Yes, from our friend Agent Robert Duffy. I sent a note to the embassy telling them I forwarded it to the Chief of Staff. He's a busy man, but I'm sure when he reads it, he'll approve. For now the Carabinieri, the Marshals Service, and your DEA will do the best job they can."

Approval may take a month, Joe thought. When the colonel wanted something done, he did it and told his boss later. This time he wanted the request to go up the, slow to react, chain of command. *I love this guy.*

"Please start, Angelo," Aldo said.

He removed a notebook from his pocket. "Miami is meeting with Omar."

Joe realized what Angelo was doing. *Doesn't want to say it's in Tunis. Good job, Ang.*

Paul turned to him and frowned. "Isn't he going out with Omar's girlfriend?"

Angelo shrugged.

"Is Miami involved in drugs?" Aldo asked.

"No, sir," Angelo replied. "Joe and I did a complete background check. Nothing on file. Never stopped or questioned by the police."

Aldo squinted and focused on the tabletop for five seconds. "Tell me about this person you call Miami."

Joe leaned forward. *Quick, what do we tell him? I need to change the subject.* Before he opened his mouth, Angelo continued and the tightness in his chest disappeared.

"Italian citizen, a patriot, good job, anti-drug, comes from a good family. Horrified when the five agents were killed."

"Are they meeting outside Italy?" Paul asked.

Angelo nodded.

Paul stared at him for a moment. "Where?"

"Didn't tell us."

"When is he coming back?" Paul asked.

Joe couldn't keep quiet any longer. Paul was fishing for information. "In a day or two."

"Traveling by plane?"

I'm not that damn stupid. The answer to the question may lead to Nina's identity. "Didn't say where the meeting was being held. We weren't told how they are getting there, or how long it would last." Joe shrugged. "Could have traveled by car, ferry, or plane."

"Miami isn't telling you much," Paul said.

Angelo leaned forward. "True. Not yet, but trust must be shown by both sides."

Sergio shifted in his chair. "Let us talk to him."

Angelo's body stiffened. "It's not going to happen."

Aldo held up a hand. "Agent Sacca and Lieutenant Lacona, your superiors may not like it, but I've made my decision. I won't place someone's life in danger. Trust Angelo and Joe and respect their request. Our first priority is to find the person leaking information. After that, we'll get Omar so you both can solve your case."

Paul raised his eyebrows and nodded. "I understand, sir. DEA told me to ask. I'll tell them to stay calm."

"Good. Anything else for me?"

"No, sir," Angelo said. "We need to discuss a few things with Paul and Sergio."

Aldo stood. When no one else spoke, he glanced at Angelo. "Call us after you debrief Miami." He left the room.

Joe and Angelo cornered the two narcotics investigators.

"Listen," Joe said. "No one is trying to cut you guys out of the investigation. The informant told us we had to keep his identity secret. I promise you'll get everything we find out. Angelo and I would appreciate you not trying to corner us in front of Colonel Aldo."

"You're speaking for both of you?"

Joe ground his teeth, his pulse raced. *I'll whip your ass if you...*

Angelo stepped in front of Sergio. "Lieutenant Lacona. When I speak, or Inspector Costa speaks, we speak for each other. I suggest you remember that, if you wish for you career as a Carabinieri officer to flourish."

Sergio took a breath. "Sorry, sir."

Paul interceded. "Both of us are being pressured. We'll handle it."

"It's best if we don't defy Colonel Aldo," Sergio said.

Yeah, if you want to keep your job.

After the meeting Joe walked with Angelo to his office. He pulled a chair, in front of Angelo's desk and took a seat. "Don't be angry at him."

"I'm not. He's doing what the academy taught him."

"What do you mean?"

"When you're an officer of the Carabinieri, you can throw your weight around," Angelo said as he grinned and tapped the captain's insignia on his uniform. "He made the mistake of doing it in front of someone whose ass is a little heavier." He removed his note pad from his pocket and placed it in the center desk drawer. "I wish we didn't have to lie to them."

"Don't worry. Their superiors feel left out when they aren't told everything that's happening. We've got to stick to our plan."

Angelo nodded. "Did you hear from Nina?"

"I told her not to call." Joe stared at him. "You didn't do anything crazy, did you?"

"No. They may watch to see if someone follows them."

"Nina's smart. She won't place herself in danger. Doesn't make me worry any less, but I can't do anything about it now."

"You're right," Angelo said. "I can't wait to pick her brain. She'll come back loaded with information. Come to dinner at my house tonight. I'll call Sofia."

"I'd love to but she'll ask why Nina isn't with me."

"Yeah. Then we must come up with more lies. We'll meet again in the morning."

Chapter XI
THE INFORMANTS

Majid got up from his desk and walked to the couch. He took his cell phone from his pocket and tapped the screen.

A deep voice with a Polish accent came over the speaker. "Are you are well today, sir?"

"Yes Gustav. Have you been to Krakow to visit your mother?"

"No. I called her this morning. She's better."

"From the sound of your message you've been busy."

"Yes, the captain is stupid."

"Tell me everything he wrote."

"Miami will talk to Omar."

"Anything else?"

"Yes. The name 'Paul', the letters 'DEA' and the words 'wants in', at the bottom of the page."

"Nothing more?"

"No, sir."

"Good work, Gustav. Miami must be a code for the person. Try to find out his real name. Check your mail in a few days. I'm sending an extra payment."

"Thank you, sir."

###

After Nina's safe return, Joe waited for her at a table in the Target restaurant on the corner of Via Modena and Via Torino, a block west of Piazza della Repubblica. That afternoon she called, and he asked her to meet him at nine for dinner.

During the week people filled the sidewalk tables and the street level dining room. Few used the one hundred-seat room down a narrow flight of stairs. He had arranged for a corner table so they would be away from other customers. An open bottle of wine and two glasses stood on the white table cloth in front of him.

Nina stepped from the stairway and headed in his direction. He stood and smiled. She wore red heels, a short skirt with a red lace blouse, and carried a large handbag over her shoulder. *Wow! Stunning. Loves red and always dresses to the nines.* What he needed at the moment was to hold her. He pulled her into his arms and they kissed. "Thank God you're back. No more trips to Tunisia, please."

"You worry too much. Everything went well, and I learned quite a bit."

He took her hand. "Glad you did but don't press your luck. I love you and don't want anything to happen. Let's have wine."

Joe sat with his back against the wall and Nina sat to his right.

She looked around the near empty dining room. "Why do you always pick a table against the wall?"

"Habit."

"Is anyone joining us?"

He slipped his hand to her knee, squeezed and watched her jump. "I told Angelo we wanted to be alone."

"Good."

"Can you go with me to his office tomorrow morning?"

"Sure, what time?"

"I'll pick you up at ten."

"There are a thousand things to tell you about the trip. I made notes."

"Besides what you told me on the phone, is anything urgent? Something we need to talk about right now?"

"Not really."

Joe smiled and took her hand. "Good. Let's enjoy the evening."

She leaned towards him, her eyes sparkling with excitement. "If I stay at your apartment you won't need to pick me up in the morning." Her hand slid to his upper thigh, and she kissed him as she lifted her handbag. "I brought everything I need."

"Beautiful Italian women are so romantic." He tickled her side and winked.

"Yes and jealous." She grabbed his chin and pulled him close to her. "For your own safety, concentrate on this Italian woman."

"I plan to, all night long."

At ten-thirty, the next morning, Joe, Nina and Angelo sat near the coffee table in Angelo's office.

Angelo read two pages of notes Nina provided him and smiled. "You did a good job listening."

"And I kept good notes."

"Angelo and I will go over them and write a report before we speak to the others. Will Monique help us?"

Nina shook her head and sighed. "No, she loves him."

Joe squinted and paused. "Is there anything we can do to turn her against him?"

"No. From what I saw, she'll do anything for him."

"That's the answer," Angelo said.

"What do you mean?" Nina asked.

It didn't take Joe long to figure out Angelo's line of thinking. He grinned and turned to Nina. "We'll use that to our advantage. If he's in danger, will she still want help him?"

"Yes. Like I said, she'd do anything."

"Good," Joe said. "If we can convince her the only way to keep him alive is to help us... she'll agree."

Nina tilted her head to the side and glanced at both men. "Maybe, but he helped kill the agents on the boat, how can he escape that?"

"He won't," Angelo said. "His fate is sealed. She's the only one who may benefit."

"I don't understand. She'll lose the man she loves."

"And she'll remain alive," Joe said. "She knows too much. The people in Majid's organization won't let her live."

Mia knocked on the doorframe and brought in a tray with three cups of espresso.

"Thank you, Mia." Nina said, as her cousin left the room.

"Did Omar say anything about Majid or his job?" Joe asked.

"No. Monique told me not to mention Majid's name in front of him. He only said he worked for him and was busy. Monique was the only thing on his mind."

"What about this lady, Ayisha?" Angelo asked.

"She's nice... we talked. She doesn't like Omar or his boss."

Joe raised a finger. "You said she might leave if given the opportunity?"

"Yes. She wants to come to Europe. Everyone in her family in Iraq is dead, except her two grandchildren." She looked at her watch. "Anything else? I have a flight to Milan and back, later today."

"Tonight?" Joe asked.

"If you pick me up at the airport."

Joe stood and took her into his arms. "I'll be there."

Chapter XII
WHO IS MIAMI

Majid leaned back in the chair and glanced around the office. Gustav seldom provided him with inaccurate information. He couldn't get their last conversation out of his mind. It worried him that Italian authorities had Omar's name and may try to use him as an informant. The problem was he had no proof, and nothing had hindered their operations. *This is not a court, I need no proof.*

Omar entered and lowered himself into a chair in front of the desk. "You wanted me?"

Majid hesitated before he spoke. "There's a problem and your name is on it."

"I've done nothing wrong."

"Someone in Italy said a police informant talked to you."

Blood drained from Omar's face as he jumped from the chair. "That's crazy. Whoever told you that is lying."

Majid locked his eyes on him. *One wrong word and you are dead.* "Sit."

Omar dropped to the edge of the chair. "When did I ever talked to anyone I haven't known for a long time?"

"Are you friends with a man named Paul?"

"An American name. No."

"What about someone called Miami?"

"Like the city? No." His eyes settled on the floor for three seconds before he raised his head. "Where did you get this information?"

"It doesn't matter. If anyone approaches you, tell me. Don't play games. Understand?"

"Of course."

Exhausted by the end of the day, Angelo sat at his desk daydreaming. Nina did a fabulous job, but he and Joe agreed she wouldn't get near Tunis or Omar again.

Mia poked her head into his office. "A man is here to clean. I told him you were busy."

"Send him in, I'm leaving." He scooped up the papers on his desk and dropped them into the two-drawer safe, spinning the combination lock as the man entered.

"Good evening, Captain."

"Hello Gustav, how are you?"

"Fine, sir."

"How is your mother? Doing better I hope."

"Much better, thank you."

"Tell her I said hello." He picked up his hat and headed to the door.

That same evening, Monique sat up in the hotel room bed, and watched television. The cell phone on the nightstand rang, and she turned on the speaker. "Hello."

"Where are you?" Omar asked.

Sounds mad. Something's wrong. "In London. Is everything all right?"

"I hope so. Are you friends with a man named Paul?"

"No."

"What about someone called Miami?"

"No. What are you talking about?"

"Nothing important. Majid wasn't friendly today. I don't know if he trusts me. He said someone in Italy mentioned my name." His tone softened. "How's my lover tonight?"

"Fine, I miss you. I thought you were mad."

"No. Did you enjoy yourself at the villa?"

"Yes, I love it there."

He hesitated. "We must do it again... maybe next month."

"I can't wait that long."

"Okay, sooner. The next two weeks will be busy. Call when you get back to Rome."

"I will. I love you."

"Me too... talk to you later."

She set the phone on the nightstand. *He didn't say he loved me.*

Nina lay on the couch in Joe's apartment and moaned as he rubbed her feet. The phone startled her when it rang. As she snatched it from the coffee table, she looked at the caller ID. *Monique.* She turned to Joe and raised a finger to her lips. "Hi Monique... Yes, give me a second." She lowered her feet to the floor and motioned for him to get a pen and paper.

He leapt to a small desk and returned with a notepad and pencil.

"Okay. Who did you say?" she asked.

After a momentary pause, she cocked her head to the side and scribbled 'Paul' and 'Miami' on the paper. "Never heard of them... why?" After listening for thirty seconds, she spoke. "Okay, tomorrow afternoon." She ended the call.

Joe glanced at the paper and froze. "What was that about... why did you write those names?"

Nina flinched and glared at him. "Monique asked if they were my friends. Why are you upset?" She paused, not taking her eyes from his. "Omar called her and asked if she knew them. He seemed to be worried. She told him she didn't and asked me if I did."

He took a deep breath and sat beside her. "In a way, you don't know them. Or I should say don't know of them."

"Do you?"

"Yes."

"How? That's impossible... you've never met Monique and haven't talked to Omar. Who the hell has the name Miami?"

Joe glanced at the blank flat screen television and shook his head. He took her hand in both of his and looked into her eyes. "You."

Her mouth dropped opened. "Me?"

"It's a long story. Angelo and I gave you that name."

Her eyes widened as she pulled her hand away. "Isn't Nina good enough? Are you both turning me into a joke?"

She slid her hand to her back as he tried to take it.

"Don't be mad. Please let me explain."

She glared at him as she leaned away and crossed both arms over her chest.

"After you told Angelo and me what you found in Monique's room, we notified Colonel Aldo and the American and Italian narcotics investigators. I told Angelo I didn't want your name in the report. I love you and don't want you getting hurt. We made up a story about a confidential informant who wouldn't talk to us if we mentioned their name. We gave you the name Miami."

Nina did not move her eyes from him for a full five seconds. "Why did you tell Aldo and the others?"

"You're now a big part of the investigation. Ang and I didn't want the others to do something stupid and send everyone into hiding. Police often give an informant a code name to protect their identity."

She pressed her lips together. "Couldn't you pick something nicer than a city name?" Nina saw him try to hide a smile. *If he laughs I'll punch him.*

"Men don't think of those things. I wanted to pick Goddess, but everyone would realize it was you."

"You're not getting away that easy. Who is Paul?"

"A DEA agent at the embassy."

She scooted next to him. "Joe... do I need to be concerned for my safety?"

"I don't think so, but remember I said this may be dangerous. I'm calling Angelo." He slid the phone from his pocket and made the call.

"I want to listen."

He tapped the screen, and they listened to the loud ring.

"Hello," Angelo said.

"You sleeping?"

"I was."

"You better get up, we need to talk. I'm with Nina and you're on the speaker."

Angelo moaned. "Okay, I'm awake. What the hell is so important?"

"Monique called Nina from London and asked her if she ever heard the name Paul or Miami."

Five silent seconds passed.

"Are you there, Angelo?"

"Yes. Did you say Nina's with you?"

"Yes," Nina said. "We're at Joe's apartment."

"Stay with Joe for a couple of days."

She shook her head. "I can't. Monique will wonder what happened and she may say something to Omar."

"Damn it," Joe said. "I'll be in your office at nine. We need to figure out what happened. Nina and I will talk about her safety tonight. See you in the morning."

Nina walked to the kitchen and returned with two glasses of wine. "How bad is it?"

"Bad. Someone is giving Majid's organization information, but you're safe."

"How can you say that?"

"Angelo and I are the only two people on earth who know you are Miami. Your notes are in my safe and the reports we wrote don't mention your name... they only refer to a person codenamed Miami."

"Then how did Omar get the names?"

Joe rubbed his chin and looked around the room. "The only people given those names are the small group that met with the colonel. The person passing information to Majid and Omar must be close to one of us."

"What should I do?"

"Nothing. Act normal around Monique and don't ask too many questions."

"At the end of the call she didn't sound concerned. I'll only see her for a short time before my flight tomorrow."

"Good. You'll be able to tell if something's wrong. Call me immediately if you think there's a problem."

Chapter XIII
IT'S ME

The next morning, Joe wasted no time. He woke Nina early, kissed her and told her to be cautious and not let Monique talk her into anything when she went back to her apartment.

He arrived outside the conference room at the same time as the colonel and hesitated before opening the door. "Good morning, sir."

Aldo nodded. "Good morning. It seems Captain Randi likes to arrange meetings with little notice."

Joe pulled open the door. "Yes, sir. This one is important."

"We'll see."

Aldo entered the room and Joe followed.

Angelo and Paul stood.

The colonel told everyone to take a seat and sat in a chair at the head of the table. He looked at Angelo. "I trust you called us because there's good news."

Angelo tightened his jaw and raised his eyebrows. "No, sir. Most is alarming."

"I've been doing this job for quite a few weeks, not much frightens me anymore, Angelo," Aldo said with a smile. "Tell us why we're here."

Joe sighed when Angelo spoke without notes or a written report. *Documents are never easy to control, even when the people in the room can be trusted.*

Angelo took a breath. "If everyone here had the true name of our informant, he'd be dead. Our leak goes directly to the Ziyad organization."

Aldo stared at him and frowned. "Are you sure?"

"Sir, the informant has not been working for us long. Last night, Joe received information that Majid asked about two names."

Heads turned and everyone looked at each other.

"What names," Aldo asked.

"Paul, and the code name, Miami. The leak is connected to one of us... including Sergio."

Aldo looked at the three men. "Where is Lieutenant Lacona?"

"In Sicily meeting with a Chief Magistrate in Palermo... he'll be back tonight," Paul said.

The colonel raised his elbows to the table, clasped his hands together, and glanced at Angelo. "The accusation you're making is serious."

Angelo's eyes widened. "Yes, sir, but I'm not blaming anyone here."

Joe leaned on the table. "Sir, may I say something?"

"Please do. Hopefully you can shed light on what Angelo said."

"We're not making accusations. But, the informant is someone we know... someone who works in this building."

Aldo pressed his hands against his lips and stared at the table. "Why this headquarters?"

"The Ziyad organization found out about the trawler operation," Angelo said. "They also knew about Saladino's pending arrest. Now they have these names, and the one place both names were mentioned was in this room."

Aldo tapped his fingernails on the table as he looked at Joe and Paul. "Don't take this personally." He turned to Angelo. "What about the U.S. Embassy?"

Joe froze in his chair. He glanced at Paul and to Aldo. "Sir, I'll answer for myself and Paul can follow. There are files in my office about the trawler case and Saladino's arrest. I also have our informant's notes. Everything is locked in my safe and I'm the only one with the combination. In the ambassador's private safe is a lockbox with an embossed lead band around it. Double-sealed envelopes containing every safe combination in the embassy are in the box." He paused and took a deep breath. "The ambassador and the Chief of Security must be present to open the box and reseal it. I'll speak with the ambassador later today." He looked at Paul.

"A large DEA file on the trawler case is in my safe. Saladino's file is next to it. Like Joe, I'm the only one with the combination." He raised his eyebrows. "The name Miami is not written on any document in my office."

Aldo looked at Angelo. "And you?"

"Two small files are in my safe along with my reports of Miami's activities. I did not keep a copy of the notes Miami provided to us."

Aldo tapped his temple with his index finger. "What I've been told is here. I suggest each of you use the same compartment, and for now, stay away from putting anything on paper. No one could gain access to one of our safes, the answer is simpler. Get your communications devices checked... today." He pursed his lips and glanced at each man. "Do what you must, I want answers, soon."

As Aldo left the room, Joe turned to Paul. "Stay, we need to talk." The door closed. "Remember I told you we'd share anything we learned?"

Paul nodded. "Yeah, you find something helpful?"

The three men sat and Angelo removed a folded paper from his pocket. "Under different circumstances I would give a copy of this to the Anti-Narcotics Group and one to you. Because of the present situation, Joe and I want it to go to as few people as possible."

Joe turned and faced Paul. "Careful with this, it can lead to the identity of our informant."

"Will I need help to act on the information?"

"Yes," Joe said. "But not from DEA or the FBI."

"There's a woman who works for Majid by the name of Ayisha... about fifty years old," Angelo said. "She's in a position to overhear details of his drug operations and she doesn't like what she heard."

"Is she involved?"

Joe shook his head. "No. She's a housekeeper in a villa he owns. It's where he entertains suppliers and dealers outside Tunis."

Angelo handed Paul the paper.

Paul spent a moment looking at the two typed sentences. "Her name, the fact she works at Majid's villa... the address and she wants to get her grandchildren to Europe. Is that all I get?"

"I'm not putting anything else on paper," Angelo said. "She's raising her two grandchildren and she'll tell us everything she knows if we can get her to Europe."

Joe raised a finger. "She may have information to put people in prison for a long time."

"You guys are asking me to get her out? What the hell can I do alone? Tunisia isn't the friendliest place on earth."

Joe grinned. "You're friends with Al Provitti. The CIA has no stake in this poker game, but they may help."

Paul pointed at Angelo. "What about your guys?"

He shrugged and raised his eyebrows. "Tunisia and Italy are trading partners with close relations. Our politicians would raise hell if we're involved."

Joe understood Paul's apprehension. Americans may be blamed for snatching an Iraqi citizen from Tunisia. *I can hear the international uproar.* The CIA Station Chief was the key to the plan. "That's why we mentioned Provitti. The Agency, more than likely, has locals on the payroll that want to make a few dollars."

Paul smiled. "You two think of everything, don't you? What other feats of magic am I supposed to do?"

"After you talk to Al, let us know what he says," Joe said.

Angelo raised a finger. "One more thing. Whatever you do, don't bring her to Italy."

"Where am I supposed to take her? You don't snatch a family out of North Africa and magically deposit them in a country in Europe. You're talking to Paul Sacca, not Harry Houdini."

"Anywhere. France, Germany, but Italy is out of the question," Angelo said.

Joe smiled. "Provitti will come up with a plan. If they can get her on a Navy ship, she can be flown to one of our bases in Europe."

Paul glanced at the ceiling. "You're not making it easy, Angelo. The ambassador will have to be told."

Joe shrugged. "Sounds like Provitti's problem."

Later that evening Angelo prepared to leave his office. He gathered the papers on his desk and shoved them into a folder in the two-drawer safe. After spending hours mulling over what he might do to find out how Majid got his information, he was no closer to an answer. He closed the safe, spun the dial and turned to his desk.

A pen and pencil caught his eye. He grabbed them and opened the center drawer of the desk. When he looked down, he saw his note pad. A pain shot across his chest as he focused on his scribbled note. He read aloud. "Miami will talk to Omar. Paul, DEA, wants in."

Time stopped and his face contorted. *I went crazy trying to figure out where the information came from and what crazy man provided it. I'm in trouble now.* He snatched the handset from the phone and dialed two numbers. "Glad you're still here, I need to talk to you."

Mia hurried to his desk. "What is it?"

"Did you go into my desk?"

Her eyes locked on his. "No! Why?"

"Things are out of place. Who has access to my office?"

She paused, glanced up, and bit her bottom lip. "Me, you, Colonel Aldo, his secretary and the cleaning crew. Those who guard the building at night may come in with the people who clean."

"Good. Thank you. Are you leaving now?"

"Yes."

"I'll see you in the morning."

Mia left the office. He pulled out his cell phone and set it on the desk.

Joe answered on the second ring. "Hi Angelo."

"I discovered the source of our leak."

"Great. Where?"

"My damn office."

"What? Who?"

"Me. Stupid me."

"Christ, Angelo. What the hell are you saying?"

"Can you come to my office, now?"

"I'll be there in half an hour."

"Don't tell anyone. We need to talk."

Angelo didn't leave his desk while he waited for Joe. *Nineteen years and it may end because of one stupid mistake.* The note kept luring his eyes to the center of the drawer.

###

Joe strode into the office. "What's this crazy story?"

"Not crazy, dumb."

"What the hell happened?"

Angelo stood and pointed to the inside of his drawer. "Look!"

Joe circled the desk and looked at the open page of the notebook. "Okay. The note you used at the meeting, what's the problem?"

"Read it... out loud."

"Miami will talk to Omar. And at the bottom, Paul, DEA, wants in." Joe's mouth dropped opened, and he looked at Angelo. "Jesus. Both of the names Omar mentioned to Monique." He looked back at the note. "That doesn't tell me how he got them."

Angelo took a breath. "After we got back from the meeting I put my notepad in the desk."

"And didn't lock it?" Joe asked.

He lowered his head and nodded.

"You tell Aldo yet?"

"Hell no. I want to catch this bastard. The colonel and I talked about having cameras installed in different places around the building. I didn't get around to it, but one will be in here before I leave tonight."

Joe focused on the desk. *Work this to our advantage.* Someone with access to the office went through the desk and passed information to Majid. *That's it.* He raised his head and clicked his fingers. "I've got an idea. Why not write another note? We can tell Majid what we want him to hear. It's our chance to get Omar."

"Omar and his girlfriend."

Joe shook his head. "Just Omar... we may need her."

"What the hell should I write?"

"We need to turn them against each other. Monique told Nina Omar's worried about Majid's questions. Let's get a coffee. We'll figure out a way to increase the pressure on both of them."

Chapter XIV
TRUST

The front door opened and Monique walked into the apartment.

"How was London?" Nina asked.

Monique turned a disgusted look to her. "I hate it. People are too serious. They never smile."

"They live too far from the Mediterranean... not enough sun. Is everything okay with Omar?"

"What do you mean?"

"Those names. Is he mad at you?"

"No. Maybe worried I'm seeing someone else. He's jealous."

"That's crazy. He knows you love him, doesn't he?"

"Yes. I'll call him. Everything is fine."

Nina watched her walk to her bedroom. *She's not upset or worried.*

###

Omar sat in front of Majid's desk. The longer his boss stared at him the more uncomfortable he became.

"Has anyone approached you?"

"No."

"Has anyone mentioned the names Paul or Miami?" Majid asked without moving his eyes from him.

"No, and like I said, I've never heard of them." He didn't like Majid's tone. *Doesn't trust me.* After hours spent trying to figure out who set him up, he was no closer to an answer.

"For your sake, I hope you haven't."

Omar's stomach churned. Images of what may happen to him flashed through his mind. *I need to be careful.* He thought about again asking Majid who told him, but remained silent.

"The next shipment is almost ready," Majid said. "Heroin is only one part of it. The other half is guns and explosives. Offload the drugs near Sicily. Everything else goes to Latakia, Syria."

"Why weapons for the Syrians?"

"The heroin comes through Iran. Bashar al-Assad is their friend... he needs help to fight those trying to overthrow him."

"The *Iran Iris*?"

Majid nodded. "Jamal is ready, see him tomorrow and make arrangements."

Omar stood and his phone rang as he left the office.

Monique ran into the living room, her face contorted in terror. "I talked to Omar."

"What happened?" Nina asked.

"He said Majid doesn't trust him. He's suspicious and asked again about the two names. It worries him because someone told Majid he met with an Italian."

Nina shook her head and took Monique's hand. "It's about drugs, isn't it?"

Monique froze and pulled her hand from Nina's. "How do you know?"

"I not stupid. Ever since the police officers were killed the newspapers are full of stories about drugs coming out of Tunis. Why don't you and Omar get away from these drug dealers? All they do is destroy people's lives."

"Omar works at the port and he may see things, but he's not involved. Anyway, only immigrants use drugs."

"What about Italian kids who get addicted to heroin?"

"They're dumb. It's their problem. Omar will soon have enough money saved. He'll leave his wife and we'll be together."

Nina raised her head. "He's married?"

"Yes, but he hates her."

"Do you realize what you're doing?"

"I love him!"

"If he's helping drug dealers and gets caught, the police will come after you."

"They're not smart enough!"

"Don't get angry. I'm concerned. You're my friend."

Monique hugged her. "Sorry."

Nina kissed her on the cheek. "I'm helping my cousin tonight. We'll be late... I'll stay at her house. Don't do anything stupid. Call me if you want to talk."

Chapter XV
THE SET UP

Joe made it back to his apartment by ten thirty and crept in the door. He spotted Nina holding a bathrobe and wearing panties and a bra at the entrance to the hallway.

"Where you been all night?"

He held her face with both hands and smiled "With Angelo. He's about to catch the informant."

"Who is it?" She put on the bathrobe.

"Soon we'll have a name. Why don't you stay tonight?"

"I plan to."

Joe led her across the living room and they dropped onto the couch. "Everything is changing fast. I want you close where I can take care of you."

"Monique's home. She talked to Omar again... he's worried."

"He should be. If they think he's talking to someone, they'll kill him."

"She doesn't realize what she's doing."

Joe shook his head. "Believe me, she knows. It's all about dollar signs."

"Maybe so, but shouldn't we show compassion?"

"My compassion is for the mothers and children of the dead agents." He grabbed her and wrapped his arms around her waist. "My passion is for you."

Nina winked. "I'm taking time off from work."

"Why?"

"Because Monique did."

He cocked his head. "Not planning anything, are you?"

"No."

"Good. Let's relax. Have a glass of wine."

She grabbed his knee, and he squirmed when she squeezed. "Time for more passion... I won't be leaving town for a few days." She pulled him toward the bedroom.

The next morning, DEA Agent Paul Sacca stepped into Joe's office. "Got good news."

"Glad someone does."

Paul dropped into a chair. "Provitti came to see me earlier about the *Iran Iris*."

Joe raised his eyebrows and leaned over his desk. "What about it?"

"Troops in Afghanistan picked up a major Taliban drug trafficker a month ago. They turned him over to the Agency."

"Is he talking?"

"Provitti said he puked all over the table."

Joe smiled. "Anything good come out?"

"The freighter is docked at Bizarte, north of Tunis... captain's name is Jamal Jalili." He handed Joe an aerial photo of the *Iran Iris* at sea.

Joe examined the picture. "Is there more?"

"Yeah. The ship will pick up guns in Croatia."

"What port?"

"An informant works on the docks in Tunis, he's trying to find out."

"What do the guns have to do with Omar and the drug case?"

"The *Iran Iris* has a long-term contract to move goods for Majid's company, MZ Shipping and Export. The only reason to make a stop in Tunisia is to pick up Majid's cargo and part of it may be drugs."

"And part of it might not," Joe said.

Paul grinned. "The puker said a large shipment of heroin left Afghanistan a week before his capture. Provitti thinks it moved through Iran and is now in Tunisia."

Joe bit his lip and stared across the room. *Got to feed him something* "We picked up information Omar is in trouble with his boss... no details yet. Who's working the gun case?"

"It's a joint European effort. The Carabinieri are involved. We'll keep an eye on the ship for them."

"We?"

"American assets, surveillance aircraft and an eye in the sky. Sergio is trying to merge the two cases. He wants to take down the drug operation at the same time they get the guns. Keep me informed about Omar." He left the office.

Joe dialed Angelo's number. "You busy? Okay, I'm on my way."

After Joe arrived in Angelo's office and told him everything Paul said, he wondered why Angelo had a smile on his face and seemed disinterested.

Angelo got up from his desk and walked to the coat rack near the door. He tapped the rack. "Come here and tell me if you can see the camera."

After examining the wood and the brass hooks, he shook his head. *What camera?* "No."

Angelo pointed to a hook facing the center of the office. "In this area."

Joe leaned over and focused on a small hole under the hook. "If there's one here, it's in this hole."

"It is."

"Damn, every year these things get smaller." They sat in chairs in front of the coffee table. "Did you get any video yet?"

"The cleaning girl came in before I arrived today... didn't open any drawers."

Joe nodded. "What did you write on the note?"

"From Miami. Omar wants out, needs money fast, help him."

"That'll rattle a few cages."

Angelo leaned back in his chair. "Did Monique tell Nina anything else?"

"No." He glanced at his watch and stood. "I'm going to be late for a meeting at the embassy. I'll see you at eight tonight, I'll tell Nina to be prepared. If what you wrote gets to Majid, things will not go well for Omar."

That evening, Joe, Nina and Angelo sat a table against a wall in a café near Angelo's office. The waiter removed their empty plates and refilled their wine glasses.

Nina stared at both men as she took a drink. She raised her eyebrows. "Everything is happening so fast. You think he'll call her?"

"I'll bet on it," Joe said.

"We need to know the moment he does," Angelo said. "The three officers outside your apartment won't get close but I need to keep them informed. This is serious. Majid will have to go after Omar. Let's hope he forgets about Monique."

"Both of you sound like my father. I'm a big girl, I'll be careful."

Joe placed his hand over hers. "Why don't you stay at my apartment tonight? You can keep in touch with her by phone."

"Please. We've already talked about that."

Angelo took a deep breath and let it out. "Pay attention to whatever Monique says."

Nina shook her head. "Will you both relax... order something... grappa."

"I have heartburn thinking about what can happen. Grappa would add to the fire," Joe said.

The next morning, Joe sighed with relief when Nina called and said Monique heard nothing from Omar.

Angelo called him before he arrived at his office and told him to be in the colonel's conference room as soon as possible. He walked into the empty room and sat.

A minute later Paul entered. "Angelo call you?"

Joe nodded.

"He sounded like he has good news... where is he?"

"Downloading a video... he'll be a few minutes."

Colonel Aldo walked in and both men stood. "Where's Angelo?"

"On his way, sir," Joe said the moment Angelo entered.

Aldo frowned. "You look like hell Captain Randi. When did you last sleep?"

"Not last night... caught the bastard." He set his laptop on the table and turned the screen toward the colonel.

Aldo motioned the others to his end of the table and Angelo started the video.

Gustav trudged into Angelo's office, glanced at the door and stepped behind the desk. He pulled on the locked safe drawer, turned and opened the center drawer of the desk. Gustav removed Angelo's notepad, took a pen and paper from his pocket, and wrote on it. When he finished, he returned the notepad to the drawer, closed it, and cleaned Angelo's desk. The video ended and everyone took a seat.

"Who is he?" Aldo asked.

"His name is Gustav Sokolski... Polish. He's part of the cleaning crew," Angelo said. "It's my fault, sir. If you wish, I'll remove myself from the case."

"Who set up the surveillance camera?" Paul asked.

Angelo took a breath. "I arranged it."

Joe couldn't allow his partner hang for his mistake. He looked at Colonel Aldo. "Sir, Angelo developed the plan, and caught him."

Aldo nodded. "Was he arrested?"

"Not yet," Angelo said. "I spent last night getting his cell phone records. Early this morning I received authority to monitor his calls."

Paul rubbed his chin. "Has he called Majid?"

"No."

Aldo sighed. "Let's make sure he doesn't."

"Sir, may I suggest we wait," Angelo said. He removed a small piece of paper from his pocket. "I wrote this on the note he copied. It will turn Majid against Omar."

Aldo read the note and looked at Angelo. "You made a big mistake, but solved our problem. You still have questions to answer about how this happened. Everyone in this room will support you."

"Thank you, sir."

Joe knew a ton of weight had been lifted from Angelo's shoulders. *He screwed up, but no one is perfect.*

"May I add something, sir?" Paul asked.

"Yes."

"The U.S. Navy and Italian Coast Guard are watching the *Iran Iris*. It will pick up guns in Zadar, Croatia and offload them in Syria. Late last night I received information it will also carry drugs. Their plan is to transfer the drugs to a small vessel somewhere near Sicily. I passed the information to the Carabinieri Anti-Drug Command here in Rome and they are coordinating with the Special Intervention Group's terrorism investigation."

Angelo's cell phone rang, and he stepped out of the room.

"Anything else?" Aldo asked.

Joe and Paul shook their heads.

Aldo looked at the door. "We'll wait to hear what Angelo says."

Angelo walked in with a smile on his face. "He called Majid and told him everything on the note."

Colonel Aldo spent a moment staring at the wall across the room. "We need to decide if we want to pick him up or let him continue sending out lies."

"His mother in Poland is sick," Angelo said. "If something happens to her, he'll leave. Once we pick him up he'll realize how much trouble he's facing. He'll do anything we ask."

"You sure?" Paul asked.

Angelo grinned. "This is Italy, not the United States."

"Arrest him." Aldo said.

"We should wait until he comes to work tonight, sir," Joe said. "If we arrest him at his house someone may call Majid."

"Good idea," Aldo said. "Thank you for the information Agent Sacca. Tell the ambassador I'll call."

Chapter XVI
THE GAME

Majid thought about what his informant in Rome told him. He made a call on his cell phone and waited.

"Hello," Omar said.

"Where are you?"

"At home."

"I need to see you tonight. My office at nine."

"I'll be there."

Majid ended the call and looked at the tall three-hundred pound African seated on the couch. A white scar sliced across the man's cheek. "Tonight, Kojo. When he leaves his house."

"And his family?" Kojo asked.

Majid shook his head. "The wife and children have no information. They can't hurt us."

"I'll call when it's done."

The man's massive frame filled the doorway as he left the room. *Everyone fears him.*

###

Angelo looked across his desk at two Carabinieri officers in dark uniforms. Both appeared as if they spent all their off-duty hours lifting weights. "U.S. Marshals Service Inspector Costa, from the American embassy, wants to watch. When he arrives, the three of you wait in the room across the hall. Once Gustav walks into my office, give me a minute alone with him, and then come in."

Joe walked into the office, and Angelo stepped beside him.

"Joe, this is Marco and Nicolas, two men from the Special Operations Group." He placed a hand on Joe's shoulder. "This is my Task Force Co-Leader, Inspector Joe Costa."

Both men nodded and extended their hands.

"Go with them, Joe, and come into my office when they do."

The three men left and Angelo moved an uncomfortable straight-backed chair to the front of his desk. He dropped into his leather chair, folded his hands, and waited. *I'm going to squeeze this guy until he pops.*

A tingle shot down his spine at the sound of footsteps. He looked at the short Polish man standing in the doorway. *The bastard that helped kill five men.*

"Sorry, sir. I didn't realize you were working late."

"That's okay, Gustav." Angelo pointed to the front of the desk. "Come in... sit. How is your mother?"

Gustav took a seat. "She is well."

"Still at home taking care of herself?" Angelo asked.

"Yes. Once a week she goes to the doctor."

Angelo nodded. "Good. I'm glad she's self-sufficient because you're going to be busy."

Gustav's forehead creased. "Busy?"

"Yes, sending messages."

"Messages?"

Angelo kept his eyes on him and nodded. "The ones I want Majid Ziyad to receive."

Marco and Nicolas, followed by Joe, rushed into the office at the instant Gustav stood. The two Carabinieri grabbed his arms, handcuffed his hands behind his back and shoved him into the seat. Both men stood behind him.

Joe sat on the couch.

Gustav's wide eyes locked on Angelo. His lower lip quivered.

Angelo rose and walked behind him. "Turn this way."

Marco and Nicolas grabbed the back of the chair and jerked it around, almost tipping it.

Gustav swung a foot to the side and stopped himself from falling.

Angelo paused, looked into Gustav's eyes and leaned toward him. "Gustav, you made a very big mistake. There is no doubt in my mind you are responsible for the five narcotics agents being killed." He removed a paper from his pocket and waved it in front of Gustav's face. "A judge issued this warrant for your arrest. Tonight you will not sleep in your soft bed, but I am not sending you to a prison in Rome." He paused and glared at him. "I'm going to find the oldest and nastiest jail in Italy. One with an underground cell just for you." He stepped back. "You will be so far underground, the jail officials will need to pump sunshine to you through a pipe."

Gustav tried to stand but Nicolas crammed him back into the chair.

"Your poor mother will find out you're living the life of a rodent," Angelo said. "I wonder if she'll survive."

Beads of sweat rolled into Gustav's bulging eyes. "Sir, please. I needed money to take care of her."

"You must love her very much. You helped kill two American and three Italian agents for her. What will she think when she's told you murdered police officers for money?"

Gustav lowered his head. "I'm sorry. All I did was pass information. No one told me they were going to die."

"It's too late. I'm not sorry for you. Life in an Italian prison may not be all you face. Look at the man seated in front of you. He's an American investigator. He told me his government wants to take you to their court where they have the death penalty." Angelo turned to Joe. "Don't they still use the electric chair in America, Inspector Costa?"

Gustav grimaced and his eyes widened. His legs and hands trembled.

Joe slid to the edge of the couch. "Florida does... two thousand, three-hundred volts. It's old, sometimes sparks come out of it. Takes a long time to die."

Angelo looked at the little man. "Of course Gustav, you'll be able to stay in a nice American prison cell before they fry your brain."

Gustav's breathing became short gulps of air. "My mother needs help."

"And now you need my help. You will do everything I tell you, and tell me everything you know, or I guarantee you will rot in a hole worse than hell."

Angelo stared at his captive and remained silent.

"What do you want from me?" Gustav asked, his voice cracking.

"For you to start talking, but not tonight. Consider my proposal. I want an answer in the morning." He motioned to the door. "Take him to his new home."

Marco and Nicolas yanked him to his feet and shoved him out the door.

Angelo walked behind his desk and sat. He opened the bottom right hand drawer and removed a bottle of Courvoisier and a pair of etched whiskey glasses. "Would you like a small drink?"

Joe smiled. "It's a sin to let fine liquor go to waste."

Angelo half-filled the glasses and handed one to Joe. "Now for our next bit of magic." He raised his glass in front of his American partner and smiled.

XVII
THE HIT

When Omar received Majid's call, the first thing that came to mind were the questions he asked about Paul and Miami. Those two names meant nothing to him. *It must be about the next shipment.* Majid was successful because he was cautious. He seldom discussed business over the phone, and when he did, they spoke with coded words. Guns going to Syria had to be what he wanted to discuss.

Omar walked from his apartment building with a smile on his face. The next trip on the *Iran Iris* would be dangerous but profitable. Majid agreed to pay him double his customary fee because of the weapon's shipment. Drug trafficking worried the Tunisian and Italian governments but guns and explosives were a concern to countless countries, including the United States, members of the European Union, and many neighbors in North Africa. *I'll soon make enough money to set myself up in business.* He wanted to keep Monique in his life, and his family at his side.

He approached his parked Toyota, stopped at the curb and unlocked the door. Before he opened it, bullets shattered the back window and slammed into the trunk. He doubled over in pain, grabbed his side, and dropped to the ground. The crack of rifle fire and the sound of bullets penetrating the car made him roll against the Toyota and press as much of his body as possible against it. Tires screeched and a black sedan sped past his car. Glass shattered and the Toyota's interior erupted in flames.

###

Majid leaned back on the couch with his eyes closed. He jumped to his feet at a knock on the door.

Kojo walked into the office.

"Is it done?" Majid asked.

"Yes. He died beside his car."

Majid nodded. "Thank you, Kojo. What car did you use?"

"A stolen Mercedes. We set it on fire when we finished."

"Good. Tell Jamal Omar had an accident, and will not make the trip."

"The captain may ask for more money."

Majid smiled. "He's done this a long time. Many people disappeared in those years. A demanding person is an unhealthy person."

"You want me to go on the ship?"

Majid seldom went anywhere without Kojo. Tunis was not a dangerous city, but his association with the traffickers in Iran made him cautious. *They is always someone who will do it for less money.*

"No, call Yassine. Tell him to find Omar's girlfriend."

Majid walked to his desk and picked up a folded paper. He handed it to the large African man. "This is her name, address and telephone number."

"What should he do when he finds her?"

"Tell him to call me. I have instructions I want him to follow."

Kojo stared at him. "I can do this for you."

Majid tapped the large man's shoulder. "Yassine is closer. You've always been at my side. I need you with me."

Chapter XVIII
NINA'S PLAN

A scream ripped Nina from a dream. She leapt from the bed and raced to Monique's room. "What happened? What's wrong?"

Monique sat on the edge of the bed sobbing, her hands pressed against her face. She raised her head. "Someone tried to kill Omar. He's hurt."

"Where is he?"

"In Tunis, he thinks it was Majid."

Nina's mouth dropped open. "His boss?"

"Yes. He has to leave Tunisia, but doesn't know where to go. He'll hide and call tomorrow. What should I do? If Majid finds out he's still alive, someone will try to kill him again. There must be a safe place to go."

Nina scanned the walls. *Joe and Angelo can't arrest people in the Middle East.* She knelt in front of Monique and took her hands. "Athens is the best place. The city is big and he'll be safe."

Monique hugged her. "Good idea. I'll meet him there."

A sickening feeling invaded Nina's stomach. *No. What is she thinking?* "Meet him! Have you lost your mind? People tried to kill him."

"I love him," Monique sobbed. "I need to help."

Nina stood. "Are you sure he'll call again?"

"Yes, tomorrow."

"Can you call him?"

"No, he won't answer his phone. He's afraid Majid can trace it." She buried her face in the pillow.

"Do nothing. I'll call a friend in Athens and ask if he can help." She ran to her bedroom, closed the door and dialed her phone. When Joe answered, she whispered. "Monique said Majid tried to kill Omar." She listened to him rant for fifteen seconds.

"No, I can't come now and don't come here. In the morning I'll meet you at your office." She pulled the phone from her ear, looked at it and listened to Joe's voice, but not his words. After five seconds, she interrupted. "I'll be at the embassy at eight thirty."

Joe didn't sleep after Nina's call and arrived at the embassy thirty minutes early. Nina stood in the lobby, waiting. "Angelo's on his way." He kissed her. "Let's go to my office."

Angelo, carrying a tie, arrived two minutes after they settled into chairs. "What the hell happened?" He looked at Nina sitting behind Joe's desk.

"Let Nina explain," Joe said.

"Did Joe tell you anything?" she asked leaning on the desk.

"Yes. Omar told your roommate Majid tried to kill him."

She nodded. "Someone shot him and he needs to leave Tunisia but has to get money first. I suggested Athens because it would be easy to hide in the city. She wants to meet him in Greece."

Angelo grinned. "You suggested Athens?"

"Yes."

"Damn, you... are... good."

She cocked her head. "Remember, I'm the quiet one who listens. Italian police can arrest him in the EU."

Angelo nodded. "We'll ask them pick him up on our European Arrest Warrant."

"Will Greece honor an Italian warrant?" Nina asked.

Angelo nodded. "They can't refuse."

Joe glanced at him. "Any good contacts with their police?"

"We won't have a problem. Is Monique still in the apartment?" he asked Nina.

"Yes, waiting for a call."

"We need to find out where he'll be," Joe said to her. "Please listen. If Majid tried to kill Omar, he may try to kill you and Monique."

"That's crazy! Why?"

"Both of you spent time with Omar just before this happened. Sooner or later he'll wonder if that night at the villa has something to do with the information he's getting."

"I've never seen Majid."

Joe sighed. "It doesn't matter. You're Monique's friend, and you were there."

"Have you noticed my men outside the apartment?" Angelo asked.

Nina looked around the room and lowered her gaze to the desktop. "I didn't realize it would get this bad." She brushed lint off of her sleeve before looking at Angelo. "I haven't seen them, but I'm glad they are watching. I look each time I leave the apartment, but no one seems out of place."

"Good, I'll add two more. Find out as much as you can without making her suspicious."

Nina walked from behind the desk. "I need to get back to the apartment. She's a wreck and didn't want me to leave. After what you told me I'll be more cautious."

Joe jumped up and took her hand. "Promise me you won't go with her."

She kissed him. "I promise."

"Stay at Joe's apartment tonight."

"As long as Monique's in Rome I need to be with her. If she leaves, I will."

###

When Nina entered the apartment, Monique raced to the door.

"He called," Monique said.

"Is he okay? Where is he?"

"Still in Tunis but I told him to go to Athens. I didn't say you suggested it because he has friends near the port of Piraeus. He'll stay at the Hotel Poseidonas for two nights."

"That's even better than Athens."

"I told him I'd arrive in the morning and booked the eight o'clock flight."

Nina frowned. "Are you sure you want to go?"

"He needs my help."

"What will you do? What about your job?"

"I don't care about the job. He'll find a safe place for us. I'm going to the bank to close my account." She walked out the door.

Nina waited five minutes before calling Joe. She turned on the phone speaker and listened to the ring.

"Embassy, Costa."

"It's me, he called."

"What did he say?"

"Tonight he'll be in Piraeus... at the Poseidonas Hotel."

"Good work."

"She's leaving in the morning."

"To meet him?"

"Yes. No matter what's said, she won't listen."

Joe hesitated. "Are you all right?"

"Yes. Don't worry, I won't go with her."

"Okay. Call if anything else happens."

Chapter XIX
IT'S NINA

Colonel Aldo stepped into Angelo's office unannounced.

Angelo leapt to his feet. "I didn't know you were coming."

"I just left a meeting."

Angelo swallowed and held his breath. "About me?"

"No... budget. Any news?"

Angelo motioned to a large chair at the coffee table. "The Americans got Ayisha out of Tunisia, Gustav is talking and Omar should be in Greece this afternoon."

"What about Majid?"

"The old woman is giving us a lot of information. If Omar stays alive he'll talk, but I need your help with Majid."

Aldo stared at him a moment. "What can I do?"

"Will the Tunisian authorities help us get him?"

Aldo rubbed his chin. "They like their status in the international community. If one of their citizens is named as an international drug trafficker, they're not going to be happy."

"Could you speak with one of your Tunisian contacts?"

"Yes. Write what you want and I'll talk with Colonel Fantar."

"Can he be trusted?"

Aldo looked at him and a slight grin appeared. "All my contacts are trustworthy. Years ago he came here for training. We attended the same class. When their government disbanded the secret police he moved to Internal Security.

Fantar's quite ambitious and has a large family. His son-in-law is Italian." Aldo glanced around the room. "Why is Omar going to Greece?"

"Our informant recommended it."

Aldo nodded and raised his eyebrows. "Your informant knows what he's doing. Are you going to tell me who he is?"

Angelo widened his eyes. *A request, not an order.* Like Joe, he trusted few, but Colonel Aldo sat at the top of his list of those held in high esteem. *He'll keep Nina's name secret.* Joe wouldn't be concerned if he told him Nina was the informant. "First may I ask you a question?"

"Sure."

"Do you remember trying to get your wife to marry you?"

"Odd question. Italian women are demanding. I can't count the number of nights I chased her around Rome trying to convince her how important she was to me."

"Then you'll understand, sir. It's Joe's informant."

Aldo tilted his head and paused before speaking. "Joe made the decision to keep the name secret?"

"Yes, sir. He didn't want to lose his future wife."

The colonel glanced at the floor and back to him. "What do you mean?"

"The informant is my wife's cousin, Nina."

Aldo sat up in the chair. "The flight attendant?"

"Yes, sir. Her roommate is French Algerian... she's Omar's girlfriend."

The colonel took a deep breath and blinked several times. "Damn. I understand."

"Joe's worried about her safety."

The colonel nodded. "He did what we all would do, lie to protect her. Is she safe?"

"My men are watching her."

Aldo stood and headed to the door. "If you need more men, call me."

"Sir?"

Aldo stopped and turned. "Don't worry Angelo. Your family secret is safe with me."

Chapter XX
MONIQUE'S TORMENT

The day before Monique's departure from Rome, Omar arrived in the port city of Piraeus. He sat in the only chair in a room at the Poseidonas Hotel. He lifted his shirt and examined the bandage on his side and the gauze wrapped around his midsection. The sound of an AK-47 still rang in his ears. *I'm lucky it didn't rip me open or hit a rib.* He stared at the television, but did not focus on the blank screen.

A blurred recollection of the last two days in Tunis did not help him answer the question stuck in his mind. *Why? Someone set me up to be killed. Who?* Jamal complained that he didn't need help to offload the drugs, and Majid wasted his money sending one of his men on the trips. *Was it him? Or the African, who thinks he's more important because he's close to Majid? The little killer in Italy? What's his name?* He clamped his teeth together as a sharp pain shot across his midsection. When it subsided, he picked up the television remote and adjusted the pillow on the bed.

An hour later, a loud crash jolted him awake. The doorframe splintered and two men in Hellenic Police officer uniforms burst into the room pointing Glock 21 pistols.

"Don't move," an officer shouted.

Omar bolted upright, raised one hand and grimaced in pain as he pressed the other against his side.

A third officer, with two days growth on his face, stepped through the doorway. "If you say one word, I will break your jaw."

Omar's heartbeat raced, and images of being placed against a wall and executed flashed through his mind. *Majid's men in police uniforms. I'm dead.*

The officer closest to him holstered his weapon and pulled him from the bed.

Omar glanced at his bare feet and handcuffed hands as they shoved him out the door. *Why didn't they kill me?*

In the hallway he came face to face with a stocky man in a suit. The man's smile looked more like a smirk.

"Good evening, Mr. Hassan. I am Carabinieri Captain Angelo Randi. We have been looking for you. I'm here with a European Arrest Warrant out of Italy. A few of my men and I will make sure you remain safe on our short trip to Rome."

A small amount of drugs. I'll be out of jail in a week.

Monique sat beside Yassine on the rear deck of the twenty-five foot boat heading to a rusted freighter. As they approached, the faded name 'Iran Iris' became clear on the front of the vessel. A steep set of steel stairs hung from the side of the ship. She looked at her high heels and short skirt. Fifteen minutes after she met Yassine, thoughts of Omar raced through her mind. *This makes little sense. He said to meet him in his room at the Poseidonas.*

"Yassine. Why did he leave the hotel?"

"It is safer on the ship with his friends."

She slipped off her heels, glanced at the stairway and the water. *Glad there are no waves.*

At the top of the stairs, a man in a white uniform waited.

The boat eased beside the ship and made contact with the platform at the base of the stairs. Yassine picked up her suitcase and motioned her toward the tiny landing below the bottom step. She tugged her skirt down and took his hand to steady herself. As she climbed the stairs she glanced at the hand holding her purse and the one gripping the handrail. Behind and below her, Yassine's head was even with her feet. *Get a good look little man. It's as close as you'll ever get.*

When she reached the deck, the man in white held out his hand and helped her from the stairway. Yassine set her bag on the deck.

"Good morning, madam. I am Lieutenant Namood Darzi, the ship's engineer. Omar is waiting."

Finally. She smiled at Namood, pulled her heels from her purse and extended the handle of her suitcase.

"Don't worry about your bag," Namood said. "Someone will bring it to you. It's best if you do not wear high heels. We must go up steep stairs."

Monique returned the shoes to her purse. They entered a steel framed doorway and Namood pointed to stairs. At the top, he led her through passageways to a cabin door and opened it. When she stepped inside, he shoved her toward the bed and pulled handcuffs from his pocket.

Her face contorted, eyes locked on the set of restraints. She raised her hands and froze. "What are you doing? Where's Omar? You said he's here and waiting for me."

The first thing to enter her mind was to stop him. She tightened her muscles and closed her fists. Her heart raced as he closed in on her. She thrust her hands against his chest to shove him aside. Namood grabbed an arm when she made contact and slapped her, knocking her onto the bed. He held her against the mattress and handcuffed one of her hands to the steel frame. Without saying a word, he snatched the purse from her hands, and ripped off her blouse. He stepped back, grinned and walked out, slamming the door.

Monique scanned the cabin and focused on a closed porthole five feet from the bed. *Why are they doing this?* She yanked on the handcuff, causing the metal to dig into her wrist. With her free hand she pressed the trembling fingers of her shackled hand together and attempted to slip from the restraint. The steel cut deeper into her wrist. *Where is Omar?* She froze. *Someone planned this... he's not here.*

The ship shuddered and the sound of steel clanging against steel interrupted her thoughts. *The anchor! Oh my God, we're leaving port.* Monique pulled the sheet from the bed and wrapped it around her body. "Help! Please, someone help me!" A sense of hopelessness overcame her and tears ran across her cheeks. She buried her face in the small pillow.

Over the next two hours, Monique lost track of time as she slipped between outright panic and light sleep. The cabin door swung open and a fat officer, in a sweat stained white uniform, threw her suitcase and purse into a corner. "I'm Captain Jamal Jalili. Your phone rang... I threw it overboard." He smiled, removed his belt and folded it in half. "Give me the sheet."

Her heart pounded and tears filled her eyes. "No! Please." She pulled the sheet tight against her body.

He swung the wide belt and struck her upper arm.

She screamed.

"The sheet," Jamal said.

Monique looked at the welt on her arm and glared at him. *This pig can't be the ship's captain.* "No! Leave me alone."

The pig swung a second time, striking the side of her exposed thigh.

Her free hand pressed against the red mark rising on her leg and she sobbed.

Jamal yanked the sheet from her and shoved her head to the mattress. He clamped a hand around the waistband of her skirt and ripped it. "You're a slave now. You will do as I say or try to swim across the Mediterranean."

"Where's Omar?"

"Forget him. You now belong to me. Take off your dress."

She pulled her torn skirt together. Every muscle in her body stiffened.

Jamal removed a knife from his pocket and opened the blade. "Do not fight. The blade is razor sharp. If I slip, you may bleed to death. The ship has no doctor." As he pulled the waistband away from her body, he slit the skirt to the hem. With one quick pull, he yanked it from her and threw it on the floor.

She slid as far back as possible, pressing herself against the bulkhead, closed her eyes and whimpered.

Chapter XXI
THE SHOOTING

After Monique left for Greece, Joe and Nina spent the morning together at his apartment. At two in the afternoon Joe suggested she pack a suitcase and stay with him until the investigation was completed and everyone arrested. *As long as Majid's free, she's in danger.*

They left the apartment and walked through the busy streets.

Joe squeezed her hand. "Angelo is on his way back to Italy with Omar. Monique will call soon."

Nina looked at her watch. "Greece is an hour ahead of us. I'm worried. She arrived at nine our time and it wouldn't take more than an hour to get to Piraeus. She should have called by now."

"If she went to the hotel they'd tell her the police arrested him. Maybe she's contacting them. Did you try to call her?"

Nina stopped. "Yes. Every call went to her voice mail. When Angelo returns, will you ask him to check with the police in Piraeus?"

"I will. Come. Let's pick up your clothes and get back to my apartment."

While they walked Joe held Nina's hand and spent a few seconds studying each person they passed. Although he knew most of the men in the Fugitive Task Force, he recognized no one.

Ten feet past the door to her building, two men leaned against a Fiat. Lowering his head to her, he whispered. "Those men may be two of our friends."

"Friends?" Nina asked.

"Carabinieri."

"They aren't dressed like police officers."

Joe smiled. "That's the idea. Angelo assigned five of them to keep you safe and I'm guessing about those two."

As they approached the door, Joe focused on a motorcycle parked along the curb fifty feet past the entrance. The man on the bike looked in their direction, put on his full face-shield helmet and started the motor. *He's staring at us and not checking the street.*

Had the man taken his eyes off them, Joe may have ignored him, at least until the engine cranked to full throttle and the bike raced toward them. He tightened the grip on her hand.

The driver pulled a pistol from his jacket pocket.

"Get down!" Joe grabbed Nina, shoved her to the sidewalk and dropped to one knee. His hunch was correct. The men near the Fiat pulled Beretta semiautomatic pistols. One officer stepped into the street, the other to the sidewalk.

Joe slid his Glock from his back waistband and raised it. One Carabiniere stood between him and the man speeding toward them. *No clear shot.* He lowered the pistol and positioned his body between the threat and Nina.

The man on the motorcycle fired two shots and hit the officer standing in the street. He swung the pistol toward the man in front of Joe and fired three times as the officer aimed his weapon.

Joe felt a sharp pain on the inside of his left forearm and leaned toward the ground.

Nina scrambled to her knees. "What's wrong?" she screamed pulling on his shirt.

Joe pushed her to the pavement. The sound of rapid shots from an assault rifle, drew his attention to the street. An officer holding a Spectre M4 submachine gun ran to his side, pointed the gun down the street and motioned to the door leading inside the building.

Joe pulled Nina to her feet. "Go!" He pushed her to the door.

Once inside, he raised his arm.

"God! Your arm... it's bleeding!" Nina stared at the torn flesh, gasped, and covered her mouth. "You need a doctor!" She burst into tears.

Joe ripped off his shirt and wrapped it around his arm. "Stay here."

"No!"

He held his hand in front of her. "Please, I need to look." He opened the door and made eye contact with the officer carrying the submachine gun.

"It's safe now," the man said.

Two officers kneeled in the street beside the injured Carabiniere. A few feet away, a bloody body lay beside an overturned motorcycle.

Joe adjusted the pistol in his waistband and looked back into the doorway. "It's over, you can come out."

Nina stepped beside him and pulled her cell phone from her pocket. "I'll call an ambulance."

Joe held up his hand. "Not yet."

"Why did he try to kill you?"

"Not me." He pressed his lips together and raised his eyebrows. "He aimed at you."

"No, please. I can't..."

An officer standing near the injured Carabiniere, walked to him. "Inspector Costa, I'm Claudio. We called an ambulance. They'll take you and our man to Gemelli Hospital. Colonel Aldo will meet you."

Joe tightened the bloody shirt wrapped around his arm. "They can take him. I'll be fine, I'll go later."

The officer shook his head. "It's best if you and the girl leave before the news media arrive. The colonel told me to tell you not to argue, he wants to talk to you before he calls the embassy."

Nina latched onto his uninjured arm. "I'm going with you."

Chapter XXII
RESOLUTION

Majid dropped two documents on his desk and looked at his watch. *Seven thirty. I stayed too late.*

A knock on the door startled him and Kojo walked into the room. "Sir, Colonel Ali Fantar is here."

Majid frowned. *The colonel always sends his men. It must be important.* "Send him in."

Ali, in a tailored dark suit, came onto the office with a smile. He motioned with his right hand. "Sorry to bother you, Majid."

Majid's eyes locked on the colonel's missing middle finger. *They died taking it from him.*

Ali pointed to Kojo. "If the big man wants a better job, send him to me."

"You can't pay him enough." Majid stepped from behind his desk. "Leave us, Kojo."

He left the room and closed the door.

"Glad to see you, Colonel. What can I do for you?"

"I'm sorry to bother you at night."

Majid nodded. "I'm always prepared to help the government. Would you like something to drink?" He pointed to a chair and sat on the couch.

"No, thank you."

"What brings you to my humble company?"

Ali tilted his head and pressed his lips together. "We have two bodies at our headquarters. You might know them or may at least recognize them."

Majid raised his eyebrows. "I doubt I can help you. I don't get out as much as I did years ago. Kojo knows all my employees and friends. Would you like him to go with you?"

"It's best if you come to see what has happened. Someone carved your name into one man's chest."

Majid wasn't surprised at Ali's bluntness. His words were meant to elicit a reaction. *Does he have information about the Iran Iris and the shipment?* He wouldn't give his old adversary satisfaction and eased from the couch. "Let me get my jacket... my driver will follow you."

Ali stood. "We're parked out front."

Lieutenant Namood and the helmsman stood on the bridge of the *Iran Iris*. Jamal Jalili sat in the captain's chair reading a book.

Namood raised his binoculars. "Italian Coast Guard, they'll pass to our stern."

Jamal looked over his shoulder. "Ahead full... keep your eyes on them."

Namood focused on the Italian cutter for two minutes. He lowered the field glasses. "They turned and increased speed."

A seaman scurried onto the bridge. "The Italians are telling us to stop and prepare to be boarded."

Jamal turned his chair towards the man. "Did you answer them?"

"No, sir."

"Don't respond."

The seaman spun around and ran.

"What should we do?" Namood asked.

The captain glared at him. "Nothing. Continue to watch them."

He raised the binoculars. "They'll soon be off our stern, port side."

"How far are they?" Jamal asked.

"One kilometer."

"Starboard twenty degrees," Jamal yelled at the helmsman. "Tell me if they turn."

Namood pressed the field glasses to his eyes as the Italian cutter closed in on the *Iran Iris*. "Five hundred meters and they are turning," he shouted and lowered the field glasses. "They're manning their deck gun!"

The seaman leaned his head through the doorway. "We are to stop or they will disable us."

The field glasses dropped from Namood's hand and bounced on the deck. "If they hit the explosives we'll be killed."

Jamal turned to the seaman. "Tell them we'll comply. All stop."

Namood's trembling hand picked up the binoculars. He turned to the captain. "We'll go to jail."

"Shut up!" Jamal yelled. "We're moving cargo from one port to another. We load what is on the manifest."

He took a deep breath. "What about the girl?"

"There is no reason to enter a cabin. Lower the accommodation ladder and quit shaking. Italy has no authority in these waters."

Coast Guard Lieutenant Falco, followed by three guardsmen carrying Fabarn FP6 shotguns, stepped from the ladder onto the deck.

"Welcome aboard Lieutenant, I'm Namood Darsi, the ship's engineer."

"I'm Lieutenant Falco." He spotted the captain rushing toward him.

"I'm Captain Jalili. What are you doing? You can't threaten to shoot at me and stop my ship!"

Falco stared at the fat officer. *Typical. He thinks he's the master of something the size of the Costa Concordia.* "We are sorry for the inconvenience, Captain. The World Health Organization reported six cases of cholera on a vessel coming out of the Port of Zadar, Croatia. Your ship recently docked there."

"No member of my crew is sick."

"Good." Falco smiled and nodded. "We'll perform a quick safety inspection and you can be on your way."

Jamal stepped close to Falco. "Safety inspection!" Jamal yelled. "You have no authority outside your jurisdiction. We're not in..."

"Italian waters?" Falco removed a handheld GPS from his pocket and tapped the screen. "Eight hundred meters inside the territorial jurisdiction... off the Cape of Otranto." He smiled and handed the GPS to Jamal.

Jamal's face turned red and contorted in anger as he looked at the GPS. "You forced my vessel into your waters?"

"You are mistaken, Captain. We gave no orders for you to change course. To do so must have been your decision. If you wish, I can arrange for you to listen to recordings of our communications and view the radar images. But, that will take two or more hours. The sooner I start my inspection, the less time I will detain you. Please tell the crew gather on the stern. You may remain on the bridge."

Falco took the GPS and turned to his men. "Carmine and Mimo, wait for the crew on the stern. Peppe, make sure the cabin passageways are clear." He stepped past Jamal. "Excuse me, captain," and walked toward the back of the vessel with the two men. *Fat man will suffer a heart attack when we tell him his run-down freighter is headed to an Italian port.*

###

Peppe paused in a passageway to check a fire hose. He hummed his favorite tune by Laura Pausini and continued along his route. As he approached the door marked 'CAPTAIN', he stopped and quit humming. *Sounds like a woman sobbing.* He squinted and looked in both directions. Unsure of himself, he shrugged and continued past the Captain's door. As he approached the next cabin, a woman moaned.

He walked to the cabin and opened the door. A woman, half covered with a blood-stained sheet, lay face down on the bed, crying. He jumped back, slammed the door and scrambled down the corridor.

When he reached the main deck, he ran to the stern.

"That was quick... you finished?" Falco asked. He stared at Peppe and frowned. "What's the matter? What happened?"

"Sir. A lady is bleeding."

"What? Where?"

Peppe caught his breath. "The cabin next to the captain's quarters."

Falco looked at the crew and his two men gathered on the stern deck. "Mimo, go to the bridge and keep your eyes on the captain and engineer. Carmine, stay with these men." He turned to Peppe. "Show me."

###

Peppe stopped in front of the cabin door and pointed.

Falco turned the handle, shoved the door open, and froze.

A woman lying on the bed turned to him. He clamped his teeth together and cringed at her blackened eye, bruised cheek, and handcuffed blood crusted wrist. *Once beautiful, but it's hard to tell now.*

Her eyes widened. She scooted into a corner and pulled the sheet over her upper body.

"My God... get bolt cutters and call for more men! Tell Mimo and Carmine what we found. Don't let the crew, including the officers, hear what you say."

Peppe raced from the room.

Falco stepped to the bed and tightened his jaw when he got a close look at the woman. *She's shaking... frightened. What the hell happened to her?* He kneeled beside the bed and kept his hands at his side. "Do you speak Italian?"

She nodded.

"Don't be scared. No one is here to harm you."

She pressed the sheet to her body and eyed his uniform.

"Where are your clothes?"

"I don't know," she mumbled through swollen lips.

He pulled open drawers until he found a clean sheet and held it to her. "Put the dirty sheet on the floor."

Her face contorted, and she pressed the blood-stained linen against her chest.

Falco unfolded the sheet and placed it next to her. "I'll turn around, cover yourself with the clean one." He turned and waited.

"Okay," she said.

He squatted beside the bed. "Try not to move. We'll help you."

She stared at his uniform. "Who are you?"

"Italian Coast Guard. I'm Lieutenant Falco. Who did this to you?"

The woman lowered her head, sobbed, and struggled to catch her breath. "The captain and another man named Namood."

"How did you get here?"

"I came to meet a friend, and they kidnapped me."

"Are you an Italian citizen?"

"No, French, but I live and work in Rome."

"What's your name?"

"Monique LaCroix."

Peppe scurried into the room holding three-foot long bolt cutters.

"Be careful. Cut the handcuff at her wrist," Falco ordered.

The young man cut the cuff, and Falco held out his hand. "Can you walk?"

"Yes."

He glanced at Peppe. "The captain and crew?"

"No one will argue with our shotguns. The engineer is with Mimo and the captain."

"Good work. We'll be taking these bastards to Brandisi."

Chapter XXIII
ALIVE AND SAFE

Two Alfa Romeo's pulled to the front of Gemelli Hospital on the campus of the Catholic University of the Sacred Heart in Rome. The drivers remained in the cars.

Three Carabinieri, in dark tactical uniforms, exited the second Alfa. Each carried a Spectre M4 submachine gun. One moved to the entrance and two secured the first car.

Angelo, in a black suit, stepped from the right front door and opened the rear door for Nina. Joe, his left arm in a sling, carried his suit jacket, got out behind her, and straightened his tie. Nina took the jacket and draped it over his shoulders.

"Thank you." He kissed her on the cheek. "This morning I considered cutting the sleeve off, but it's a five hundred and fifty euro suit."

Two officers walked beside them as they headed to the entrance.

Angelo led the group to a bank of elevators and when they reached the third floor, he allowed one officer to lead. The group walked to a large waiting room.

Nina glanced around the room, turned to Joe and raised her eyebrows.

Joe leaned to her. "Are you sure you want to see her?"

"Yes. She needs to know her life has changed."

"It's not your fault, she wouldn't listen."

"What will happen to her?" she asked Angelo.

"That depends. If she agrees to testify, the government will not charge her with a crime." His cell phone rang, and he left the room.

"Monique's lucky," Joe said.

Nina frowned. "Why do you say that?"

"Because she's alive and may be given an opportunity for a better life."

Nina focused on the floor and took a deep breath. "I hope so. No one should have to face what she did."

Angelo returned with a smile on his face. "Colonel Aldo called."

"Everything okay?" Joe asked.

"He wants us in his office at ten tomorrow morning. Nina also needs to come."

"Why me?"

"I don't know. You played a big part in this case, it must be important." He looked at Joe. "He went to Tunis to identify Majid. Someone cut him into pieces, so I should say to identify his body, after the Tunisians put it back together."

Joe scooted forward in his chair. "Who killed him?"

Angelo shrugged and rolled his eyes. "An investigator said thieves robbed him and he fought for his life."

"Convenient."

"It's odd. Aldo said a police colonel and government officials now have control of his business and property." He held a hand to Nina. "Ready?"

"Yes." She stood, adjusted the one carat pear shaped diamond ring on her finger, and looked at Joe. "Don't tell her I'll be moving in with you."

He nodded, and they followed Angelo to a door.

"Both of you go. I'll talk to her later," Angelo said.

Nina and Joe strolled into the room. It took a moment for them to adjust to the dim light.

Monique's eyes remained closed, a bandage covered one side of her face. Blood stained thick gauze circled one of her wrists. Two IV bags, connected to needles in her arm, hung beside the bed.

Nina's eyes widened. *My God. They beat her.*

Monique opened her eyes, began to cry, and fought to catch her breath. She grabbed Nina's hand.

"You're safe. Everything will be okay now," said Nina.

Her fingers touched Nina's ring, and she looked at it. "You got married after I left?"

"No, engaged." She motioned Joe closer to the bed. "This is my fiancé, Joe."

"Hi, Monique. Talk with Nina. I'll wait in the hall."

She sat on the edge of the bed and held Monique's hand. "I wish you had listened and not gone to meet Omar."

"No one could have stopped me."

This time pay attention. "Do whatever the police say. Find a new life... forget Omar."

Monique sobbed and squeezed her hand. "I loved him... I didn't realize what kind of man he was."

Nina"s brow furrowed. *Sure you didn't.* "Those people have no respect for women or life. Look at what they did to you."

Monique wiped her tears. "You're right. They planned everything before I left Rome. The man that met me at the airport said Omar was hiding on a ship. He lied, but I didn't realize it. I still don't know where he is."

Nina handed her another tissue and rubbed her arm. "Soon you'll get out of the hospital and start a new life. I'm leaving for a month and will be moving. Later you'll meet Carabinieri Captain, Angelo Randi. I asked him to help you find a new apartment. He'll talk to you about Omar and Majid. You need to help him with the investigation."

Monique's eyes widened. "Where's Omar?"

"He's in jail. Someone in Tunisia murdered Majid before they could arrest him."

"I didn't want to see Omar go to jail, but at least he's still alive. Tell Captain Randi I'll help him."

"Good."

For the next thirty minutes they spoke of what would happen in the months to come.

Nina kissed Monique's cheek. "When I return I'll call you." She left the room.

Chapter XXIV
YOUR PLACE IS HERE

Joe and Nina held hands and walked along the corridor to Colonel Aldo's office. Nina tugged Joe's hand and stopped. "Are you hiding something from me? What's this about?"

Joe raised his eyebrows and shrugged. "I don't know. I'm as curious as you."

"Why does he want me here?"

"Like Angelo said, you helped us close this case. He may have a letter thanking you for what you did. If not, I have no idea."

"Did he say anything more to you?"

"No. We're both in the dark. Whatever it is, we'll be surprised." *The colonel wants to surprise her.*

They stepped into the office and stopped near the door.

Colonel Aldo, Angelo, his wife Sofia, and Mia stood in the center of the room talking. They quit speaking and turned toward the door.

Joe squeezed Nina's hand and whispered. "They're here for you."

"Come in, please," said Aldo.

Sofia and Mia rushed to Nina, hugged her and kissed her cheek.

"Show us the ring," Sofia said.

Nina grinned and held out her left hand, the pear shaped diamond sparkled in the light.

Joe approached Colonel Aldo. "Good morning, sir."

"Glad you could come."

"I didn't think I had a choice."

"True." Angelo said.

Aldo moved to the front of his desk and looked at the three women. "Everyone, I have an important announcement."

Joe and Nina joined Angelo, standing between Sofia and Mia.

Aldo took a moment to glance at each person. "For the past two months I've investigated a matter I consider important." He looked at Joe. "The investigation concerns you, Inspector Costa."

"Me?" He looked at Angelo, rigid and expressionless between the two women, and turned back to the colonel. "Did I do something wrong?"

"No," Aldo said. "Not you. It concerns your family in Italy and the United States." He turned to his desk and picked up multiple pages stapled together. He held them up for everyone to see an official Carabinieri investigation report. "One year after your birth, your father, Amadeo Costa, went before American immigration officials and swore he intended to renounce his Italian citizenship." Aldo tapped the papers. "A copy of the form with his signature is attached."

Joe glanced at Nina and back to Aldo. "I can explain. That was so he could become an American citizen."

Aldo raised a hand. "Not now. If you wish to explain in a few moments, you may. Four years later he became a citizen of the United States. The document isn't so important, the dates when this occurred are significant." He set the report on the desk and picked up a large envelope. "Inspector Costa. Have you done anything similar to what your father did? I mean, at any time during your life, did you declare you intended to renounce your citizenship?"

"No, sir." Joe glanced at Angelo and raised his eyebrows.

"Good. Since your date of birth is before your father renounced his Italian citizenship, I took it upon myself," he reached into the envelope and removed a paper, "to complete the process of reinstating your Italian citizenship. It is registered in Campania, in the commune of Giffoni Valle Piana, where your family lives." He handed the document to Joe.

Joe and Nina were the only two not smiling. Stunned, they studied the paper and the official seal at the bottom.

Joe read aloud. "Certificate of Citizenship. This official record certifies that Joseph Anthony Costa is an Italian citizen. Rome, 14 May 2015."

Everyone applauded. Angelo stepped in front of Joe and held out his hand. "Congratulations. You always said you were Italian, now it's official."

Aldo pulled an Italian passport from the envelope. "Here is your passport, you need to sign it and a few documents. A friend at the embassy got the photo from your file."

Joe took the passport. "Thank you, sir."

Aldo slapped him on the side of his shoulder. "If you wish to spend the remaining years of your career in Rome, I'll make it happen. I'm sure your Department of Justice will agree."

"What if they don't?" Joe asked.

Aldo raised both hands. "I can find someone who will explain the importance of Italian-American law enforcement cooperation. If they disagree, you can retire and work for me."

Nina pressed herself against him. "I'll go wherever you want, but it would be nice to stay here."

"Angelo told me Nina's favorite restaurant is the Target near Piazza Repubblica," Aldo said. "I arranged for a large table to be waiting for us at eight tonight. We will toast her for the help she provided us. Without her quick thinking, Omar Hassan would still be a free man and more drugs would flow into Italy."

Sofia tugged on Angelo's sleeve. "My cousin helped you with the investigation?"

"Yes. I'll tell you about it later."

After everyone congratulated Joe he approached Aldo with his hand extended. "Sir, thank you for what you've done. Nina and I are looking forward to tonight."

"Tonight we celebrate. We'll talk again in a few days. Angelo has the papers you need to sign."

Joe caught up with Angelo in the hall. The women walked in front of them. "Did the colonel tell you about this?"

"Of course."

"And you kept it secret?"

"I had to."

"Why?"

Angelo grinned. "I wanted to see your expression."

Chapter XXV
A RAY OF SUNSHINE

Gustav wasn't a happy man. *I gave them information. Why am I still here?*

He had told the captain everything he knew and Randi promised to move him to a new jail when the colonel signed the papers. The authorities now said the colonel had sent the transfer papers to a general for approval. *How long can that take?*

Gustav paced beside the rust pitted bars of the filthy six by ten feet windowless cell. The uneven concrete floor and stained walls revealed its decades of use. He glanced at Omar sleeping on the upper bunk. Prior to being moved into this cell, he had never met the man who now spent most of his days sobbing, moaning, and asking to see his girlfriend.

In the center of the ceiling a single bulb glowed inside a thick plastic fixture recessed in the cement.

He walked to the center of the room and looked up at an open four-inch wide pipe protruding from the concrete. A drop of water fell from the mold at the end of the pipe and landed on his forehead. He squinted and focused on a distant, weak glimmer of sunlight barely visible at the other end of the pipe.

THE END

Out of Naples

When you have to kill
a man, it costs nothing to
be polite.

–Winston Churchill

Chapter I
HOME

U.S. Marshal Service Chief Inspector Joe Costa sat at his desk in the Rome U.S. Embassy. He gazed at the small cardboard box he had received in a diplomatic pouch. Three weeks earlier, the U.S. Attorney's office in the Southern District of New York asked the Italian government for their assistance. The Rome Embassy received a copy of their request and forwarded it to the Italian Ministry of Justice. He smiled as he picked up the German-made switchblade lying beside the box and pressed the lever, allowing the polished Solingen steel blade to spring open.

With his thumb and index finger holding the tip of the blade, he guided it along the tape securing the package. Inside lay three sealed espresso pods. He removed one, stared at the wrapper and began to rip it open, but stopped. *Five hundred and sixty dollars, I'll wait for the meeting.*

When his cell phone rang, he dropped the packet into the box, tapped the screen and the speaker icon. "Pronto."

"What do you mean pronto? Only Italians answer their phone that way and you saw it's me," his wife Nina said.

"True, but one of my passports is red, and Italian Republic is printed on the front cover."

"How does it feel being a man with two countries?"

Actually good. The embassy restricted his travel to places in Eastern Europe and Southwest Asia. Americans needed to be cautious, and travel was less risky on a European Union passport. "The same as it did when I had one. Today I'm here, and next week you and I will be in New York City."

"That's why I called," Nina said. "How long are we going to be there? Sofia asked Angelo, but he couldn't tell her. We both need to plan what clothes we'll take."

"Anything you pack will do, as long as it is sexy."

"The lingerie is already in the suitcase, but it would be nice to know how to dress when we leave the hotel. I want to see the Statue of Liberty and other places in New York City."

"I'm meeting with Angelo and Colonel Aldo in an hour. We plan to ask for two or three extra days to do the tourist thing. You and Sofia always look nice. Whatever you pack will be fine, but remember we'll be doing a lot of walking. I'll call when I know how many days we'll be there."

"Okay. Tell Angelo my cousin is worried about the long plane ride."

"Has Sofia been on any long flights?"

"Only short trips. She and Angelo have traveled throughout Europe... nothing like crossing the Atlantic."

"We'll be in business class, everyone will love it."

Nina chuckled. "You're lucky I work for Alitalia. You owe me for the upgrade."

Joe lowered his voice to a whisper. "Take it out in trade."

"Is that all you think about?"

He smiled before he answered. *Why not!* "If you married you, it would also be the prominent thought of your day."

"I'm not complaining. You can make the first installment on your debt when you get home. Don't be late."

"I may be early. I love you."

"Love you too, I'll be waiting."

Nina ended the call, and Joe looked at the framed photo taken at the Target Restaurant the night they met. *Hello, Beautiful. In those red heels you are just the right height.*

Proud of his recent promotion, he lifted the carved wooden nameplate at the front of his desk and turned it. *Chief Inspector Costa. Someone is looking out for me.* After replacing it, he glanced at a document to his left. *Wow. Almost two hundred grand a year. All that, just for ducking bullets, and arresting bad guys.* "I love this job."

Joe slipped into his suit jacket as he left his office. At six foot two, he easily tapped on the top of the door frame at the office next to his. "You ready, Paul?"

DEA Special Agent Paul Sacca, a quiet man more dangerous than he looked, picked up his coat, and they headed down the hall. After Paul spent two successful years' undercover trading drugs for weapons going to the IRA, the Drug Enforcement Administration allowed him to pick his next assignment. He chose Rome hoping he'd be able to reconnect with his family in Verona.

As they neared the elevator, they ran into FBI Special Agent Robert Duffy. *Of all the guys I want to see today, he's the last.* Joe didn't dislike the man. Robert had a good attitude, but took his job, and himself, a little too seriously. *He's a pain in the ass.*

Agent Duffy was the same height as he and Paul but thirty pounds lighter. *Runners aren't built for throwing their weight against immovable objects.*

"You training for next month's marathon?" Paul asked.

"Yeah, why?"

"Looks like you lost a little weight."

Robert shook his head. "No. I gained two pounds this week."

"Fooled the shit out of me," Paul said.

Agent Duffy was like everyone's pesky unwanted little brother. With only four years in the FBI, his assignment to Rome resulted from his important connections. Having an uncle who was the Executive Assistant Director for Science and Technology at FBI Headquarters, had its perks.

"Where you guys headed?" he asked.

"A meeting at Colonel Giuseppe Aldo's office," Joe said.

"Got something going?"

Paul nodded. "DEA's coffee case out of New York."

Joe smiled. *The guy horns in on every investigation he can find.*

Duffy's eyes widened. "I heard about it from the agents handling the racketeering side of the prosecution. Call me if you need any help."

"DEA and the Marshals Service have it covered, but if we get in a bind, and need the Bureau's help, we'll call," Joe said.

Duffy looked at the small box in Joe's hand. "What's in there?"

Joe raised the box. "Coffee... espresso pods."

Duffy lifted his eyebrows. "Is it any good?"

Joe tapped the box. "This shit makes the Colombian and Brazilian Arabica blend taste like pulverized wood."

"I'd love to try it," Duffy said. "Save a few packs for me."

"Expensive stuff," Paul said. "If there's any left we'll bring it to you."

The elevator door opened. Paul and Joe stepped in and waited until it closed before they spoke.

Paul shook his head and shrugged. "He doesn't have a clue."

"He's harmless," Joe said. "I'm surprised a young Italian fashionista hasn't latched onto his ass yet."

"Wouldn't last long."

Joe tilted his head and shot him a quizzical look.

"She'd get bored hearing about the exploits of the FBI. I wouldn't want him anywhere near my sister."

Joe furrowed his brow. "Why not?"

"The Feebs always want to stick their fingers in things."

Chapter II
EXPENSIVE COFFEE

Joe, his partner, Carabinieri Captain Angelo Randi, Commander of the Fugitive Task Force, and Paul, waited for the colonel at the polished chestnut wood conference room table. The narrow room was furnished with the table that sat eight, and an Italian flag standing in one corner. It wasn't anything like the colonel's large office, meant to impress or intimidate his visitors.

"After you get back from New York, I won't bother you," Paul said to Angelo. "But I'd appreciate it if you'd keep me informed."

Angelo nodded. "No problem. I'll make sure you get a weekly update. If we get our hands on any of them or something out of the ordinary happens, Joe or I will call."

Angelo stared at the wall and tapped his pen on the table.

"What's wrong?" Joe asked.

"I can be a hard ass. As soon as I open my mouth, the Neapolitans will hear my Roman accent. They won't trust me. You, on the other hand, will get away with murder down there. We may need your Southern Italian charm to get people to talk."

Joe grinned. "So, you're promoting me?"

"Yeah, from partner to close partner and mouthpiece, but don't expect a pay raise."

The door opened and Colonel Giuseppe Aldo entered the conference room. Everyone stood. He motioned for the three men to take their seats and sat in the chair at the head of the table.

Joe gazed at the stubble on his face and his bald head. *Needs to shave twice a day but not one hair on his head.* He caught the colonel's eye and rubbed the side of his cheek. "Looks like you started early today, sir."

Aldo grinned. "One AM. The Carabinieri never sleep." He pointed at the box in front of Joe. "Is that what we've been waiting to get from New York?"

"Yes, sir." He removed one of the tiny espresso pod packages. From his pocket he pulled the switchblade and pressed the lever. "Shall I?"

Aldo nodded.

Joe ripped open the packet and dropped the circular pod onto a piece of paper on the table. He slit open the filter paper and raised a small mound of white powder on the tip of the knife blade. "One packet, seven grams of cocaine, sold for five hundred and sixty to six hundred dollars on the streets of New York."

Angelo raised his eyebrows. "Leave it to the ingenuity of the Neapolitans to come up with something like this. When the Naples command closed the Camorra coffee manufacturing facility, they arrested ten people. They're still in jail awaiting trial."

Paul leaned forward. "The trial for the drug dealers arrested in New York is scheduled to begin next month. All the defendants are on bond because the judge wouldn't consider their flight risk. He said Italians have close-knit families... must have thought they had relatives in the city. Three of them are now missing. He should have asked where their families lived."

"They came home?" Aldo asked.

"Yes, Sir," Paul said. "Our informant said they returned to Naples." He raised his eyebrows. "The metropolitan area is smaller than Rome but they have almost a million more people. It may be difficult to find them."

Aldo looked at Angelo and smiled. "Think your men can handle it?"

"The Neapolitans don't trust people from outside the region of Campania. If we can get someone to talk, we'll find our fugitives."

"Let's discuss New York. You're making arrangements to go there and meet with the investigators?" Aldo asked.

"Yes, sir. Joe is taking Nina on the trip, and with your permission I'd like to take Sofia. We thought we'd extend our stay two days and visit the 9/11 memorial."

"Of course," Aldo said. "If I had the time, I'd go with you. Who will you be meeting?"

Joe removed a paper from his pocket. "DEA Supervisor Al Sarno, NYPD Inspector Michael Cleary, and Marshals Service Fugitive Squad Inspector Harry Walters."

"If you hadn't told me where you were going, I'd assume you'd be staying here in Europe," Aldo said.

Angelo's brow furrowed, and he looked at his boss. "Why is that?"

"Sarno, Cleary and Walters. Italy, Ireland and England. Although, the last time I was in New York City, it was like taking a trip around the world." Aldo placed his elbows on the table, clamped his hands together, and paused. He pointed at the three men. "Remember, what you hear from the investigators in New York relates to the Mafia, not the Camorra in Naples. Earlier I said the Carabinieri never sleep. The clans of the Camorra never close their eyes. They refer to themselves as 'O Sistema, The System' in

Neapolitan. Before you look for anyone down there, we need to have another conversation."

"Yes, sir," Angelo replied.

Aldo looked at Joe. "I don't know if I should let you go with Angelo on this one."

"Sir. Please don't take this the wrong way." Joe took a deep breath. "I didn't take this job to sit on my ass in an office in Rome. Angelo and I are cautious. We rely on each other's instincts before we act. Neither of us will do anything stupid."

"I know that. But I worry about the ramifications if an American gets injured in a raid on Italian soil. The other problem is you may have to shoot someone to protect yourself. Members of both governments would jump onto my desk with both feet. I had people nipping at my ass when you got shot during the trawler case."

Angelo interceded. "Sir, I'll protect him as I would any member of my family. He looks Italian, speaks the language fluently, and wears our tactical uniform on operations. I allowed him to place a U.S. Marshals patch beside our patch. If he is to pass for one of us, we'll remove it."

Aldo shrugged. "Our government has already given him permission to carry his weapon. I've been doing this job for a long time... controversy doesn't bother me. But let me think about it."

When he slid his chair back, the others stood.

"Call me later today, Angelo," Aldo said before leaving the room.

Paul tapped Joe on the shoulder. "I envy you, but don't be surprised if the Ambassador doesn't go along with it when he's asked if it's okay for you to work the operation."

Paul was right. Although his boss in Washington didn't worry, the hierarchy at the embassy would want to cover their asses.

Joe grinned. "Who's going to him to ask permission?"

Chapter III
THE CITY

After a long day of sightseeing, Joe, Nina, Angelo and his wife Sofia, crossed the lobby of the Trump International Hotel and Tower next to Central Park. They entered the well-lit bar and sank into leather chairs.

"What did you think of the statue?" Joe asked.

"I didn't know it was that big," Sofia said. "Before we came, I read about it. Lady Liberty, it's a wonderful name."

"It is," Nina said. "When we looked at the exhibits at Ellis Island, I couldn't believe how many Italians came to this country."

Joe nodded. "I read somewhere that between 1900 and 1930, three million Italians, many of them from the south, immigrated to America."

A waitress took their drink orders.

"Most of the day tomorrow you girls will be on your own. Joe and I are meeting with police officials," Angelo said.

Sofia looked at Nina and grinned. "We'll go shopping."

"I'm sure Angelo and I will be back before five. Don't get lost."

They finished the drinks and headed to their rooms.

The two men arrived at DEA Headquarters on 10th Avenue at eleven the next morning. They walked into an upper floor conference room overlooking the Hudson River and the Chelsea Piers Sport Complex. One of the three men standing at a panoramic window motioned to them. "Come here, it's a good view of the river."

These guys are huge, well over six feet. Joe glanced at Angelo, who at five-eleven, was the shortest in the room.

The man who spoke introduced himself and extended his hand. "I'm DEA Supervisor Al Sarno." He motioned to the two men beside him. "NYPD Inspector Michael Cleary, and Marshals Service Fugitive Squad Inspector Harry Walters."

"Nice to meet you. I'm Chief Inspector Joe Costa." He motioned to Angelo. "This is Carabinieri Captain Angelo Randi." Everyone shook hands and took a seat at a table with a pitcher and glasses in the center, and notepads and pens in front of each chair.

"When did you arrive?" Walters asked.

"The day before yesterday. We took time to see a few sights." Joe replied.

Walters turned to Angelo. "Is this your first visit to New York?"

"Yes. Impressive."

"Did you get the package I sent?" Sarno asked.

Joe picked up on his southern drawl. "Yes. It matches the ones seized in Naples. You're not from New York, are you?"

"Been here ten years." Sarno grinned. "Can't shake New Orleans out of my system."

"You're Italian?" Angelo asked.

"Yeah. My grandparents emigrated from Sicily. There's a large Italian population down there and I stay in close contact with my podnas."

"Podnas?" Joe wrinkled his brow.

Cleary smiled. "It takes time to get use to his colloquial expressions. A podna is a friend."

Angelo shook his head. "English is difficult enough. I'll never figure out the local dialects."

Walters handed Angelo and Joe manila folders. "These are the Marshals Service Wanted Posters with information on the guys that skipped town. After the judge issued UFAP warrants, the Marshals Service asked the Justice Department to request your fugitive task force get involved. Your reputation proceeded you."

Angelo glanced at Joe and furrowed his brow.

"UFAP," Joe said. "Unlawful Flight to Avoid Prosecution."

Both men opened the folders and looked at the first page.

"Santo Esposito, aka The Saint," Joe said.

"His involvement matches his size, small time," Walters said. "He's five-six... short and skinny. Wears all black and could pass for an undersized priest. Family is from Naples."

Angelo and Joe flipped to the second page.

"Dominic Capasso, he's called Heads," Angelo said staring at the paper.

"He's the least dangerous of the three... the money guy, and leader of a small group in the Greenwich Village crew," Cleary said. "Short... another peewee. Also five-six, but heavier than The Saint."

They turned to the last page and Joe's eyes widened. "Who's this giant?"

"Francesco Russo. Six four and three hundred plus pounds," Cleary said. "On the street they call him Poco Tonno."

Angelo leaned forward. "Little Tuna? The Japanese only wish half of them were this size."

"He's the midget in the family," Walters said. "See the bottom of the page? His older brother, Johnny, Grande Tonno, is six seven and a little over four hundred pounds. Francesco is the one you need to watch."

"Why?" Joe asked.

Al Sarno tapped the table. "We didn't know the full extent of his involvement until we cultivated an informant. Little Tuna is the enforcer... weapon of choice is the Walther PPKS, 22 long rifle. Killing isn't his only enjoyment in life."

"What else can we look forward to?" Angelo asked.

"The snitch was at his apartment when Francesco cut up a body in the bathtub," Cleary said. "He told us the creep ordered pizza and opened the door in a blood-stained apron... told the delivery guy he was making sauce."

Angelo raised his shoulders and cringed.

"A real nice guy! Is there a complete file on each of these mopes?" Joe asked.

Angelo looked at him and raised his eyebrows.

"Sorry, Ang. A mope is police slang for an unsavory character. We also use the terms dirt-bag and low-life."

Al nodded. "Before we leave for lunch, I'll get the three files off my desk."

When the meeting ended, at a little past one, a black Chevrolet Suburban took them to Pellegrino's restaurant on Mulberry Street, in Lower Manhattan's Little Italy.

Inside, a young man led the five investigators to a round table in an alcove halfway into the narrow dining area. The table could not be seen from the street.

Michael Cleary, in fluent Italian, told the waiter to bring two bottles of red wine and to make it Cabernet Sauvignon.

"You speak Italian well," Angelo said.

"Half Irish and half Italian. My mother is from Naples. She was a school teacher and met my father when he served a tour of duty there. I grew up a few blocks from here."

A man in a white shirt and tie, trailed by a waiter, walked up to the table and looked at Cleary. "Hi Mike. Glad you could come. Who are your friends?"

"Nice to see you again, Tony." Cleary introduced everyone to Tony LaRocca, the manager of Pellegrino's.

Tony nodded to the group. "May I suggest you start with a fine antipasti... the Prosciutto e Melone. The Linguine alla Sinatra, with half a lobster, shrimp, clams, mussels, pine nuts and mushrooms, is excellent as is the veal and filet mignon."

Everyone agreed to let Cleary order the appetizers. "We'll split two orders of Prosciutto e Melone, and two of Mozzarella Della Casa." He nodded to the others. "It's fresh and smoked buffalo mozzarella, tomatoes, roasted peppers and basil."

While Michael Cleary ordered, Joe noticed a man wearing a well-tailored suit and carrying a fedora walk in to the restaurant as if he owned the place. He headed in their direction. *Confident air about him. He looks important... might be the owner.*

Tony saw the gentleman, nodded, and stepped back to let him pass.

When the guy reached their table, Joe saw him turn his head, getting a good look at the five cops. He continued to a corner table at the back of the restaurant.

Tony motioned the waiter to his side and placed a hand on his shoulder. "Enzo and his assistant will serve you. The wine is on me."

Cleary stood. "Thank you." He leaned to Joe and Angelo. "I'll be back in a few minutes. It's been a while since

Tony and I talked." The two men headed to the front of the restaurant.

While they waited for the appetizers Al Sarno and Harry Walters asked Angelo questions about the Carabinieri.

"My wife and I were in Rome two years ago," Sarno said to Angelo. "Your guys on the street didn't smile much. I tried to trade a DEA hat and patch for an exploding grenade pin on one of their hats. They wouldn't even discuss it."

Angelo nodded. "Not all of us are unfriendly. It's the image we project that counts. You asked the wrong guy. That pin is difficult to get, but I'll see if I can steal one for you. Give me your address before we leave."

Cleary returned to the table when the appetizers arrived.

Joe started on the delicious food and watched Enzo talk with the well-dressed man. He leaned forward, "Who's the guy in the back of the room? He took a good look at us when he passed the table."

"Vincenzo Rizzo," Cleary said. "He's the Greenwich Village capo in the Genovese family. They call him Vinny No Words. He's quiet and keeps to himself. When I got to the front of the restaurant with Tony, two of Vinny's men were drinking coffee at an outside table. He's a regular here, nothing out of the ordinary. The chef is from the same town in Sicily."

"Is the chef connected?" Joe asked. He noticed Angelo looking at him and the American investigators.

Cleary shook his head. "No. He's religious... kept his nose clean."

"Not connected, but has a clean nose?" Angelo asked. "I don't understand."

Everyone at the table laughed.

"I'm sorry, Angelo," Cleary said. "American idioms are hard to follow. He's not involved with the Mafia and hasn't been in any trouble. Vincenzo helped him get the job. His cousin went to school with him in Sicily."

The five men finished their meal, and over drinks, discussed law enforcement agencies in Italy. At four thirty they drove Joe and Angelo back to Trump Tower.

Chapter IV
TOURIST

The next morning Joe, Nina, Angelo and Sofia got out of the Lincoln Navigator on Vesey Street beside One World Trade Center.

Joe leaned into the passenger's side and spoke to the driver before he closed the door. "I'm glad there are Uber drivers with big cars. We'll call you an hour before we want to be picked up and meet you here."

They walked past the entrance to the one hundred and four story building, passed under many of the four-hundred trees surrounding the memorial pools and approached the north pool of the 9/11 Memorial.

Angelo looked back at the tall silver structure and took Sofia's arm. "You want to go to the top before we leave? The observatory is on the hundredth floor."

Sofia pulled him close and everyone looked to the top of the massive building. "How do we get there?"

"Take the elevator at the entrance we passed," Joe said.

Nina looked at Sofia. "Flying doesn't bother me, but riding to the top of that isn't something I want to do."

Sofia raised her eyebrows and nodded. "The plane ride wasn't as bad as I thought it would be, but the elevator doesn't have Business Class. I'll keep my feet on the ground."

"I don't blame you," Angelo said.

Joe took Nina's hand. "Come on."

They walked to the wall surrounding the pool and stared at the names inscribed into the bronze parapets.

"My God. How many names are inscribed here?" Nina asked.

"On this one," Joe pointed at the south pool, "and that one, there are 2,983 names of the men, women, and children killed in the attacks."

"Is this where the buildings stood?" Angelo asked.

"Yes. It's the exact footprint of the two towers. We'll walk to the other one and then go to the museum."

When they turned away from the pool, Joe spotted a man in a black jacket for the second time. *He's the same guy who passed us in front of the building. It's cool but not cold.* He shrugged, but made a mental note of the guy's black combed-back hair.

As if descending into a gigantic tomb, they took the escalator seventy feet below ground.

Nina turned, wide eyed, to Joe. "Not one person has a smile on their face."

"I can understand why."

They stepped into a cavernous room cut out of the earth. A gigantic graffiti covered pillar stood before a section of the original foundation wall.

Angelo turned to Joe. "How big is this place?"

"The museum covers one hundred and ten thousand square feet." He tilted his head and paused. "That's a little under two times the size of the field at the Olympic stadium in Rome. I've heard people say it they took five hours to see everything." He took Nina's hand. "Let's get started."

They walked toward the sixty-foot high exposed section of the World Trade Center's slurry wall that held back seepage from the Hudson River. Joe's eyes came to rest on a black jacket. *Why the jacket? Maybe he's from down south... Central America.* He stopped, shook his head, and turned away from the man.

"What's wrong?" Angelo asked.

"Don't anyone react to what I say. Act like we are having a normal conversation and please do not turn toward him. Directly behind me, near the wall, there's a man in a black jacket. I've seen him three times since we got out of the car."

"Are we being followed?" Angelo asked.

Joe shrugged. "I'm not sure. Let's walk past the next three exhibits and then stop. We'll see if he stays with us."

"Okay." Angelo stepped in front of Nina and Sofia. "Don't make eye contact with him. If you turn in his direction, focus on something to the side."

They stopped beside a fire truck partially destroyed when the buildings fell.

Joe asked the others to stand beside the truck for a good camera shot. Out of the corner of his eye he noticed the man standing thirty feet behind the exhibit. He moved to the side and raised his Nikon so he could position the stranger in the background of the photo.

"Everyone smile." With the camera pointed at the group he zoomed in on the man's face and took two pictures.

Angelo stepped in close. "Did you get a good picture of him?"

"Yeah, a great shot of his face."

Angelo raised his eyebrows. "What are you thinking?"

"Someone wants to find out more about us." Joe said. "Remember the guy at the restaurant? He's the key to this. People on Mulberry Street in Little Italy need to live with the wiseguys. When they go into a restaurant and ask questions, they expect an answer. I'm sure by now they know we're here, but they may not know why."

"And if they do?"

Joe shrugged. "They might pass the word to friends back in Italy."

Angelo pondered and rubbed his chin. "The Saint and his friends aren't stupid. They realize we'll be looking for them."

"True, but one thing bothers me."

"What?"

"Are they going to be told who's doing the looking?"

Chapter V
WISEGUYS

The waiter at Nougatine, inside the Trump International Hotel, set the after-dinner drinks on the table. "Are you sure you don't want dessert?"

Joe glanced at Angelo and the women. They all shook their heads. "No thank you, we're fine. Everything was excellent."

He handed Joe the bill. "Thank you for coming to Nougatine," and walked away.

"What time does the plane leave tomorrow?" Sofia asked Nina.

"At four-twenty. We'll fly all night and land before seven the next morning. Want to get up early and go to Times Square?"

Sofia looked at Joe. "Do we have time?"

"Sure. We need to leave for the airport by twelve-fifteen. Michael Cleary from the New York City police department will meet us in front of the Alitalia counter at two." He slid cash into the bill folio and they left the restaurant.

###

That evening two men in suits walked into the lobby of the hotel and stopped at the reception desk. Ralph, the taller man, motioned to the desk clerk, while his partner turned and observed the lobby.

"Excuse me." He pointed at the clerk's nametag. "Stephen. How ya doing?"

"Fine, sir. How may I help you?"

"Earlier today, my boss noticed two Italian guys in the lobby. He thinks he may have met one of them in Rome." Ralph handed him a photo of Joe and Angelo. "Could you give me their names?"

Stephen bit his lip. "I'm sorry, sir. For security reasons we may not give out that information without the guest's permission."

Ralph opened his hand, unfolded a pair of hundred-dollar bills, and slid them toward the clerk. "I understand, Stephen, but my boss is a powerful man, and he doesn't like hearing the word no. Maybe you should make an exception for him."

The clerk glanced to an office door at the end of the counter. "I don't want to lose my job, sir. Sorry, I can't help you."

"That's too bad." Ralph motioned toward the lobby. "Mr. Trump must be a wonderful employer and pay you well. Does he offer hospitalization insurance? Something to pay the bill should you have an accident on the job? Ya know, like one or two broken legs." He slid the bills closer to the clerk.

Stephen took the money. "One moment, please." He shuffled through a card file, scribbled on a piece of paper and pushed it across the counter.

Ralph lifted the paper. "Angelo Randi and Joseph Costa. Yes, I believe he knows Mr. Randi." He shoved the paper into his pocket. "Thank you, Stephen. My boss and I wish you good health." Ralph pointed to Stephen's wedding band. "Also your wife, and kids, if you have any." Both men and left without looking back.

Vincenzo Rizzo held a Coke glass half-filled with red wine. He sat on a couch in the back room of a bar in

Greenwich Village. On an end table next to him lay a plate piled high with a variety of savory cheeses. He seldom missed a Rangers game and stared at the television on the wall.

Ralph stepped into the room. "Hi, Vinny. I got the names you wanted." He handed his boss the paper.

"Good." Vinny scanned the note. "Over at Pellegrino's, Enzo said one of them was a Carabinieri Captain... powerful man. Ya don't wanna fuck with him. The other *chooch* is a U.S. Marshal. One of those *mamalukes* who hide the snitches."

Ralph scrunched his eyebrows. "Hide snitches?"

"Yeah. Remember, Sammy the Bull, and Joe Dogs Iannuzzi, the cook? Them guys... the snitches."

Ralph's eyes widened. "The G's protection program for rats?"

"Yeah. I'll call Dante in Naples tonight. He'll wanna know they're here asking questions."

Chapter VI
THE BLUEPRINT

A week after he and Angelo returned to Rome, Joe sat in on a meeting at Colonel Aldo's conference room.

In attendance were the colonel, Angelo, DEA Special Agent Paul Sacca, Sacca's counterpart Lieutenant Sergio Lacona of the Carabinieri Counter-Narcotics Group, and FBI Special Agent Robert Duffy.

After the group spent thirty minutes discussing the case, Aldo glanced at the five men. "Are there questions about Angelo's report of the New York trip?"

They all shook their heads.

"Coordinating the investigation could become a problem," Aldo said. "I spoke with the colonel at the Counter Narcotics Group. Lieutenant Lacona and his men will monitor the case here in Rome. The Fugitive Task Force will take the lead and attempt to make the arrest in or around Naples." Aldo motioned to Duffy. "Agent Duffy, this is your first case with us. Again, I want to welcome you to our group."

"Thank you, sir. I'm looking forward to providing you with the FBI's help."

"We welcome all the help we can get, but for now you and Agent Sacca will stay in Rome. Sergio assures me you'll both get access to the Counter Narcotics Group."

Duffy took a deep breath. "But, sir. The FBI has the ability..."

The colonel interrupted him. "There are no butts in my office Agent Duffy. We are flexible, and will use all the resources of the FBI and DEA should my Fugitive Task Force need them. Until that time, Captain Randi, Inspector Costa, and their men will work the case in Naples."

"Yes, sir," Duffy replied.

"Good. I don't want any of the problems that arise when different agencies compete against each other. Questions anyone?"

The men remained silent.

"Thank you, gentlemen. I need to speak with Angelo and Joe."

Sergio, Paul and Duffy left the room.

When the door closed, Colonel Aldo continued. "Back to what we discussed before your New York trip." He looked at Angelo. "I will allow Joe to work the case with you. I told Agent Duffy there were no butts in my office, but I have a few instructions you are to follow."

"Thank you, sir," Joe said. "We'll abide by any rules you set."

"Both of you listen. I want to make sure nothing happens during this operation that will embarrass us. Joe's not to dress any different than you and your men... nothing that could identify him as an American."

Angelo smiled. "A week ago he picked up new Carabinieri tactical uniforms to include boots. The bullet-proof vest he brought from America is in his office and I gave him one of ours."

Aldo turned to Joe. "Put your Glock with your American vest. Angelo, issue him one of our Beretta pistols. Take submachine guns. I seem to recall you and your men received the new H&K MP5?"

"Yes, sir."

Aldo raised his eyebrows. "Don't ask for another one to give to Joe. Tomorrow I'll bring in the one I keep at my house."

Wow. He's putting his ass on the line. Joe leaned over the table. "Sir, you don't have to do that."

"I know." Aldo stared at him. "I wouldn't if I didn't trust you. Remember you are not dealing with structured Mafia families that have a defined chain of command. The Camorra is composed of formless and autonomous clans. Honor plays no part. Control is imposed by force... often violent. The members do not worry about their next birthday celebration. You both need to learn more about them before you start your operation. Now, tell me what you and Joe plan to do."

"We're going to Naples for a few days to get familiar with the surroundings. During that time, we'll formalize a plan. When we return, we'll brief you and the others and then go back with a team from the Task Force."

Aldo nodded and stood. "Be careful." He looked at Joe. "Do you know the motto of your Special Forces?"

"Yes, sir. *De Oppresso Liber,* to liberate the oppressed."

Aldo grinned. "Forget it. The oppressed don't want to be liberated. Best if you follow the motto of the Special Air Service, *Who Dares Wins.*"

Chapter VII
THE ADVANCE

Angelo and his wife Sofia arrived at Joe and Nina's apartment at eight that evening. They spent the next three hours sitting around the dining room table talking, drinking and eating the appetizers Nina prepared.

The conversation remained light. Neither man wanted to alarm the women with details of their planned trip, but both wives knew they were leaving in the next few days.

Joe glanced at Angelo. *Got to tease him a little.* "When we get back are you going to invite Nina and me to San Lorenzo so we can visit with your neighbor, the Pope?" Joe asked.

Sofia raised her eyebrows. "You've never been to Castel Gandolfo?"

"I have, but Joe hasn't," Nina said.

Angelo laughed. "Sure, we'll have you come to dinner. The Pope's residence is nearby but I hope you aren't expecting a personal invitation from His Holiness?"

Joe looked at him and smiled. *Come on, Angelo.* "Why not? You have connections with the Swiss Guard. I'll bet the Pope never met a U.S. Marshal."

"I have friends in high places," Angelo said, "but few of them are that close to heaven." His phone rang. "Excuse me." He walked away from the table.

A minute of casual conversation passed and Angelo called Joe's name.

He walked into the living room. "What is it?"

"One of our men believes he saw The Saint in Naples."

"A guy on our Task Force?"

"Yes." He tilted his head toward the dining room. "We need to tell them we're leaving tomorrow."

###

Early the next afternoon Joe and Angelo pulled into the driveway of a safe house twenty miles outside Naples. Angelo stopped the car and waited for the automatic gate to retract allowing access to the property. He then drove a hundred feet to a villa on an oversized lot.

Upon entering the house, Joe saw Claudio, one of the Task Force officers involved in the shooting in Rome. "Hi Claudio. Haven't seen you in six months."

"The day you stopped a bullet with your arm," Claudio said. "Have you had any problems with it?"

Joe raised his left hand and flexed his fist. "No. Everything still works, but it left me with a hell of a scar."

Angelo introduced him to two other Task Force officers. Gennaro appeared to be a short teenager, but shook Joe's hand with the grip of a flyweight wrestler. Sabatino was the largest of the three. The muscular six-foot tall man had hands larger than Joe had ever seen. The first two knuckles bore thick calluses.

Angelo led everyone to a room with a large table and eight chairs. A white dry-erase board hung on one wall. A table with a laptop and two projectors stood in the corner.

Once everyone took a seat, Angelo broke the silence. "What do you have planned for us in the morning, Claudio?"

"Two days ago, in the town of Sant'Antonio Abate, thirty minutes from here, Gennaro and I saw a man that fits Santo Esposito's description."

"Where?" Joe asked.

"We've been watching a market, a bar, and a few more locations frequented by the clan. He came out of a local market one block from a bar that's known as a clan hangout. The place is called Caesar's Bar. It appears to be a typical local business... coffee, liquor, pastry, small meals, and gelato. We didn't go there. They would have known we're from out of town."

Angelo spent a moment staring at the table and then looked at Claudio. "Are you sure it was him?"

"No. Later I'll set up the computer and projector and show you the photos we took."

"Did Santo go into the bar?" Joe asked.

"No. He stopped outside and said something to a man coming out the door. They spoke for five minutes, then he turned down an alley and we couldn't follow him without being seen."

"Okay," Angelo said. "When we're done here, I want to take a drive past that bar."

Two hours later Angelo turned his gray Alfa Romeo onto a narrow street in Sant'Antonio Abate. Joe sat in the front and Claudio in the back.

Joe glanced to the back seat. "How far is it from here?"

"One kilometer. It will be on the left."

Joe studied the road in front of the car. *Not very wide.* "Is this street always crowded with cars, Claudio?"

"Yes, but late at night there's not much traffic. Cars may park on the right side. You'll seldom find a vacant space."

An empty feeling developed in Joe's stomach. The driver's side mirrors on the parked cars were folded in to allow passing vehicles a few more inches. "Glad you're not driving a big Ford or Chevy, Ang. This Alfa barely squeezes through here."

Angelo laughed. "The road has been here longer than America has been a country."

Joe looked at the two and three-story buildings lining the street. The three-foot-wide sidewalks in front of the structures provided little room for people to stop and talk while others passed. Many of the people talking stood in the small space between the parked cars. It would tempt fate to step off the sidewalk on the left side of the street.

"How much farther?" Angelo asked.

"A hundred meters," Claudio replied.

Joe scanned the buildings ahead.

"Up there, on the left. The sign is above the door." Claudio said.

Angelo slowed as they passed the entrance to the bar. Two men, leaning against the wall near the doorway, looked at the Alfa Romeo as it passed. Joe glanced over his shoulder and noticed one of them pointing at the car.

Fifty feet past the bar, a bullet shattered the back window and tore into the center console.

Claudio threw himself down on the seat and Joe ducked as Angelo hit the gas.

Later that night Joe sat with Gennaro and Sabatino in the makeshift conference room at the safe house. No one spoke. Gennaro shuffled through a stack of papers and Sabatino cleaned his fingernails with a pocket knife.

Joe stared at the wall and took a deep breath. *We haven't started yet and already someone takes a shot at us. The colonel was right. These bastards are dangerous. We need more firepower than handguns.*

Angelo and Claudio walked in and sat at the table. Angelo turned to Gennaro and Sabatino. "Did Claudio and Joe tell you about our back window?"

Both men nodded, their eyes locked on their boss.

Angelo tapped the table with his fingers. "This will not go unanswered." He looked at Claudio. "Get two more men and two of our marked Land Rovers. I want these bastards to know they are dealing with the Carabinieri. We'll raid the bar at ten tonight."

Sabatino raised a finger. "How did they figure out it was you in the car?"

"I don't think they did," Angelo said. "The car attracted their attention. It may be unmarked, but an Alfa Romeo with three men in it, and two of them in suits, was something they've seen many times. Carabinieri may not be written on the side, but, when they looked at it, that's what they saw."

Someone is protecting the place, Joe thought. "The round didn't come from street level. It had to be fired from a rooftop to end up in the console."

"Joe's right," Angelo said. "The five of us will take the bar, have to others in street clothes and tell them to get to the top of the highest nearby building."

"Tactical gear?" Gennaro asked.

Angelo nodded. "Vests, masks, and I want each of us to carry a MP5."

Joe smiled. *What's that old saying? God protects children and fools. The MP5 will even out the odds.*

Chapter VIII
CAESAR'S BAR

At 9:30 that night, Joe watched Angelo glance into the rearview mirror at the police car behind their Land Rover. Blue flashing lights lit the dark street.

"This is a good spot. Even though we have one of our men with the local officer, I don't want them getting any closer," Angelo said. He stopped, stuck his hand out the window and pointed at the ground.

The sedan turned and blocked the street. The officer and Carabiniere got out.

"They won't let any cars pass until we tell them. We'll wait until the street clears and Claudio calls," Angelo said.

Joe pointed the barrel of his MP5 at the floorboard and placed the weapon between his legs. He set his balaclava face mask on his thigh and tightened one strap of his protective vest. *Hope this goes well. Never seen Angelo this angry.* The bullet that shattered the rear window of Angelo's car wasn't meant to hit anyone. Someone wanted to intimidate them. *This will be interesting. Ang will kick ass.*

"Say nothing in English while we're there."

"I won't." Joe smiled. "I'll try to keep my mouth shut, look mean and make sure everyone is safe." He glanced to the back seat. "You ready, Gennaro?"

"Yes, sir."

The radio crackled and Claudio's voice blared from the speaker. "Moving now."

Angelo pulled the mask over his head and put the Land Rover in gear.

Claudio's SUV came from the opposite direction and skidded to a stop in front of the bar. He and Sabatino, with two other Carabinieri leapt out seconds before Joe and Angelo came to a stop.

Two men standing on the sidewalk dashed into an alley. A young man bolted out of the bar and Sabatino stuck out his arm. His rigid forearm slammed into the man's jaw.

Joe's mouth fell open, and he froze. Everything seemed to move in slow motion. He cringed as the guy's head stopped when it met Sabatino's muscular forearm. *Holy shit!* The man's feet continued to race from the scene. Both of his legs left the ground, and for a split second his prone body hung three feet above the concrete. The man dropped and moaned when his back and head hit the sidewalk. *That hurt!*

Sabatino dragged the body from the entrance, placed a boot on the unconscious man's chest, and smiled.

Joe and Angelo jumped from their vehicle.

"Stay behind me!" Angelo yelled.

They left an officer to secure the vehicles and cover the alley.

Sabatino and Gennaro followed Angelo and Joe into the bar.

Angelo looked at Joe and pointed to a frail, gray-haired woman sitting at a corner table. "Watch her." With Sabatino and Gennaro leading, he headed to a back room.

Joe lowered his weapon, moved away from the door, and glanced around the stale smelling room. Dusty tables, and two near-empty pastry and gelato cases caught his eye. One tub of ice cream, and two small trays of broken cookies were the only items on display in the cabinets. Four shelves behind the bar held only three bottles of whiskey. *This bar isn't selling anything.* He focused on the old woman. "From the looks of this place, there's not much business."

The woman shrugged. "You're from Naples."

"No. Milan. All of us are dressed for the late night opera at the La Scala Theater."

She laughed. "If you wanted me to believe that, you should have written it on paper. The sounds of Naples came out of your mouth."

Angelo returned. "A meeting room. Two slot machines, card tables and a big television. Everyone in there ran out the back door." He walked to the woman. "Where is the owner?"

"You're speaking to her. The bar closed last year."

"Where do you live?"

She hesitated. "In the apartment upstairs."

"Why do you have slot machines?" Angelo asked.

"Entertainment. They pay no money, only a paper with a score. My friends come here to enjoy the soccer games on a large television."

"Your friends weren't interested in the rest of the game. They left their drinks on the table when they ran."

The woman raised her palms in front of her and shrugged.

Sabatino came out of the room. "They're gone. The street out back and the alley are clear."

"You and your men wait here until the local police arrive," Angelo said. "Don't allow anyone to touch the box of receipts and credit cards near the slot machines." He turned to the woman. "Stay in that chair, the Financial Police will want to speak to you when they arrive."

The woman leaned forward and spat.

Angelo took a step back and glared at her. "Signora," he said in a sarcastic tone. "Was it your mother who taught you to spit on the floor?"

He headed to the door, paused and turned to Sabatino. "Please call the local health service. Ask them to inspect this woman's apartment to make sure it's livable. She has the bad habit of discharging body fluids on the floor."

The woman stood and stared at him with a contorted expression that turned to a smile. "You have beautiful eyes, Carabiniere."

Angelo glared at her. "Be careful, old woman. Imagine what will happen if I tell your neighbors and friends we had a long friendly conversation about their activities."

Joe followed him out the door.

During their drive to the safe house, Joe kept quiet. *Ang is pissed!* After ten minutes, Angelo's hands relaxed on the steering wheel. *He'll talk now.*

"Did you hear what she said, Ang?"

"Yes."

"You know that wasn't a compliment she gave you." Joe said.

"I know. It isn't the first time it's happened. As soon as she spoke I knew what she meant. It was a curse... the evil eye." Angelo looked at him, faked a shiver and grinned. "I'm worried."

Joe shook his head. "When people down here do that, I get nervous."

Angelo couldn't hide his smile. "Do you have a horn for protection?"

"Yes, on a chain. It's in a drawer in my bedroom."

Angelo raised his eyebrows. "Can I borrow it when we go home?"

"Hell no, Ang. Buy your own. I'm putting it on as soon as we get to Rome. What are you thinking?"

"The one thing they respect is force. I want them to see the power of the Carabinieri Fugitive Squad. Tomorrow we'll go back to Rome. You get your horn, and then we'll brief the colonel."

Chapter IX
NO MEN OF HONOR

Colonel Aldo motioned Angelo and Joe into his office. He pointed to the leather couch in front of the coffee table and they took a seat. Angelo set a thick folder between them.

Joe leaned forward and rubbed his hand across the table. *Black marble with veins of gold... beautiful.*

Aldo sat in an armchair across from them. "How long have you been back?" Aldo asked Angelo.

"Three days."

The colonel pointed at Joe. "Do you still want to help Angelo on this case?"

"Yes, sir. The Camorra may be dangerous, but they're too smart to do something as dumb as shooting an officer. One bullet through the back window of our car was their attempt to frighten us."

"I agree, Inspector Costa, but be careful. You and Angelo are working a case against organized crime, but like I said, it's not the Mafia you face."

Joe scratched his cheek and squinted. "What do you mean, sir?"

"The Mafia thinks of themselves as honorable men. Have you heard that term?"

"Yes, sir."

"Their criminal organization accepts only full-blooded Italians as members... most from Sicily. Their men spend years working and waiting to become members of the family. They are loyal to a 'Don', the head of the family."

"I understand that, sir," Joe said. "But the Camorra, in its own way, has the same structure."

"That is where you are mistaken. The Camorra draws its members from the streets. Have you read anything by Isa Sales?" Aldo asked.

"No, sir."

"He's an expert on Italian organized crime. He said, 'Camorra soldiers come from the lowest socio-economic echelons, the urban sub-proletariat.' Unlike the Mafia, anyone can join a Camorra gang. Sales described the Clans as having no central organization. Their loyalty is to crime and money."

"Isn't that the same as the Mafia?" Joe asked.

Aldo shook his head. "No. When we go after the men, or the head of a Mafia family, they don't take it personal. They may threaten law enforcement officials, but they seldom act on the threats."

"What about Giovanni Falcone, the judge and prosecuting magistrate? The Mafia killed him with a bomb in 1992," Angelo said.

Aldo nodded. "Yes, in Sicily. A half-ton of explosives in a culvert under the road. By early 1993 the boss responsible for the murder, Salvatore Riina, they call him The Beast, paid for it. We arrested him and brought his family to their knees."

"I remember the case," Angelo said.

Joe looked at Colonel Aldo and tilted his head.

"You don't know about Falcone's death?" Aldo asked.

Joe shook his head. "No, sir."

"Angelo, tell him about it later. The government went after Riina's organization. The Mafia learned a lesson, but the Clans in Naples didn't pay attention. Men of the Camorra, from the war-torn countries of the Middle East and Africa, don't value life as we do. Many of them have sworn allegiance to terrorist groups. They don't care who they kill."

"The difference is interesting," Joe said, "but I still want to help the Fugitive Squad. I helped create it."

Angelo shifted his position on the couch. "Sir. Has anyone brought up the shooting in the trawler case?"

"Not for a while. The politicians worried after Joe got shot in the arm. When I spoke to the Director of the Marshals Service, he told me Joe is safer here than on the streets of Chicago or New York City." Aldo paused, rubbed the stubble on his chin, and stared at both men. "Both of you be careful. Now, what's your next move?"

"Three of my men remained at the safe house. We'll brief the other twelve men I'm taking." Angelo said. "I'll contact Naples Carabinieri Command, and if more men are needed, I'll speak with the State and Municipal police."

Aldo waved a hand. "No. I want you to be more cautious. I'll arrange for you to meet with Colonel Ferrara. Brief him, and no one else. Contact no other police until the moment you need their help. The local officers live and have families in those communities. One passing comment about Carabinieri from Rome looking for three fugitives could be disastrous."

"Angelo and I will put six men in plain clothes on the street. Does Colonel Ferrara need to be told?"

"Yes, but I'll make the call. All raids are to be conducted in tactical uniforms. I don't want one Clan to think another started a war. Anything else to discuss?"

Angelo tapped the folder next to his leg. "Yes, sir. We received information from DEA in New York. They provided us with family addresses of the three fugitives. The men working undercover will check out each location."

"Anything more?" Aldo asked.

"No, sir."

"We're leaving the day after tomorrow," Joe said.

"Watch out for that big guy," warned Aldo.

Joe grinned. "Francesco... Little Tuna?"

Aldo raised his eyebrows, "Yeah. Little lard-ass tuna."

Chapter X
CAMORRA EYES

That night Joe and Nina finished dinner in their apartment. After clearing the dishes, they relaxed, sipping cold yellow Limoncello liqueur from shot glasses. He looked across the table at his wife. *I never get tired of looking at her, she's so beautiful. I'm a lucky man.*

"Angelo and I are going to Naples in two days, and we'll be there about a week."

Nina tapped her fingers on the table and frowned. "Not another trip out of town. Are you trying to find more fugitives?" She took a sip of her drink.

"Yeah. The three from New York. Remember the case I told you about while we were there?"

Nina shook her head. "I thought you would have found them by now."

"I wish it was that easy," Joe sighed. "What's your flight schedule?"

"The day after tomorrow I fly to Miami for one night. The return flight comes into Milan and I transfer planes to get back to Rome. After that I have three days of flights to different places in Europe. If you're not back by then, I'll call Sofia and we'll go shopping."

Joe smiled. "So, we'll be out of town at the same time. Miami returns to Miami."

"Don't bring up the Omar Hassan case. I'm still mad at you and Angelo for giving me that name."

"It worked." Joe chuckled. "Thank God they didn't find out your real name." He tapped his glass against hers. "I'll always love Miami."

Nina stuck her tongue out at him and then downed the last drops of her Limoncello.

Neither Bruno, nor his cousin Josef, thought much about the Camorra. They didn't sell drugs or engage in any activities they considered criminal. Helping The Scorpion keep members of his gang in line was nothing more to the cousins than a well-paying job. The police did little when they found a drug dealer with two broken legs or a thief beaten half to death in an alley. Bruno could not recall the Carabinieri ever taking time to investigate the murder of a Camorra soldier. *We're doing them a favor.*

Bruno pulled onto a narrow street in the Campo Marzio section of central Rome. He slowed the old Fiat in front of the apartment building and noticed a vacant parking space. *Amazing... a place to park at night in Rome. This place is worse than Naples.* He pulled into the spot and turned off the engine. *Let's not attract attention.* He pointed to the door of a building across the street. "That's the entrance. The apartment is on the second floor."

"The American, Costa?"

"Yeah."

Josef nodded. "What's his wife's name?"

"Nina Belsogno. She's Italian. They married here in Rome."

"What about the other one?"

"Angelo Randi. Nico said he's a corrupt Carabinieri captain. His wife Sofia is also a Belsogno... the wives are cousins. Nico doesn't want us to tell anyone we know about them. One of D'Arco's men told him about a telephone call from a Mafioso in America." He started the engine.

"Okay," Josef said. "Where does the captain live?"

"In San Lorenzo, not far from Castel Gandolfo. We'll drive there now."

"An apartment building?"

"No. A villa. Carabinieri captains are well paid."

The next morning, sixty-year-old clan leader, Dante D'Arco sat at his desk in a cramped bedroom he had converted into a home office. The old wooden desk wasn't large but served its purpose. *I'm the boss.* The faint sound of opera came from a stereo on a bookcase against a wall.

Nico Basso, the leader of his largest gang, slouched in one of two chairs in front of the desk. Dante didn't like the man. He tolerated him, but head strong Nico seldom thought before he acted.

Dante stared at a black and green tattoo of a scorpion on the young man's neck. The pincers and fearsome tail clearly visible, and ready to strike. *Why would anyone want a bug on his skin?* "You said you'd have that tattoo covered."

"The scorpion? It's my mark and the reason everyone fears me. I don't know anyone who isn't afraid of them. The three Americans even keep their distance."

"They are not Americans, Nico." Dante glared at him. "Our friends once lived in New York but they are Italians, and their families work for me."

Nico took a deep breath and nodded. "Sorry. Santo will be here in a few minutes. They're lucky they weren't at the bar when the Carabinieri went there."

"Tell everyone to stay away from the old woman's place. The neighbors have been talking. It seems she spent a long time with the officers."

Santo walked into the room and Dante pointed at a chair.

He sat, shot a questioning look at Nico, and turned back to Dante. "Good morning Mr. D'Arco."

"Good morning, Santo. Are your friends safe?"

"Yes. We are staying at Francesco's brother-in-law Gino's house."

Dante waved a hand toward Nico. "Thank you for arranging this meeting. I'll have someone drive Santo back to the house."

As Nico left the room, Santo's eyes lingered on the doorway.

"Is something wrong?" Dante asked.

"No. I'm uncomfortable around him."

"Many people are," Dante said. "Tell the others to stay away from him and his men. One of them shot the window out of an Alfa Romeo near Caesar's Bar. The dumb bastard said it looked like something the Carabinieri would drive and he wanted to screw with them."

"I'll bet it scared the shit out everyone in the car. Did you get any news from New York?"

"Yes. Vincenzo Rizzo called me. Two police officers from Italy met with New York cops. We're sure it was about you and your friends. He thought they were both Italian, but one is an American who works at the embassy in Rome. His name is Joseph Costa, and he's helping a Carabinieri captain named Angelo Randi."

"Are they the same ones who raided the bar?"

"I don't know. We have photos from across the street but they all wore masks."

Santo sighed. "Should we leave town?"

"No. You're safe here. My men are watching for any Carabinieri vehicles." He stood and Santo left.

Chapter XI
LITTLE TUNA

Few people would guess Francesco Russo had the street name Little Tuna. It made no sense for a man who stood six foot four and topped three hundred pounds. He and The Saint sat at the kitchen table in his sister Maria's house.

She stood in front of-the stove preparing pasta and asparagus in a frying pan. The smell of cooked garlic and tomato sauce permeated the room. Chicken breasts and mushrooms sizzled in a pan on the back burner.

Santo scooped two slices of prosciutto, capicola, soppressata, and a ball of buffalo mozzarella onto his plate. Franco filled their glasses with red wine, emptied the plate of sliced meat and took two balls of the soft white cheese. He passed a basket of sliced homemade bread to Santo.

"Will the old man continue to help us?" Francesco asked as he stuffed prosciutto into his mouth.

"Yeah, but he wants us to stay away from The Scorpion and his crew."

Asshole, Francesco thought as he took a bite of bread, and spoke with a full mouth. "That scorpion meatball wouldn't last a week with Vinny and our crew back home. If he tries to break my balls, I'll crush him like a bug."

"The guy's a nut case. Better if we avoid him."

Franco nodded. "What's the skinny with the American cop? NYPD?"

Maria placed a bowl of pasta in front each man.

Francesco put his hands together as if praying and raised and lowered them. "Jeeze, this all I get?" He stared at the plate piled high with macaroni.

Maria smacked him in the back of the head. "Christ, Franco, finish that first. I'm making enough chicken to feed the priest and his altar boys, then you'll get salad."

"Thank you, Maria," Santo said.

She rolled her eyes and returned to the stove.

"The American cop." Francesco prompted.

"Oh, yeah. He works at the U. S. Embassy... must be a feeb. No way will they find us here."

"Good. When we're done eating, let's go for pizza."

Gennaro, wearing civilian clothes instead of his usual uniform, had spent the last four hours in and out of shops on a side street closed to vehicles. He was one of four men Claudio had assigned to various parts of town, hoping one of them would see the fugitives. *It's getting crowded.* His stomach growled at the instant he spotted an inviting sign. *Pizzeria Mezza Luna... perfect.*

He walked into the restaurant, stepped to the counter, and nodded to the man in a dough and tomato stained white shirt. Four precooked pizzas lay on a slab of marble behind a glass partition. "I'll take a large slice of the Margherita."

"Something to drink?" the man asked.

"No, and I'll take the pizza with me."

The man cut a generous slice, wrapped it in butcher paper and handed it to him. "Two Euros."

He dropped the money on the counter, stepped back, and bounced off the man behind him. Gennaro, turned. His eyes focused on the black button of a massive tan shirt. *A friggin giant.* He raised his head, his heart fluttered, and he quit breathing. *Holy shit. Little Tuna!*

"You done, little man?" the giant said.

Gennaro rocked from side to side and glanced at the man standing next to the big guy. *Black pants, black shirt, black sports coat. It's The Saint!*

Santo motioned with his thumb to the man behind him. "Dance with Gino. Move so we can get something to eat today, not tomorrow."

"Sorry." *Damn! Three of them, get out now.* He hurried out of the restaurant. Ten feet past the door, he stopped, leaned against the building, unwrapped the pizza and took a bite. *Should I follow them?*

That afternoon, Joe nodded to Angelo, Claudio and Gennaro as he entered the living room at the safe house and took a seat. He smiled at Gennaro. *I've got to ask him.* "Is he that big?"

"Jesus, sir. You ever hear the ancient Greek story about the mythological giant Mimos?"

"Sure. He's buried under Mount Vesuvius."

"Well, the bastard escaped. And when I saw him at that pizzeria, he looked hungry."

"Anything else?" Angelo asked.

Gennaro shook his head. "No. I wish I could have followed them, but they got a good look at me. If they had seen me after I walked out the door, they would have been suspicious."

"And you're sure the three of them were together?"

"Yes. The Saint didn't hesitate when he pointed at the third guy."

"Gino? Right?" Angelo asked.

"Yes."

Angelo lifted three file folders from the coffee table. He set two aside, opened the third and scanned the pages. "Is this the guy?" He handed Gennaro a police mug-shot.

"Yeah."

"Gino Di Napoli," Angelo said. "Little Tuna's brother-in-law. He married the fat guy's sister, Maria." Angelo flipped through two pages and stopped. "He works on the docks in Naples."

"Is it close to where they made the coffee pods?" Joe asked.

"Yes. Three blocks away."

Angelo turned to Gennaro. "And you didn't see Dominic Capasso?"

"No, the place was crowded. He could have been sitting at a table."

Angelo handed the folder to Claudio. "The sister's address is in here. Make sure the family still lives there. If they do, assign two men to take pictures of the house. Call headquarters in Rome and find out if we have any recent aerial photos of the house and the surrounding area."

"Think they would be dumb enough to stay with family members?" Joe asked.

Angelo smiled. "They left Italy twelve years ago. I'm betting they see Naples as it was back then and don't realize the Carabinieri uses the latest technology like the rest of the world."

"You thinking about raiding the place?" Joe asked.

Angelo nodded and grinned. "If we can verify they are staying there. If not, we'll be nice and knock on the front door."

Chapter XII
COMMANDO NAPOLI

The next morning, Joe smiled as a junior officer led him and Angelo to Colonel Ferrara's office at Carabinieri Command in Naples. Angelo wore his uniform, and he wore a dark gray suit. Joe allowed Angelo to do all the talking since they arrived. *No one knows I'm American.*

In a wide hallway with framed photos of retired officers lining the walls, the young man pointed to a doorway and stepped aside.

Joe and Angelo walked into the colonel's outer office and stopped in front of the secretary's desk. "I'm Captain Randi." He motioned to Joe. "Chief Inspector Costa, we're from Rome."

Joe smiled at the slim well figured woman in a tight white dress. *Early to mid-thirties.*

"Welcome to Naples. Colonel Ferrara is waiting for you." She led them to a door and opened it.

Colonel Mauro Ferrara met them in the center of the office and shook their hands. "Come in, Angelo." Mauro pointed to a round table with four chairs in the corner of the office and looked at Joe. "And you must be U.S. Marshal Chief Inspector Costa."

"Yes, sir. Please call me Joe."

Mauro wasn't a tall man, but he was stocky and had streaks of gray peppered through his wavy black hair and goatee. Joe scanned the office. *Not as elegant as Colonel Aldo's, but nice.* A large carved wooden insignia of the Special Intervention Group hung on the wall behind the colonel's executive desk. He noticed the paratrooper badge above Mauro's breast pocket.

Everyone sat, and the colonel looked at Joe. "Welcome to our command. Few visitors from American law enforcement come here."

Colonel Aldo must have told him. "Thank you, sir. It's a pleasure to meet you."

"It's my pleasure to meet someone from near my home."

"Boston?" Joe asked.

"No. Your family in Italy... the Province of Salerno."

Joe's eyes widened. "I thought I recognized the accent. Where do they live?"

"Vietri Sul Mare, not far from the port. The Ferrara family owns the largest ceramic shop in town."

Joe smiled. "A beautiful little town. The Amalfi Coast is one of my favorite places in Italy."

Mauro turned to Angelo. "Your boss and I had a long conversation. He told me about the case. You're looking for three men who fled to Naples following their arrest in New York City?"

Angelo nodded. "Yes, sir. My men located two of them near the town of Sant'Antonio Abate."

Mauro stared at the table and then raised his head. "The D'Arco clan. We arrested six of them when we discovered where they were manufacturing the coffee pods filled with cocaine. They're a large group... many Africans and people from the Middle East. Besides drugs and counterfeit products, they're implicated in illegal hazardous waste disposal."

"These three would stick to trafficking drugs." Joe said. "But at the moment, I'd guess they're only thinking about keeping themselves out of an American jail."

"Arresting them will not be easy, Captain Randi."

Angelo looked at Mauro and raised his eyebrows. "We discovered that when we had a window shot of our car."

"I heard. I doubt D'Arco had anything to do with the shooting," Mauro said. "He'll help your fugitives, but he will not lose money because of them."

"What do you mean, sir?" Joe asked.

"D'Arco's not stupid. Shooting at a Carabinieri vehicle only makes us more determined. In the past he's shut down activities to avoid conflict with the police. The three who spent years in New York may not be as accommodating."

Joe focused on the colonel. *He may be right.*

Angelo leaned over the table. "We discovered they may be staying at one of the fugitive's sister's house. I have two men watching the residence. If they are inside, we plan to raid the place."

Mauro looked at him and paused. "I'm not comfortable having your task force running operations in my jurisdiction without the help of my men. Colonel Aldo asked me to give you some leeway, and for the time being I will."

Joe interceded. "Sir. We don't want to put you in an unfavorable position. Colonel Aldo speaks highly of the Naples Command, and we'll do whatever you believe is best."

"Continue on your own, but you'll soon need our help. D'Arco's clan is organized. There are many places to hide the fugitives, and your men are unfamiliar with the area. Be careful."

"We will, sir." Angelo replied.

Joe and Angelo stood when Colonel Ferrara pushed himself away from the table.

"Keep me informed, Captain Randi."

Chapter XIII
MARIA'S HOUSE

That night at the safe house, Joe listened to Angelo lay out his plan. They would raid Little Tuna's sister's house in the morning. The key to the operation was to wait for Claudio to tell them if he saw any of the fugitives at the residence.

The next morning, Claudio's call came at eight. Little Tuna had come out, smoked a cigarette, and then went back inside the house.

Thirty minutes later, Sabatino climbed into the Land Rover. He drove. Angelo sat next to him.

Joe took a deep breath. *Hope we have enough men.* He and Gennaro sat in back. Five officers manned the lead vehicle. All the officers wore ominous-looking dark blue tactical uniforms, balaclava full-face masks, and vests with CARABINIERI printed in large white letters on the front and back. Each man carried a holstered Beretta semi-automatic pistol, and an MP5 slung across his chest.

Sabatino slowed the SUV as they approached the house. He waited until the five men in the first vehicle turned into an alley adjacent the residence. Their goal was to secure the back and sides of the house so no one would escape.

Sabatino stopped in front of the single-story house. Joe and the others jumped out of the vehicles and ran to the door.

Gennaro rang the bell and pounded on the steel door frame with a crowbar. "Carabinieri! Open up!" he yelled glancing at Angelo for guidance.

After five seconds with no answer, Angelo nodded.

Gennaro slammed the crowbar into the space near the deadbolt. With a loud crunch the lock popped, and he jumped aside.

Sabatino kicked in the door and Angelo and Joe raced in. Angelo spun from the foyer to the living room and leveled his MP5 on Gino and Maria, huddled in a corner. "Don't move!"

Maria, fell to her knees beside Gino, squatting against the wall, and clamped a hand around her husband's arm. She jabbed a finger at Angelo. "What are you doing?" Tears ran down her cheeks as she turned away from the officers and sobbed.

Gino glared at Angelo and pulled Maria close to his side. "Why are you doing this to us," he yelled.

Joe followed Sabatino, down a hallway to the back of the home.

Sabatino opened a door leading to the small yard. Three uniformed men entered. "Clear each room while Joe and I check on the captain."

Gino and Maria now sat on the couch, their eyes locked on Angelo. She wiped tears from her cheek.

"You people are crazy! We've done nothing wrong!" Gino screamed. "You'll pay to have our door replaced."

Joe wondered if Angelo was smiling under his mask.

"Maybe, but that depends on what we find," Angelo said.

"I told you no one is here. I don't know where my brother-in-law is."

A young officer walked into the room with a grim expression on his face. "You need to take a look at what we found," he said to Angelo.

Angelo looked at Sabatino and pointed to Gino and Maria. "Stay with these two." He and Joe followed the man.

As soon as they entered a bedroom, Joe stopped. He scanned the clean windowless room, furnished with a double bed, and a tall five-drawer dresser. A large crucifix hung on the wall above the dresser. *Something is odd.* He looked to the left at a four-foot-long and three-foot-deep closet cut into the wall. *Never seen an American style closet in an Italian home.* On the floor, outside the closet, lay a brick size chunk of metal with a handle attached.

One officer picked it up and held it in front of Angelo. "It's a strong magnet," he said. He lowered the magnet to the floor at one end of the closet. When the metal came within an inch of the floor, it slammed against the hardwood planks. He pulled and the entire floor of the closet rose.

Joe's eyes widened and he and Angelo moved to the opening. Speechless, both stared at a set of stairs leading below ground.

"Did anyone go down there?" Angelo asked.

The officer nearest him nodded. "I did. It leads to a basement full of junk. There's a locked door framed into a rock wall."

"Follow me, Joe." Angelo motioned to his men. "Two of you come with us."

At the bottom of the stairs, one officer pointed toward the door.

"Where's the crowbar?" Angelo asked.

"With Gennaro, out front," an officer said.

"Get it." Angelo turned to Joe. "A door in a stone wall? Looks odd, doesn't it?"

Joe nodded. "My grandfather had a door in his basement that led to a wine cellar. Made of old solid planks of oak, and he kept it locked to keep the kids out."

"If we find barrels of wine behind this door, I'll buy you dinner tonight."

When the officer returned, everyone stepped to the side and trained their weapons on the door while he crowbarred it open.

Joe and Angelo looked down a stone and brick tunnel that appeared to be thirty feet long.

"Just what I thought." Angelo said. "It's wide and high enough for that fat ass." He motioned for one of his men to lead the way.

At the end of the passageway a set of stairs led up to ground level.

Joe stepped from the stairs into a garage. The door opened to a street behind the Di Napoli house. He and Angelo glanced at a white Fiat parked across the street. The driver's side window was open, but the vehicle appeared to be empty.

Joe turned to Angelo. "They must have gone through the tunnel and had a car in here."

A gun shot reverberated through the garage.

"Jesus!" Angelo grabbed his calf as he fell to the floor.

Joe turned his MP5 toward the Fiat as a pistol pointed at them from the driver's side window. He fired three rounds, and before he could take cover, saw a muzzle flash.

A bullet slammed into his stomach with the force of a professional player's baseball bat. The impact knocked him on his ass. The last thing he heard before hitting the floor was screeching tires, and a long burst from an MP5.

Chapter XIV
RETURN TO ROME

Four hours after the raid, Joe stood in front of a bathroom mirror in the safe house. He cringed in pain as he removed his bulletproof vest and then his shirt. He examined the three-inch round bruise on his stomach. Bright red blood pooled just below the skin in the center of the welt. Joe touched it with his little finger and flinched. *Jesus that hurts! I'd be dead if it wasn't for the vest.* He put on his shirt, buttoned it over the ugly wound, and walked to the living room.

Angelo sat on the couch with his injured leg resting on a coffee table. A Carabinieri doctor kneeled in front of him and cut the end of five stitches. "You're lucky it only grazed you." After he bandaged the leg, he turned to Joe. "I'm Doctor Fausto Nepi. I understand you're injured."

Joe unbuttoned his shirt and looked down at the bruise.

The doctor raised his eyebrows. "Does it hurt?" He pressed his finger against the center of the wound.

Joe leapt back. "Jesus! Yes, it hurts! All you had to do was ask."

"Sorry. It will be sore for a while... severe pinpointed trauma." He glanced at Angelo. "Why didn't you go to the hospital?"

"That's a long story about Americans getting shot when they're not supposed to be in the line of fire," explained Angelo.

The doctor's eyes narrowed, and he turned to Joe. "You're an American?"

Joe buttoned his shirt, leaned toward the doctor and lowered his voice. "American and Italian. The American side need not hear about this."

Dr. Nepi sighed and rubbed his temple. "Now I know why Colonel Ferrara sent me here and told me to forget what I saw."

###

Two hours later Angelo hobbled out of the kitchen carrying his cell phone. "Talked to Colonel Ferrara. He's mad as hell."

"At us?" Joe asked.

"No."

"Me?"

Angelo shook his head. "The three fugitives. New York City street thugs. Shoot first, ask questions later."

"What's he going to do?"

"Don't know yet. He said he might put pressure on the D'Arco clan. I told him we're going back to Rome for a few days. What did you do with your vest?"

"Left it in my room."

"Give it to Sabatino. Colonel Ferrara said he'll replace it with a new one."

Joe pulled out his cell phone. "Okay. I need to call Nina. She's going out of town."

Angelo raised a hand. "You won't tell her, will you?"

"Hell no! I'll say I was clumsy, had an accident." He headed to his room, sat on the bed and listened to the ring on the speaker.

"Hi, Joe. Where are you?" Nina asked.

"Still in Naples, but I'll be home tomorrow around noon."

"Damn. I fly to Berlin and then to London tomorrow. I'll be back on a direct flight the next day. Will you be at the apartment?"

"Yes."

"I'm not looking forward to the trip."

"Why?"

"I'm flying with two male flight attendants. Both of them think they're comedians."

"What do you mean?"

Nina sighed. "They like to play games. About an hour ago I got a call. When I answered a guy asked if he was speaking to Nina... I think I recognized the voice. I said yes, and he said 'thank you, see you later', and ended the call."

"Assholes." Joe said. "Tell them your husband isn't a friendly guy."

"I already did, and it worked for a while. I'll remind them again."

"What time will you get back to Rome?" Nina asked.

"Before noon. Meet me at the house for lunch at one."

###

Two days later, Joe stood in his kitchen, cut mortadella and capicola, and placed the slices in the refrigerator. He slit two sub rolls, set them on the counter and looked at his watch. *One fifteen.* He walked to his desk and turned on his computer. *The flight must be delayed.*

He checked his email and signed in to the secure section of the U. S. Embassy web page. He answered the non-classified messages, logged off the site and looked at his watch. *Damn! Two ten, she's over an hour late. What the hell is happening?*

Joe grabbed his cell phone from his pocket and tapped Nina's number. The call went to voice mail. He called

Alitalia flight information and waited until a woman answered.

"Good afternoon. I need to find out if Nina Belsogno was on the flight from London that was due to arrive in Rome at eleven fifty-five?"

"Sir, I'm not allowed to give out that information."

He shook his head. "I understand, but she's a flight attendant on that plane, and she's my wife."

"I have no way to verify that."

Joe rolled his eyes. *Everything's a secret.* "Thank you." He ended the call.

On the Alitalia Airlines website he checked the arrival time of flights from London. An empty feeling came over him and adrenalin rushed through his veins as he stared at the entry for the last flight from London. The plane landed on time. *She should have been home by now.* He hit Angelo's number twice.

Angelo answered on the second ring. "Hi, Joe."

"Ang, I need a favor!"

"Sure. What's wrong? You sound worried."

"Nina should have come home at one and she's not here yet. The flight from London landed a little before noon, and Alitalia won't tell me if she was on the plane."

"Stay calm and give me a few minutes. I'll call you right back."

Joe pushed himself away from the desk and walked into the kitchen. He opened a bottle of beer, sat at the table, and stared at his phone, willing it to ring for fifteen long minutes.

When it rang, he jumped. "Yes, Ang, what did you find out?"

Angelo paused and lowered his voice. "The supervisor said a man called and told him he was her husband. He said she couldn't work the flights because she was sick."

Joe's jaw tightened, and he pressed his lips together. "Damn it, Angelo, I didn't make that call! It's a setup. Oh my God! If she didn't take the flights, it means she's been missing for two days."

"Let's stay calm, we'll find out what happened. I'll brief Colonel Aldo."

Joe couldn't calm down, but realized Angelo was right. "I'm going to the embassy to tell the security staff, then I'll meet you at your office."

Joe had spent the last few hours in high gear. At three-thirty, he arrived out of breath at Angelo's office. *I lost it at the embassy. Keep your cool.* "Sorry, I came as soon as I could."

Colonel Aldo and Angelo sat near a coffee table. Joe pulled a chair in front of them and dropped into it.

"What is the U.S. Embassy going to do?" Aldo asked.

Joe couldn't answer that question. The embassy had contacted the National Security Agency and the Central Intelligence Agency for assistance. The means by which they gathered information was classified. "I don't know. The Deputy Chief of Mission and the Security Chief were meeting when I left." He shrugged and looked at the two men.

"I have men examining every frame of the surveillance tapes from the security cameras at the central train station, and the one at the gate for that flight," Angelo said. "It'll take a few hours... they'll call us the minute they find anything."

The ring of Joe's phone interrupted them. He held up his hand. "Excuse me, I need to take this. Hello... yes, read it." His facial muscles tensed as he listened. "Damn it! I'm at Angelo's office now. I'll tell them. Let me know if you hear anything else." He hung up, pulled himself together, and shook his head. "The embassy just got an email they can't trace. Nina was kidnapped! The message said they wouldn't harm her if we quit looking for the fugitives from New York."

Colonel Aldo pressed his lips into a fine line and leaned forward. "Anything more?"

Joe took a deep breath and fought to keep his composure. "Yes, sir. They want the Italian government to tell the New York police they will no longer help with the investigation, and they want it printed in the newspaper... la Repubblica. Once they see that, they'll release her."

Colonel Aldo's face turned red. "These Camorra bastards don't tell the Italian government what to do!"

Joe cringed as his stomach twisted. His tongue stuck to the roof of his dry mouth. He spun his wedding band around his finger. "Sir, that's not all they said. We need to think about this before we do anything. You said these bastards are dangerous. Nina is Sofia's cousin. They said if we don't follow their instructions, she will be next."

Angelo jumped from his chair. "I'll kill every damn one of them!" He clenched his fists and turned to his boss. "Joe and I will go to Naples—"

"No you won't," Aldo said. "Both of you are letting your emotions get the better of you. That could get Nina killed. Sit down and listen. I know what we need to do to have her released."

Chapter XV
MAURO'S TURF

The next morning Carabinieri Colonel Mauro Ferrara tugged on his uniform jacket as he walked into Dante D'Arco's large living room. *He'll know how serious we are when he sees me,* he thought.

A sergeant came to attention.

Mauro nodded.

The sergeant pointed to a hallway. "Sir. He's in the room at the end of the hall."

Mauro passed three bedrooms and two baths on his way to the door at the back of the house. He entered a small office and scanned the room. A single pedestal desk and office chair stood near the back wall. Two wooden chairs stood in front of the desk. *A converted bedroom.*

Two Carabinieri officers in tactical uniforms and balaclava masks came to attention when he looked at them. One held an MP5 pointed at the floor. Mauro nodded, and they relaxed. "Leave us and close the door." He glanced at the sound system on a bookcase against a wall and listened to the music. *Puccini's aria. Pavarotti. At least he likes good music.*

He pulled a chair away from the desk and placed it in front of Dante, sitting on a footstool against the wall. *He's sweating. The biggest set of balls will win.* "Good morning Mr. D'Arco. I am Colonel Mauro Ferrara, Provincial Commander of the Carabinieri. Do you know why I'm here?"

Dante looked at him and hesitated. "No. I've done nothing wrong."

Mauro sat and removed his hat. "Let's not bullshit each other. I'm well aware of your position in the community and guarantee you it's about to become untenable. At this moment ten of my men are at your family's grocery store. It is closed, and will stay closed until they complete their search for drugs and counterfeit products. There is no doubt in my mind they will find something after they examine every product, and every container, in the building."

Dante hands trembled. "Why are you doing this? I'm only a businessman supporting my family."

Mauro cocked his head to the side and smiled. "It's sad you and your family must suffer because the local clan kidnapped an American cop's wife, and threatened a woman named Sofia, the wife of a Carabinieri captain. I would think the members of O Sistema had more brains than to shoot at my men and seize a woman off the street in Rome."

Dante furrowed his brow and rubbed his hands on his pant leg. "I don't know what you're talking about!"

I have him where I want him. Mauro stared at him for ten seconds. "Then I cannot help you. When we finish looking at everything you have touched in the past five years... including the fine lace panties in your wife's dresser drawers, the Financial Police will begin. They'll want to see the books for every business you are associated with."

Dante's nostrils flared, and he stood. "Why would I do anything to a woman in Rome?"

Mauro stared at him. *Think you intimidate me?* He remained seated, lowered his voice and pointed at the stool. "Sit down Mr. D'Arco. My men are outside the door. I can arrange for us to continue this conversation through the bars of a cell in my headquarters."

Dante sat, slumped forward, and covered his face with his hands.

Mauro leaned toward him. "At the moment I'm not sure how involved you are, but it won't take long to get the answer. I find it odd that while we are looking for three fugitives in Sant'Antonio Abate, the wife of an investigator helping us is kidnapped. Now our men in Rome are told to stay out of Naples and to cease looking for the three wanted men. The only conclusion I can make is that the men who left New York, like obedient puppies, followed your orders."

"What fugitives are you talking about?" Dante yelled.

Mauro stood. "If you don't know, then our conversation is finished. I promise one thing. It may take me a week, a month, or a year, but rest assured, a long prison sentence is in your future. Should the woman be released unharmed in the next forty-eight hours, I could return my focus to what I was doing yesterday. Then you can continue to provide for your family. If not, plan to spend most of your time speaking with every government agency I can bring down on your ass." Mauro got up, walked to the doorway, stopped, and turned. "One more thing. If you desire more children with your wife or girlfriend, work on it during the next two or three days. After that someone else will play games in the little bush."

By three that afternoon the two men Dante called, after the colonel left, had arrived at his home.

Nico Basso and Dominic Capasso walked into his office with wide darting eyes. Both men glanced around the room before they sat in wooden chairs in front of the desk. They looked at Dante and remained silent.

The clan leader glanced at the scorpion tattoo on Nico's neck and shook his head. "Which one of you decided to kidnap the American's wife in Rome?"

Nico and Dominic glanced at each other. "Both of us talked about it," Nico said. "We thought it would be a good way to get them to quit looking for Dominic and his friends."

"And who threatened the Carabinieri captain's wife?"

Dominic shook his head. "We didn't!"

"Does the name Sofia sound familiar?"

Nico's eyes widened, and he froze. "We didn't know she was married to a captain."

Dante tensed his muscles and ground his teeth. "Don't lie a second time, Nico!"

Dominic shifted to the edge of his chair and waved a hand. "Wait, a minute. No one told me about threatening a woman named Sofia."

Dante tightened his jaw and glared at Nico. "Is that true?"

"Yes." His eyes lowered to the floor, and he took a deep breath.

The old man's face turned red and a pain shot across his chest. Heat flushed through his body and he wanted to be some place else. Anywhere but here with the walls closing in on him. He leaned on the desk and glared at the two idiots sitting in front of him. "I asked you who thought it was a good idea... who decided to go after the two women?"

Nico raised his hand. "I did. The police were close to arresting our friends at Gino Di Napoli's house."

Dante glared at him. *This asshole may cost me my life.* "When you walked into my home, did you see my wife cleaning the mess the Carabinieri made?"

"Yes."

"A colonel, not a sergeant or a lieutenant, but a fucking colonel, and his men, just spent hours in my home looking for a reason to arrest me!"

Nico squirmed in his chair. "I didn't think the—"

"I don't give a shit what you think! Has she been harmed?"

"No."

"Where is she?"

"At a farmhouse, outside Rome."

Dante stood and pointed at Nico. "I want her released in the next twenty-four hours, and she better not have a scratch on her body. And one more thing. If anyone touches the other woman, I will feed them their balls. Get out of my house. When it's done, come back to tell me how it went, and it better be good news. Don't call me! I want you to come here and tell me she was released and is in perfect health. Do you understand me?" he yelled.

"Yes," Nico replied in a low voice.

Dante leaned across his desk. "Get out of my house before I get mad."

Nico ran out of the room.

Dominic stood.

Dante raised a hand. "You stay. We have something to discuss."

Dante rubbed his temples to ease the headache as he stared at the man called *Heads*. "You and your friends are a pain in my ass. Do you want to stay in Naples?"

Dominic nodded. "Yes, our families are here."

Dante paused and tapped his fingernails against the desk. "Our friends in New York City do things differently. If you want to continue enjoying the company of your relatives, I suggest the three of you forget everything you learned there."

Dominic eased air from his lungs. "Please don't worry, we will."

"Italy has changed since you left. We don't like to attract attention from the government." Five seconds passed while Dante stared and pondered his decision to help the three men. "How is Little Tuna?"

"He's fine… the bullet didn't hit the bone. It's still in his leg, but the doctor fixed it."

"Where are you staying now?"

"A vacant apartment above a bakery, not far from Caesar's Bar."

Dante stood. "Tell the others everything I said. Should there be one more problem, I will fix it myself."

Later that afternoon Dominic sat on a timeworn couch in a dingy apartment above the Regina Bakery. He shook his head and looked at Little Tuna and The Saint. "You guys wouldn't believe how mad he was. The Scorpion came close to pissing his pants."

Little Tuna rolled his eyes. "The Scorpion," he mimicked in a high-pitched voice. "I call him the fucking bug." He slapped his knee and grimaced in pain. "Son of a bitch! D'Arco better never try to break my balls. I'll step on him."

"Be careful you'll tear those stitches," Santo said. He raised his hands. "Half of these assholes wouldn't last a week with the wiseguys back in the Village. I don't give a shit what D'Arco says, I'm not spending the rest of my life hiding in this shithole. Why does he want the broad released? She's our insurance policy."

Dominic pressed his lips together and raised his eyebrows. "The old man ain't gonna take the heat for us."

"Tough shit if he doesn't like it," Santo said.

Dominic rubbed the back of his neck and sighed. "Don't piss him off, Santo. He didn't get to be the boss just by providing cannolis to the old ladies at his local church."

Chapter XVI
AGONY

Nina, sat on the ground for hours shivering in the cool dampness. A blindfold, soaked with tears, covered her eyes. Ropes secured both hands behind her back and clamped her legs together at her ankles. When she pushed a hand to the floor, her fingers dug into dirt.

She sensed the emptiness but called out. "Hello! Is anyone here?" The sound of the words rang hollow in her ears. *A shed or a basement.* She tried but couldn't push away thoughts of what had happened last year to her roommate Monique. The horrors swirled through her mind. *How did Monique survive what they did?* She couldn't hold back her sobs.

Thoughts of Monique and Omar continued to bounce around in her head. This must be about drugs, but Joe said she shouldn't worry because everyone in the trawler case was out of the picture. Omar was in jail. Monique now worked as a travel agent, and someone had killed Majid in Tunis. *It could be the guy who took Monique to the ship. What was his name? Yassine, that's it! Joe said they never caught him.*

She heard footsteps. *Wooden stairs... two people.* "Who's there?" No response came as the steps got closer.

A hand touched her ankle and someone untied the rope. "Stand up and turn around," a woman ordered.

As Nina struggled to stand, she saw a brief flash of light flicker through the bottom of the blindfold. *A candle.* She took a deep breath through her nose. *Oil, a lantern.*

The woman spun her around, untied one hand, and retied both of them in front of her body. Firm fingers grabbed her arm, digging into the flesh. "This way. When I tell you, step up the stairs," the woman said, pulling her forward.

Nina focused on the woman's voice. *She's from Naples.*

When they reached the top of the stairs, she inhaled fresh air that smelled of flowers. Nina's feet shuffled through dry grass as the woman pulled her. Her heart raced and thoughts tumbled through her mind. The black cloth covering her eyes kept her from seeing anything.

The woman yanked her arm. "Stop," and released her grip.

Nina heard the metallic sound of a door sliding open.

"Get in the van. Reach up and you'll feel the seat," a man said.

Another one from Naples. It can't be Yassine. She found the edge of the floorboard with her foot and hesitated. "No!"

Two hands shoved her forward. "Get in!" a gruff voice ordered. "Now, or I'll throw you on the floor."

She pulled herself onto the seat.

"Move over," the man said.

Nina slid to the far side of seat and felt him sit beside her. "Where are you taking me?"

"Shut up and don't move until I tell you."

She furrowed her brow. The door slammed shut, and she listened to another door open and close. The engine started and her head thrust back when the van lurched forward.

During what seemed like an hour drive, she contemplated her fate. *Why are they doing this? Where are we going? Will I ever see Joe again?*

The time spent in a dark space was hellish, but so far no one had threatened or hurt her. No one told her why they seized her on the street in front of the apartment, or what they wanted.

The van stopped, and she felt the man move from her side. The door slid open.

"Get out and be careful. I don't want you to fall." He pulled her hands, and she scooted across the seat.

When she stepped from the van she froze. *Fish! I smell fish. We're near the water or a fish market.* She trembled, and her knees weakened while she listened for any sound. *Nothing, must be night. Please don't put me on a boat.*

The man grabbed her arm and forced her to walk a short distance. *Cobblestones.*

"Stop," he ordered. "Step up and turn around."

She did as he instructed, turned and sobbed. "Where am I?"

"I told you to shut up. Don't press your luck. Reach to the ground and sit."

With her hands still tied together, she eased them toward the ground, and felt damp concrete. She sat and wiped her fingers on her blouse.

"Listen and do exactly what I say." His breath, inches from her face, smelt of stale cigarettes. "I placed something beside you. Sit here and do not move for two minutes, count to one hundred and twenty. We're watching you."

A door on the van closed. The vehicle drove away.

One, two, three, four. She paused. *I'm near a port or a fish market. It stinks. Fifty-five, fifty-six, fifty-seven. They're gone, but who's here? Ninety-one, ninety-two. Stop!* She yanked off the blindfold, saw her purse beside her, and realized she was one block from her apartment building.

Joe sat at the kitchen table and poured an ounce of Crown Royal. He stared at the caramel colored liquid, shook his head and half-filled the glass.

After he returned to Rome, he tried to make sense of what happened to Nina, and how he might have prevented it. He tapped the edge of the glass against the table top and glanced at his watch. *Three AM. It's been four days. I need to trust Aldo and the colonel in Naples, but for how long?*

During the last few days he had many conversations about Nina with Angelo and Colonel Aldo. Both men told him that no organized crime group had ever kidnapped a police officer's wife. Even the old Red Brigades, a left-wing paramilitary organization of the seventies and eighties, never targeted family members. In 1981, when they kidnapped U.S. Army Brigadier General James L. Dozier at his home in Verona, they left his wife bound and chained in the apartment.

He recalled Aldo's words. "Colonel Ferrara passed the word to other major clan leaders. He told them the problems they were about to face resulted from D'Arco's stupidity." Then he assured Joe no one would harm Nina, and she would soon be released.

Joe finished half his whisky and checked his watch for the hundredth time. *Three twenty. I hope it works.* In ten years working Witness Security, and during the last five chasing fugitives around the world, he had never sat on the sidelines. He slammed his hand on the table, grabbed the whisky bottle and added more to his glass. *No more sitting on my ass. Tomorrow I rattle cages.*

He jumped when the doorbell to the street entrance of the building rang. "Wrong apartment, asshole." He took another drink. The last thing he wanted was to deal with a person who had forgotten their key and rang his bell to be let him into the building.

The bell rang three more times and Joe pushed his chair back. *Who is this dumb ass?* On his way to the door, he paused at a small table when he saw the Glock pistol. He picked up the weapon, opened the door and walked to the edge of the stairs. As he focused on the landing at ground level, he heard the electronic deadbolt on the door to the street unlock. *Dummy.* He turned back to his apartment and yelled over his shoulder. "Next time use your damn key before you ring the bell!"

"Joe!"

His heart stopped, and he turned. "Nina!"

Nina raced up the stairs before he could process what happened.

His heart pounded as he sprang down three stairs at a time to meet her on the landing.

Tears streamed down her face as she leapt into his open arms and sobbed.

Joe and Nina slept little that night. They spent their time talking about everything that had happened. When she finished, he filled her in on what he had done since he found out about the kidnapping. The two subjects he did not bring up was taking a bullet to the vest and Angelo being shot in the leg. Once both of them calmed down, Joe called Angelo, and Nina spoke with him.

The next morning, on their way to Colonel Aldo's office, Joe wouldn't let Nina leave his side. After what she had told him at the end of their conversation, he realized she needed to slow down and take care of herself. *I need to convince her to quit her job.*

Joe looked at her oversized gray shirt, tight black jeans, and gray heels. *My God, she is beautiful.* "You look nice today... you look nice every day. I don't know what I'd do without you." He kissed her.

She squeezed his hand and laid her head against his shoulder. "After four days without a bath, two hours in the tub last night helped."

When they entered Colonel Aldo's office, Angelo wrapped his arms around her and kissed her cheeks. Aldo pecked one side.

"Angelo told me what you said on the phone last night." Aldo said. "I'm glad you weren't hurt." He motioned toward the couch.

Angelo and the colonel took the two large armchairs on one side of the table and he and Nina sat on the couch facing them.

Aldo looked at Nina and smiled. "I hope you're not planning to work another case with us. The government will have to pay you a salary."

Nina chuckled. "No. There's much less stress at Alitalia." She pointed at the cane leaning against Angelo's chair. "What happened?"

"I sprained my ankle."

"You and Joe need to take better care of each other."

"What do you mean?" Angelo asked.

"The bruise he got on his chest when he slipped and fell against the railing of the stairs. Both of you are clumsy."

Angelo raised his eyebrows and smiled. "I told him the floor was wet."

"Is it still sore?" Aldo asked Joe.

"A little... I'll get over it."

"Good." Aldo said. "I spoke with Colonel Ferrara earlier this morning. I thanked him for what he and his men did. They helped get you released."

Nina took a deep breath and nodded. "The next time you talk to him, tell him I'm sending an expensive bottle of grappa with Joe, and buying myself a bottle of champagne to celebrate."

Aldo grinned and then raised his eyebrows. "We must remain cautious. I'm assigning men to guard your apartment and Angelo's house. Let's hope D'Arco can control his men."

"What did the gang think they would gain by kidnapping me?"

"We believe none of the clan bosses knew about it," Angelo said. "The three America fugitives may have convinced local gang members to take you. Their only demand was for us to stop looking for them."

"That's crazy!" Nina said. "I know you and Joe won't stop looking."

Aldo nodded. "D'Arco and the other clan leaders aren't stupid. People thought they could take matters into their own hands. They may have brought about their own downfall," Aldo said.

Joe's brow furrowed. "What do you mean?"

"D'Arco doesn't want his clan being targeted by law enforcement. He needs to prove to the other bosses he still controls his men. This could start a war between clans. Someone will pay, and I hope you and Angelo can use it to your advantage."

Chapter XVII
THE MESSAGE

Dante D'Arco's driver pulled to the curb and stopped in front of the TRI Electronics store in Torre Del Greco, south of Naples. Dante sat on the right side in the back of the black Audi A6. A short Asian man, with a crooked scar across his cheek, came out of the store, walked around the car, and took a seat next to him.

Dante wasn't comfortable with the little man. People on the street referred to him as The Ghost, but no one called him that to his face.

"Hello, Luca." *Why the hell did he pick an Italian name?*

The man nodded, and Dante handed him a photograph. "His name is Nico Basso, on the street he's called The Scorpion."

Luca paused. "Where and when?"

"As soon as you find him." He slid an envelope across the seat. "The money and my instructions."

"Will I need to call you when it's done?" He picked up the envelope.

"No. Do as I ask, and I'll hear the news."

"I will." The man got out of the car and the driver pulled away from the curb.

Dante had thought twice before he contacted the little killer. No one knew his real name or where he came from in Asia. The man had no loyalty to any clan. He offered his services to gang leaders and clan bosses throughout the Naples area. His fee was as high as his reputation. He never missed his target. Dante leaned toward the driver. "Take me to the church."

"One nearby?" the driver asked.

"No. Go back to Sant'Antonio... Santa Maria la Nova. The priest needs more money for the ladies' cannolis."

Colonel Mauro Ferrara walked into his office the next morning at seven. Lieutenant Savio Vasta followed him carrying a folder. Mauro sat at his desk and Savio waited for him to speak.

"Tell me how it happened, Savio."

"At five this morning, two men coming to work noticed a white sheet at the corner of a building two blocks from here. They went to pick it up and saw blood stains. Under the sheet was a body."

"Man or woman?" Mauro asked.

"A man, sir. In his twenties."

"How did he die?"

"A single gunshot to the back of his head. It must have been a small caliber... no exit wound."

"Anything else?"

"Not much, except there's a note." Savio removed three photographs from the folder and handed them to Mauro. "Two pictures of the body and one of the paper pinned to his shirt. The close-up of his face shows a tattoo on his forehead." He set the folder on the edge of the desk. "This is the file on the dead man."

Mauro placed the photos beside each other and stared at them. His brow furrowed. "Why is there so much blood around the tattoo?"

"They cut it off the side of his neck and laid it on his forehead."

"Any idea why?"

"Yes, sir. I believe they wanted to make sure we could identify him. As soon as we saw the scorpion tattoo, we realized it was Nico Basso."

Mauro set the third photo on top of the other two and focused on it.

"We can't figure out what the note means, sir."

The colonel studied the photo of the note. He looked at the lieutenant and grinned. "I understand it, Savio. Leave these."

Savio came to attention, turned, and walked out of the office.

Mauro removed his cell phone, laid it on the desk and dialed a number. He tapped the speaker icon.

"So, we are both in the office early this morning," Aldo said.

"When you reach our age, what more is there to do? I have news for you."

"Good, I hope," Aldo said.

"It is. Remember when I told you about the meeting I had with Dante D'Arco?"

"Yes. The day he denied knowing anything."

"When I walked into his office, music was playing in the background. He was listening to classical opera, Puccini's Turandot... Luciano Pavarotti singing *Nessun Dorma*."

Aldo chuckled. "Good taste, but what's the point?"

"This morning he sent me a note."

"In the mail?"

"No. A dead man delivered it."

"Nothing that dramatic ever happens in Rome," Aldo said. "What did it say?"

"First, I must tell you who delivered the message. We found it pinned to Nico Basso's shirt. He's one of D'Arco's gang leaders. Suffered massive brain trauma when a bullet bounced around inside his skull."

"It must be an important note."

"It is. I'll read it to you. 'Wives and children have no parts in the opera.' I don't think we need to worry about another kidnapping."

Aldo remained silent for a few seconds. "You think Basso had something to do with Joe's wife being taken?"

"I do. We know the guy well... have a thick file on him. Everyone on the street called him The Scorpion... thought of himself as a bad ass."

"Why, The Scorpion?" Aldo asked.

"He had one tattooed on his neck but the killer removed it."

"How do you know?"

"It was sitting in the center of his forehead. I'll send you the photos."

"Only in Naples, Mauro. D'Arco may be safe for a few days, but I'm sending Angelo and Joe back down there. They'll come to see you when they arrive."

Later that morning Joe and Angelo sat in Colonel Aldo's office.

The colonel relaxed in a large armchair on the other side of the coffee table. He slid two typed pages onto the table. "Thank you for the report, Joe. They didn't give her an opportunity to see anything so I understand why she can't tell us much."

"The only time she could move around was when they took her to the bathroom. The woman removed her blindfold, but kept her own face covered so Nina didn't get a good look at her," Joe said. "But she'd make a good investigator."

"Why do you say that?" Aldo asked.

"One day, after she scooted across the floor, the woman came down the stairs and told her she'd tie her to the wall if she moved again." Joe raised his eyebrows. "Although she never spotted a camera, at that moment, she knew they were watching her. I don't know what D'Arco said, but it worked. They dropped her off outside a fish market a block from our apartment."

Aldo grinned. "You're right, she would be a good investigator. Now let's get back to the dead guy they found in Naples."

"Why did they kill him?" Angelo asked.

"D'Arco realized he had to appease Colonel Ferrara. Mauro took men off of other cases and focused on Dante's criminal organization. Sooner or later it would have led to the other clans taking advantage of the situation and moving in on his territory."

"So. D'Arco did the one thing that would protect his organization. He got rid of the man that created the problem," Joe said.

Aldo nodded. "Yes. He's not stupid. The Carabinieri have kept pressure on the clans but rarely focus on one group. There are over a hundred of them with close to seven thousand members. Mauro's men are spread thin trying to watch everyone."

"Let's hope the fugitives get no more help." Angelo said.

Aldo nodded. "We'll see. I told Colonel Ferrara you and Joe would return. Go to his office when you get there. He plans to reduce the pressure on D'Arco and send him a message. He'll tell him we want the guys we're looking for, and he should quit protecting them."

"We'll leave in the morning," Angelo said.

Aldo raised a finger. "One more thing. Colonel Ferrara formed a group of fifteen officers. Five of them will work undercover in the area where the wanted men are hiding. The other ten, and any equipment you need, are available for you to use. Take a small contingent from your task force."

Chapter XVIII
LAST RIGHTS

Joe and Angelo met with Colonel Ferrara and coordinated using the colonel's men in the area where officers had seen the three fugitives. After the meeting, they spent the next few days in the safe house outside the city.

Each day, Claudio received updates from the undercover officers, but could provide Joe and Angelo with little information about the fugitives' whereabouts. On the third day he received information they could use. That afternoon, he sat with Angelo and Joe at the kitchen table.

"It happened outside The Saint's mother's home," Claudio said. "At first the officer thought someone in the family had died when a priest came there. A half hour later two men came out and got into a car. He didn't recognize the men but followed them."

"What made him suspicious?" Joe asked. "Something had to draw his attention."

Claudio nodded. "Nothing at first, but then he noticed the one that looked like a priest... you know, dressed in black, didn't have a white clerical collar."

"Did he get a good look at the man's face?" Angelo asked.

"Not initially. He followed their car for twenty minutes until it stopped in front of the Regina Bakery, close to Caesar's Bar. The two men sat there and talked for ten minutes."

Joe's brow furrowed. "Is that when he identified Santo?"

"No," Claudio said. "Our guy walked into the bakery to buy bread and when he came out, he passed the car. As he did, he got a good look at the two men. He's positive... it's The Saint."

"Good work," Angelo said. "What happened next?"

Claudio smiled. "Santo got out of the car and went into a door next to the bakery. We've confirmed it's the entrance to an apartment above the store. It was for rent two weeks ago, but the sign in the window was removed." He opened a folder and slid one page in front of Joe and one to Angelo. "This is the advertisement made by the rental agency."

Angelo and Joe scanned the paper. "Perfect," Angelo said. "A complete description and drawing of the floor plan." He looked at Claudio. "Have everyone here tonight at six for a briefing. We'll hit the apartment at seven tomorrow morning."

Joe got Claudio's attention. "Tell Gennaro and Sabatino to continue gathering information from the undercover officers. We need to know if they leave the apartment tonight."

"And since the apartment is not at ground level, we won't need to worry about a tunnel, and the floor plan doesn't show another exit," Angelo said. "One way in and one way out."

The next morning, before leaving the safe house, Angelo checked the men and their equipment. Colonel Ferrara's ten men would use two Land Rovers. Joe and Angelo would ride in a marked sedan driven by Claudio. Everyone wore tactical uniforms, masks and carried an MP5.

Claudio led the vehicles to Regina Bakery. He slammed on the brakes, stopping with the front of the car on the sidewalk between the bakery and the door to the apartment. Two people standing near the bakery entrance ran up the street.

Joe leapt out of the back door as the first Land Rover turned onto a street along the side of the building. The second vehicle stopped next to the sedan and five Carabinieri jumped out. Claudio and the other drivers remained with the vehicles to protect them and keep anyone from approaching the building.

Angelo stood to the side of the door leading to the apartment stairway, turned the knob and pushed. "Locked!" He pointed at an officer. "Break it open."

A large officer stepped in front of the door and another steadied him from behind as he thrust the bottom of his boot against the wood below the handle. The frame shattered, and the door slammed against the stairwell wall.

Two officers slipped past the broken door.

Joe, Angelo and the remaining two men followed as everyone worked their way up the narrow staircase.

An explosion shook the stairway and the walls. Everyone froze and Angelo cringed as he looked to the officer at the back of the line. "Jesus! Find out what happened!"

As the remaining men crept toward the landing, a hand holding a pistol appeared from behind a wall at the open apartment door.

"Gun!" Someone shouted.

Joe dropped and slid up against the wall when he saw the first muzzle flash of three shots. He raised his MP5. *No clear shot, damn it!*

The officer leading the group moaned and pressed himself against the stairs. The man behind him fired six shots toward the door and then turned to his wounded partner. "You okay?"

"Yes. It's my arm, keep going!"

"Get out of here! Claudio will help you," the lead officer said and then turned to Angelo. "He'll be okay. Step over him and follow me."

Angelo and Joe worked their way past the injured officer who held his hand against his blood-stained shirt. At the top of the stairs a pool of blood spread across the floor at the apartment entrance.

"Wait!" Angelo ordered. He pointed at two of his men. "Once we're inside, you two clear one room at a time." He looked at the third officer. "Cover them and watch the other doors along the hallway. Joe, stay with me."

Joe stepped into the living room and kicked a pistol away from Santo, lying on his stomach. Both of Santo's limp arms lay at his side, his face squished against the wall. Joe raised his eyebrows when he saw blood seeping from under the body. He leaned toward the floor. *Damn! Eyes are still open.* He pressed two fingers against the fugitive's neck, but felt no pulse. "He's dead."

Claudio strode into the apartment. "One of those bastards threw a grenade out a window overlooking the side street. The driver and another man were injured. Ambulances are on the way."

Angelo spun toward him. "How bad is it?"

Claudio took a deep breath. "Thank God, the vehicle blocked most of the blast."

"Sir! Come in here!" an officer yelled from a room at the back of the apartment.

Joe followed Angelo into a bedroom where two officers stood next to an open door.

"What the hell is that door doing there?" Angelo asked. "It's not on the plans."

One man pointed. "It's a stairway leading to a vacant storage room at the back of the bakery. A door down there opens to the alley behind the apartment. We checked but saw no one. What happened to the men covering the back?"

Joe shook his head. *These assholes think of everything!*

Angelo glared at the narrow stairway. "A grenade stopped them!" He stomped out of the room. "Come on, Joe. We need to check on our men and talk to the people in the bakery."

Joe tapped him on the shoulder. "One minute, Ang."

Angelo stopped and turned. "I know. This won't work."

Joe nodded. "We need to change our tactics. I have an idea."

Chapter XIX
CUT THE CARABINIERI

After the fiasco at the bakery, Joe could sense Angelo's vile mood.

He stayed out of his partner's way and pondered what had happened since they came to Naples. *Three raids. Lousy results,* he thought. Caesar's Bar turned out to be nothing more than a place for Camorra soldiers to relax and watch soccer. In Little Tuna's sister's house, the tunnel surprised them, and the team left empty-handed. The operation at the apartment above the bakery worried him and Angelo the most. *If they have grenades, they can get larger weapons.*

When he stood in the dingy apartment, and looked down the flight of stairs leading to the storage room, Joe realized the fugitives had an advantage over Angelo's men. Gang members were hard to identify. Task Force officers wore uniforms and drove marked cars. *These guys grew up here... know everyone in town. We're the strangers on the street.*

After the failed raid, he and Angelo sat in Colonel Ferrara's office.

"Thank you for your report. You're lucky none of the three men were seriously hurt," Mauro said. "Tell me about this idea you've discussed."

"Sir. Prior to leaving Rome, Joe and I spent hours talking about the Camorra with Colonel Aldo. After what happened to us here, we thought about the advantages the Clans have over the police in and around Naples."

"In Boston, the Marshals Service faced a similar problem to the one we find ourselves confronted with," Joe said. "We often looked for fugitives in areas we referred to as The Projects."

"Explain the term, projects," Mauro said.

"Groups of government subsidized or low-rent apartment complexes. Many are multi-story... separated by space, a wall or a fence."

Mauro pressed his lips together. "Okay, but that isn't the problem here."

Angelo leaned forward. "Sir. Joe isn't speaking of the buildings, it's the social structure around those complexes that makes our job difficult... almost impossible."

"Explain."

"Gangs control areas." Joe said. "They call it their turf. Many times they use lookouts... even children, to watch for the police or strangers."

Mauro smiled.

"You know where this leads don't you, sir?" Angelo asked.

"Yes, but let Joe finish."

"Thank you, sir. Here we're facing that problem, but on a much larger scale. Clans, with thousands of soldiers, control vast areas in and around Naples. If they have something to protect, they only need to surround it with sentries."

Mauro nodded. "Who report any police in the neighborhood."

"And when they see two or more Carabinieri vehicles together, they know something is about to happen and send out a warning," Angelo said.

"What do you propose we do?" Mauro asked.

"Quit using marked vehicles," Joe said.

"It's a simple fix but also a challenge," Angelo said. "The vehicles can't attract attention. Painting cars and trucks with fake business names won't work. They'd be out of place and the locals would know."

Mauro interrupted by raising his hand. His eyes narrowed, and he glanced around the room. "We'll never get a local business to help us. You need undercover vehicles that the people will accept as commonplace. I think I have an answer to your problem." He walked to his desk, sat and dialed a number. "Good morning. I need information about your repair projects. Is there any cable work being done near Pompeii or Sant'Antonio Abate?" he paused. "Hold on, let me get a pen." He pulled a pad of paper and pen from the side of his desk. "Okay, where?" Mauro scribbled on the pad. "Okay. What work are they doing?" Mauro listened for almost thirty seconds. "Thank you. I'll call you later. Tell your mother I said hello." He ended the call and returned to Joe and Angelo.

Mauro glanced at the notepad. "My nephew, Carlo, is a security manager for Sky Italia. They're upgrading optical cable along the A3 Autostrada east of Pompeii. The D'Arco Clan controls that area. Let's meet Carlo for lunch near the Archeological Museum. I'll tell him to pick a place."

Joe, Angelo and their men, spent the next four days at a warehouse in Benevento, forty miles northeast of Naples.

"You think this will work?" Angelo asked Joe.

"It depends. The people in and around Sant'Antonio know what Sky Italia is doing. The key to the operation is to make our men look like Sky workers. That means they need to be working on the cable or the junction boxes."

Angelo pressed his lips together and spent a moment focusing on the floor. "When do the two cable workers arrive from Milan?"

"Later today. They're bringing forty sets of work pants and shirts."

Angelo shook his head. "Five people wounded, including us. Remind me to tell everyone to be careful."

Colonel Aldo had arranged for two white Sprinter vans and a smaller Mercedes Viano van to arrive from Rome. It took a day to add Sky Italia graphics to each vehicle.

After inspecting the vehicles, Joe and thirteen officers gathered at a table in a section of the warehouse. Each man held a submachine gun with the stock folded.

Angelo raised a weapon. "The MP5K, with the stock extended, is sixty centimeters." He pressed a lever and folded the stock. "Now it's thirty-seven centimeters." He looked at Joe. "For my American partner that's fourteen and a half inches."

Joe rolled his eyes. "I know."

Everyone chuckled.

Angelo lifted a short canvas sling. "With this sling you can hang it from your shoulder so it rests just below your armpit. Don't celebrate yet. When we finish this operation, these guns go back to the paratroopers of the Tuscania Regiment. Everyone will get gray pants and a Sky Italia shirt baggy enough to conceal the weapon. Make sure you wear a tight undershirt. Keep your vests in the vans." He looked at Claudio. "Did you cover Carabinieri on the front and back of each vest?"

"Yes, sir. With black cloth tape." Claudio pointed to a box on the end of the table. "What's in the box, sir?"

Angelo smiled. "Since we're wearing civilian clothes, we'll need a pistol that's easier to conceal." He pulled a

Beretta XP4 Storm Subcompact semi-automatic from the box and held it above his head.

Joe laughed when he heard oohs and aahs from the men. *A bunch of kids waiting for toys.*

"It's small, but it holds thirteen rounds in the magazine and one in the chamber," Angelo said. "Claudio, you have the honor of issuing one to each man. Sadly, I must collect them when we complete the operation."

The prior oohs and aahs turned to boos.

Angelo grinned and shrugged. He removed two folders from the table. "Tomorrow Gennaro will lead one group to the south side of town. Sabatino, your men will cover the north side." He handed the envelopes to the two men. "Divide your groups in half. Rotate taking breaks so they can move around and mingle with the locals. Chief Inspector Costa, Claudio, and I will stay at the safe house. A portable radio, for every two men, is in each van. Keep us informed."

Chapter XX
THE WAIT

By the third day in the safe house, Joe noticed Angelo had become antsy and paced the living room, staring aimlessly at the floor and walls.

Joe shook his head as he sat on the couch watching Angelo trudge from one side of the room to the other. *He's driving me nuts.* He pointed to an armchair. "Ang! Sit down and relax."

Angelo dropped into the chair and raised both his hands. "Nothing. No one has seen them. They're like ghosts."

"It's not as if our men can walk around asking people if they know where these mopes are hiding," Joe said.

"I had my doubts from the beginning."

"What do you mean?"

"Remember what we talked about earlier... central Rome?" Angelo said. "People know their neighbors, their customers, and those who work in nearby businesses. When someone moves into an apartment, or a business hires a new employee, everybody knows it."

Joe shrugged. "It's like that in tight neighborhoods, but what does that have to do with our men?"

"When people in Rome see strangers, they notice them, but think little about it. It's not like that here... the people are different."

"Sure they are," Joe said. "Neapolitans are more family oriented... a closer knit society."

"That's the point, tight-knit, full of mistrust and skepticism. It's worse in a small town like Sant'Antonio. I'll bet half the people are related."

Joe laughed.

"What's funny?"

"You know where my family lives in Italy?"

Angelo nodded. "Yes, Salerno."

"Well, a small town about thirty minutes outside the city... population of about two thousand. Ninety percent of them are my relatives. Let's give it more time, something will develop."

"I hope so." Angelo looked at his watch. "It's seven. That small lunch wasn't enough." He stood. "Let's go for pizza... we'll wear our Sky Italia shirts."

They walked outside and jumped into the white Mercedes van. Angelo drove and turned left at the road in front of the property.

Joe tilted his head back. "Where are you going? There's a place that makes good pizza back the other way."

Angelo looked at him and raised his eyebrows. "Gennaro said the food in *Pizzeria Mezza Luna* was good."

"Are you crazy?" Joe sat up straight in his seat.

"No, but I am bored. Who knows what we may find?"

"What the hell are we going to do if Little Tuna and two of his friends show up for a slice of pizza?"

Angelo shrugged and smiled. "We'll figure something out."

Angelo found a parking space near the pizzeria and they walked into the restaurant. A young waitress, dressed in black slacks and a red shirt, guided them to a table.

Ten or twelve tables, Joe thought looking around the room. *Not busy tonight.*

"Would you like wine or coffee?" she asked after they sat.

"Two glasses of the house red wine," Angelo said.

"Water?"

"Yes. Natural, non-carbonated."

She glanced at the letters SKY embroidered on the front of their shirts. "Are you with the men working on the cables?"

Angelo nodded. "Yes, we have two crews in town."

"Both Internet and television?" she asked.

Angelo nodded. "Yes."

The girl jumped. "Good. How fast will the Internet connection be?"

Angelo hesitated.

Oh shit! Nothing gets past these people. Joe turned to her. "Once we've installed the fiber cable, we'll offer a speed pack at a reasonable cost... up to three hundred and fifty megabits."

She squealed. "Finally we're getting what they have in Milan."

Why quit now, Joe thought. *Make her day.* "There may be other options that are even faster."

The girl giggled. "Everyone will start gaming." She covered her mouth with her hand. "Sorry, back to your order. Would you like pizza or calzone?"

"Pizza Margherita?" Joe asked Angelo.

"No, a Marinara," he said.

Joe smiled at the girl. "One Margherita, and one Marinara." He watched her run to a man standing behind the counter. The young guy pointed at him and Angelo.

Joe caught the waitress's eye and motioned her back to the table.

"Yes. Is there something else you want?" she asked.

"The man behind the counter looked confused. Is there a problem with our order?"

She smiled. "No. He streams movies to his laptop. I told him what you said about new cable."

Emilio had worked in his family's pizzeria since he turned ten years old. After the Second World War, his grandfather opened the business with a loan from the local Camorra boss. Not much had changed over the years. D'Arco's men came to collect his payment on the first Monday of each month.

He snuck glances at the two men from Sky Italia. *I've seen both before, but where?* During the last few days, the only strangers that came in to eat were the men working for the cable company. *They look familiar.*

A customer set a ten Euro note beside the cash register. Emilio took the money and rang up the bill. As he reached for change in the open drawer, his eyes focused on a photo laying on top of the bills. He slid the photo aside and handed the man his change.

Emilio looked at the grainy image of two men and two women standing near a black wall with inscriptions on it. He studied the faces, then took a quick look at the two sitting at the table. His heart fluttered and eyes widened. *That's them!*

Emilio shoved the picture in his pocket and headed to a door leading to the kitchen. On his way, he passed two cooks making pizzas. "I'll be back in a minute." He hurried into the kitchen, pulled out his cell phone and the photo. At the back of the room he leaned against a refrigerator and dialed a number. *Why is everyone looking for them?* "Hi, it's Emilio. Remember the photo you gave me... the two men you wanted to find?" He listened a moment. "They're here in the pizzeria. I recognize them from the picture." He wiped beads of sweat from his forehead and concentrated on the man's voice. "Yes. I'm positive. They're the same guys." He almost dropped the phone when he heard the man's response. "Carabinieri? Hell no! Both work for Sky Italia." He took a deep breath and shook his head. "Okay. The pizzas aren't finished. They'll still be here when you arrive."

When he left the kitchen he saw two more men wearing Sky Italia shirts talking with the two seated. *If he's right, they're all cops.* His eyes widened, and he stopped breathing. *I hope nothing happens in here!*

Sabatino surprised Joe when he and one of his men walked into the pizzeria. After a brief conversation, they ordered slices of pizza and left.

Angelo shook his head. "Still nothing! Where are these guys?"

I wish he'd relax, Joe thought. "Don't get discouraged. Sooner or later someone will see them. You can't miss the fat guy."

The waitress brought their pizzas and refilled their glasses with wine from a carafe. "Can I get you anything else?"

"No," Angelo said.

The girl slid the bill on the table and walked away.

Both men remained silent as they dug into a slice.

"I must admit the best pizza in Italy is made in Naples," Angelo said.

"You can thank Raffaele."

Angelo frowned. "Who the hell is he?"

"The guy that made the first Margherita pizza in honor of the Queen Consort of Italy."

Angelo rolled his eyes. "How do you know this shit? What Queen Consort?"

"Margherita Maria Teresa Giovanna," Joe said with a smile.

"Oh, The wife of King Umberto the first. She's buried in the Pantheon in Rome. I forgot the story."

Both of them were laughing when Joe saw Little Tuna's brother-in-law, Gino, walk through the door and stop at the counter. *Jesus, Joe, don't react.* He looked at Angelo, quit smiling, and raised his eyebrows. "Don't turn now, Ang. Gino Di Napoli just walked in... he's at the counter."

"You sure it's him?"

"Yes."

Gino asked for coffee and headed to a table against the back wall. He took a seat facing Angelo and Joe.

Angelo leaned across the table. "Maybe he wanted a coffee. Quite a few locals come here." He looked into Joe's eyes. "I'm glad we were wearing masks when we raided his house. There's no way he could recognize us."

"We've got to ignore him," Joe said. "You think he's waiting for Little Tuna or Dominic Capasso?"

"Could be. Did you bring your weapon?"

Joe nodded and widened his eyes. "Yeah, the Storm... wish it was the MP5."

"Let's take our time, eat, and see what happens."

The waitress took an espresso and a glass of water to Gino's table.

Joe caught glimpses of Gino watching them. "He keeps looking this way."

"Now you're worrying," Angelo said.

Five minutes later Gino got up and strolled out the door without a glance their way.

They finished their meal, paid the bill, and left.

On the way back to the safe house Angelo wouldn't stop talking. "I can't believe it. The first time we go there, someone involved in the case decides he wants a coffee. I'll tell Claudio to coordinate with both crews and have people go the pizzeria more often."

"Good idea," Joe said, "but don't overdo it. They may get suspicious."

"No. All they need to do is rave about the pizza being the best in Naples. Everyone will love them."

Chapter XXI
THE WAIT ENDS

Gino pulled to the side of the road before he reached his house. He picked up the photo on the seat next to him and studied the image of two men and women in New York City. *It's them. The captain and the American cop.* "I bet they're the bastards who came to my house." *Better call Little Tuna.* He yanked his cell phone from his pocket and dialed.

"Francesco, it's me. Emilio was right. They're the two cops in the photo. I arranged for two kids on motorcycles to follow them when they leave the restaurant. One of them will call me later and tell me where they went." He listened to his brother-in-law and frowned. "Give them a hundred Euros? They're teenagers... that's too much." He pulled the phone from his ear when Francesco yelled. After Francesco stopped shouting, Gino shook his head. "Okay, okay! I'll call and tell them. It's your money. You want me to call the boss?"

Gino cringed when his brother-in-law screamed again. He held the phone six inches from his ear and let him finish his rant. "Yes, I know you don't like him. I won't tell anyone."

###
Twenty-four hours after they saw Gino, Joe and Angelo had made arrangements with their men to spend more time in *Pizzeria Mezza Luna*. Angelo told Sabatino to move his team from the north side of town to a large cable junction box closer to the restaurant.

Joe noticed Angelo was more relaxed and confident as they waited for someone to report seeing the fugitives. Joe occupied his time answering emails from the embassy and from Nina.

At eleven that night, both of them sat on the living room couch and watched the late international news on the RAI News 24 channel. Joe finished cleaning his Beretta Storm and reassembled the pistol. He checked the 9mm rounds in the magazine and shoved it into the weapon. Chambering a round in the pistol, he set it next to his leg.

A newspaper on the coffee table caught his eye. He picked it up, saw it was a day old, and tossed it on top of the Beretta.

Angelo's head nodded. He yawned and rubbed his face.

"Tired?" Joe asked.

"A little. Waiting for something to happen is driving me crazy."

Joe laughed. "Me too. The embassy Deputy Chief wants to know what the hell I'm doing down here."

"You didn't tell him, did you?"

"Hell no. I'm getting good at stretching the truth. Told him we were helping the Naples Command setup a mini task force to catch the fugitives."

"You think he'll believe you?"

Joe shrugged. "Sure. Typical ass-covering politician. Hasn't seen me for over a week and needs something to tell the ambassador should he ask."

Angelo's cell phone rang. "Hello." He paused and listened. "Okay, Joe and I are both awake. We'll see you in a few minutes."

"Who was that?"

"Claudio. He's on his way. He and his men will start again at seven in the morning."

"What about Gennaro and Sabatino?" Joe asked.

"They won't come for at least a half hour." Angelo headed to the kitchen. "Want anything?"

"No thanks."

Angelo returned with a bottle of water and set it on the coffee table just as the doorbell rang. "Who the hell is that? I didn't hear a car. I'll bet Claudio forgot his key."

Joe shrugged. "Might have, he's got a lot on his mind."

Angelo grinned, walked to the door and yanked it open.

Joe froze when Little Tuna barged in with a revolver pointed at Angelo's head. He forced Angelo back into the room.

"Don't do anything stupid, Captain Randi," the fat guy said.

Joe didn't have time to react before a skinny guy ran in and pointed a gun at him.

"Don't move!" the kid yelled.

Joe raised both his hands to chest level. *Holy shit! We're in trouble.*

Little Tuna pointed at the couch. "Sit with your American friend," he ordered.

How the hell does he know who we are? Joe tightened his jaw. *Well, they knew about Nina.*

Francesco and his friend stepped back and looked at them.

Francesco lowered the revolver to his side. "Both of you have been causing a lot of problems. Who shot Santo?"

Joe answered. "We didn't. Must have been someone from another clan."

"Sure, guys on the street in Carabinieri uniforms. I'm not that dumb."

Joe stared at him. *Yeah, fat ass, whales are smart.* His muscles tensed and he eased his hands to his lap. *Be careful, this guy is dangerous.*

"What do you want?" Angelo asked.

"For both of you to disappear... forever. No way am I going back to New York to be locked in an American shit hole."

"It's better than sitting in an Italian jail," Angelo said. "We can help you get a reduced sentence."

Francesco laughed. "You're not listening. I don't plan to see the inside of any jail. In a few weeks, I'll fly to Canada, get a new name, and then cross the border." He turned to his accomplice. "See if they have wine in the kitchen... we'll toast their departure."

Angelo placed both his hands on his thighs.

Does Ang have his pistol? Joe wondered.

"Every police officer in Italy will look for you," Angelo said. "There's no way for you to escape."

Little Tuna laughed. "We already made plans. Dominic and I will be in Albania in a few days. The police can waste their time searching every house in Italy."

Doesn't look good. He's giving up too much information. Joe bit his lip. *The bastard's gonna kill us.*

Francesco looked toward the kitchen. "What the hell you doing, making the wine?"

"There are no clean glasses!" his partner yelled.

Little Tuna took a deep breath and stared at the door to the kitchen. "Just bring the damn bottle!"

Now! It's my only chance, Joe thought. He glanced at the newspaper, moved his hand to his side and slid it under the paper. In one swift motion he wrapped his hand around the pistol grip, raised the weapon, and fired two shots into Francesco's chest.

The big guy staggered back. His bulging eyes locked on Joe as he raised his pistol.

Joe fired a third shot, hitting the fugitive in the center of his throat. Francesco grabbed his neck and blood spurted through his fingers.

Shouting came from the kitchen. "Francesco, you okay?"

Joe jumped from the couch.

Little Tuna floundered, flailed his arms, and fell, with a loud thud, to the floor.

Angelo leapt from his seat, knocking the coffee table aside. He dove to the pistol clutched in Tuna's hand.

"Francesco!" The skinny guy screamed as he bolted through the kitchen doorway with his gun held in front of him. His face contorted when he saw Tuna on the floor. He pulled the trigger as he swung the weapon toward Angelo.

Bullets whizzed over their heads.

Joe dropped to one knee and raised his Beretta with both hands. He fired three shots into the man's chest.

"Jesus!" Angelo yelled.

Joe approached the body sprawled on the floor outside the kitchen. He figured the guy was dead but touched his neck to check for a pulse.

Angelo stood over him. "Christ, I thought we were dead! Where did you get the gun?"

"After I cleaned it, I laid it on the couch. It was under the newspaper. Almost forgot it was there." Joe took a deep breath and exhaled. "The next time we pass a church, we'll stop and light candles."

Angelo placed a hand on Joe's shoulder. "I'll never forget this."

"Neither one of us will." Joe pointed at Little Tuna's body. "That bastard made up his mind, we were both going to die."

Angelo pulled his cell phone from his pocket. "I'll call Colonel Ferrara. You call Gennaro and Sabatino. Tell them to bring their crews here as soon as possible."

Joe's muscles tensed, and he glanced around the room. "Why wasn't Dominic with him? If more of them are outside, they had to hear the shots!"

"Damn!" Angelo's eyes widened. He raised the twenty-two caliber pistol he had taken from Little Tuna. "This thing is worthless." He threw it on the table. "Give me your Storm and get two submachine guns. I'll lock the door and close the windows. We have the advantage as long as we stay in the house."

Joe handed him the Beretta.

"How many rounds are left?"

"Seven." Joe bolted down a hallway.

When he returned, he held an MP5 and a small canvas bag in each hand. *Angelo's been busy.* An oversized armchair blocked the front door. The couch, with the coffee table turned over on top of it, sat to the side of the room. He handed Angelo a weapon and bag. "There are six extra magazines in the bag."

"Did you make the calls?"

"Yeah." Joe chambered a round in the MP5 and removed the magazines from the bag. "Claudio is five minutes from here. The rest of them will take a half hour or more."

"Did you tell them what happened?"

Joe raised his shoulders and eyebrows. "Only that we had a one-sided gun battle with Francesco, and he lost. Claudio will park down the road and check if anyone is near the house. When he meets the others, he'll send me a text. What about Mauro?"

"It will be over an hour before he and his men arrive." He walked to Joe and shook his head. "He would have taken a drink of wine and pulled the trigger."

The words made Joe shudder. *He's right!* Little Tuna didn't worry about the ramifications. He and Dominic may have gotten out of the country, but someone would have found them. *We wouldn't be there to see it.*

Chapter XXII
BORING TRIP

Two days later, Joe, DEA Agent Paul Sacca and FBI Agent Robert Duffy sat in Angelo's office in Rome.

"Now that Dominic Capasso turned himself in, tell us what happened," Paul said. "We heard there was a shootout."

"One of my men shot The Saint, Santo Esposito, when we raided an apartment in town. He died before we got to him," Angelo said. "Francesco Russo, Little Tuna, and Dominic, got out by going down a hidden flight of stairs."

Duffy furrowed his brow. "Little Tuna was the fat guy, right?"

Joe nodded. "Yeah. The reincarnation of Mimos, the giant."

Duffy tilted his head to the side and looked at the three men. "Mimos? Who the hell is he? I thought you were only looking for three fugitives?"

Joe smiled at Duffy. *You can't help liking this guy.* "Mimos is the mythological giant buried under Mount Vesuvius."

"Oh! Never read that story," Duffy said. "So you refer to Little Tuna as a giant?"

"If you saw him you'd understand. He was that big," Angelo said.

"The first time we got close to them, one of our men put a bullet in Francesco's leg," Joe added.

"Any of your men get injured?" Paul asked. He looked at Angelo. "You were limping, and Joe said he bruised his stomach."

Angelo didn't wait for Joe to answer. "Nothing bad... small accidents. A few of my men took fragments... Joe and I are clumsy."

"So, Francesco is dead. How did that happen?" Duffy asked.

"He showed up at the wrong place with a pistol. An officer on the task force shot him," Joe said.

Angelo stood. "That's it. When we finish writing our report we'll send you both a copy."

Paul and Robert left the office.

"We can't give them the same report we're writing for Colonel Aldo," Angelo said.

"I know. If the Ambassador finds out everything, he'll tie me to my desk."

Angelo headed to his desk. "Let's get started. We meet with Colonel Aldo the day after tomorrow."

Chapter XXIII
THE GIRLS

That night Joe, Angelo and their wives finished dinner in the candlelit downstairs dining room at the Target Restaurant.

Sofia looked at both men. "I'm glad you don't need to go back to Naples. Nina and I are tired of being alone and having guards watch us twenty-four hours a day."

"Did you catch all the men you were looking for?" asked Nina.

Joe glanced at Angelo and smiled. During the three hour drive back to Rome, they discussed what they would tell the women. They both agreed there was no reason to bring up what had happened at the safe house. "Two of them gave us no problem when we took custody of them. A day later, the third guy turned himself in to the Carabinieri."

Sofia turned to her husband. "When can we get rid of the guards around the house?"

"Joe and I spoke with Colonel Aldo. They won't be back tomorrow."

"What about our apartment?" Nina asked Joe.

"Don't worry. Today's the last day. The asshole that planned your kidnapping is no longer a free man. The people who held you were threatened with the same fate."

"I hope you'll both be spending more time at home," Sofia said to Angelo.

"We will."

Nina smiled at Joe. "Sofia and I want to go to Saturnia's thermal baths." She glanced between Angelo and Joe. "Will you take us?"

Joe raised his eyebrows. "The hot springs in Tuscany. The water is a hundred degrees."

Sofia raised a finger. "And we want to stay at the Wellness and Spa Center... at least three days."

Joe looked at Angelo. "You ever been there?"

"No, but I heard the Center is luxurious, and exclusive."

"We won't let either of you say no," Nina said.

Sofia pointed at her husband. "You and Joe have been enjoying yourselves running around Naples and eating good pizza and Neapolitan pastries. Now it's time you both work hard to please your wives."

Angelo grinned. "Okay. When we meet with Colonel Aldo, I'll ask him for a week vacation. I'm sure Joe can get away from the embassy for a while."

Chapter XXIV
TELL US

After Colonel Aldo returned from a trip to thank his friend Mauro, Joe, Nina and Angelo met him in his office. He had asked Joe to bring his wife so they could further discuss what had happened while being held.

Angelo convinced him to not to mention his and Joe's injuries.

"Did you get a good look at the people when they took you?" Aldo asked Nina.

"No. I came out of my apartment building and two men behind me grabbed my arms. They put a black cloth bag over my head and shoved me into a van."

"Are you sure it was a van?" Angelo asked.

"Yes, a white one. I saw it parked in front of the door when I walked out."

Aldo nodded. "Then what happened?"

"We drove for a long time... at least an hour. When we stopped, they took me to a room down a flight of stairs. They removed the cover from my head, but I didn't see a thing. There was no light in the room. Someone wrapped a dark cloth across my eyes and tied my hands and feet."

"Could you tell what direction they drove?" Angelo asked.

"No. I couldn't see through the cloth. While in the room, no one talked, but someone put a water bottle to my lips and allowed me to drink. They didn't give me anything to eat the first day. I sat there for the longest time, lowered myself to the dirt floor and fell asleep. After that, they gave me a bowl of pasta and chicken each day."

"Are you sure the floor was dirt?" Aldo asked.

"Yes. I dug my fingers into the soil."

"Based on what she told me, it may have been the basement to a house," Joe said.

Nina looked at him and nodded. "It was damp and smelled musty."

The conversation continued, but Nina provided scant details. She didn't realize how long they held her, but later found it was for four days. She couldn't tell them much about her captors, except for their accents.

A tear rolled down her cheek. "All I thought about was what happened to Monique on that ship. Can we continue this later?"

"There's no need to," Aldo said. "We have Joe's report. If you think of anything more, tell him."

Nina pulled a tissue from her purse and dabbed her eyes.

Joe stood and helped her to her feet. He wrapped his arms around her waist, then stepped back and looked into her eyes. "You better tell them what else has happened."

Angelo and Aldo stood.

Angelo took her hand. "Is it important?"

Nina nodded. "Yes."

"We need for you to tell us where, when and how it happened. Every detail is important," Aldo said.

Nina stared at him. "I'm sorry but I can't give you the exact details, but I know how it happened."

"Try to do the best you can," Aldo said.

Nina raised both her hands and her eyebrows. She took Joe's hand and squeezed it against her chest. "I'm pregnant!"

THE END